CONVICTED

CONVICTED

…With one smooth move, Deacon pulled Lisa into his arms and onto his lap. She didn't fight him.

"No," he said. "You're not crazy. And all this stuff that's been happening to you is not your fault. It's just someone with a sick sense of humor trying to rattle you for some reason."

She put her head on his shoulder, letting him hold her. "A lot of people seem to think it's you."

That didn't set well with him at all. "Like who?"

"Terry," she mumbled. "My parents."

"They don't like me anyway," he told her. "And Terry's jealous."

She nodded against his neck. "Don't you think he has the right?"

"To be jealous—sure," Deacon said. "But not to go around accusing me of stalking you."

"He hasn't gone around accusing you of stalking me." The soft touch of her breath on his skin was driving him nuts.

"I have an idea," Deacon told her. "Let's not talk about Terry any more, okay? Or your sister. Or your parents."

She pulled away to meet his gaze. "You'd rather talk about what kind of koi to put in the pond?"

"I'd rather," Deacon said, "not talk at all."

Her mouth was sweet and welcoming, and she returned his kiss eagerly. It had only been a little over a week since the last time he'd had her in his arms, but it felt like an eternity. Suddenly he couldn't have been happier to be working late…

ALSO BY MEGAN HART

CONVICTED

BY

MEGAN HART

AMBER QUILL PRESS, LLC
http://www.amberquill.com

CONVICTED
AN AMBER QUILL PRESS BOOK

This book is a work of fiction. All names, characters,
locations, and incidents are products of the author's imagination,
or have been used fictitiously. Any resemblance to actual persons
living or dead, locales, or events is entirely coincidental.

Amber Quill Press, LLC
http://www.amberquill.com

Layout and Formatting provided by: ElementalAlchemy.com

PUBLISHED IN THE UNITED STATES OF AMERICA

*Special thanks to Officer Tom Nicklas of the
St. Mary's Police Department for all his help. A million hugs and
tons of gratitude to my family and friends for all their support.
Of course, as always, to DPF, who
makes it all possible.*

CHAPTER 1

Lisa Shadd put down her menu and stared up into the face of the man she'd sent to jail three years before.

"I guess it really is hard to find good help these days," quipped her sister Allegra from across the table. She tilted her head toward the man waiting to take their order and added a laugh that made Lisa wince.

"Al." Lisa shook her head.

"Are you ready to order?" Deacon Campbell spoke the words with incredible dignity considering the circumstances.

Lisa studied him. His sleek dark hair was shorter, trimmed around his neck and ears. His face was thinner; his deep brown eyes a little harder. Three years had changed him, but not for the worse. If anything, time and circumstance had aged his previous good looks into an almost feral beauty that reminded Lisa of the wolf-dog hybrids Harry Keller kept on the outskirts of town.

Allegra laughed again. "I'll have the grilled chicken breast and a Tequila Slammer. Oops, I said slammer!"

Allegra's poor attempt at humor made Lisa cringe. She turned to her sister with a warning look that, thankfully, Allegra chose to acknowledge. Allegra got up from the table with a pout.

"I'm going to the ladies room," she said with a fixed glare at Deacon. To Lisa, she said, "Keep an eye on my purse."

Throughout it all, Deacon's expression had not wavered. His pen remained poised over his notepad. Only the tightening of his full mouth gave Lisa the suspicion her sister's words had affected him.

Lisa cleared her throat and tried to sound light. "How long have you been…back?"

Deacon met her stare steadily. "I got out two months ago."

"I hadn't heard." Lisa surreptitiously wiped her moist palms on her skirt. She'd thought a hundred times of meeting him again. In a town the size of St. Mary's, there'd be no way to avoid it. She just hadn't expected to see him here.

Deacon cocked his head to the left and raised one eyebrow in the way she still remembered so well. "Sorry, I guess my press agent forgot to send you the notice."

His casual but slightly bitter reply made her cheeks flush. Lisa finally dropped her eyes. She couldn't blame his bitterness. He'd spent the past three years in jail because of her testimony. She wasn't exactly his best friend.

The restaurant's owner, Tom Lee, appeared from behind Deacon and smiled nervously at Lisa. "Is there a problem here?"

"No, of course not," she began, then spotted Allegra standing across the room. When her sister noticed she'd been caught out, she looked anything but apologetic.

"Deacon was just taking my order," Lisa said firmly. "No problem at all, Tom."

Tom flashed Deacon a wary look as though he expected the much taller man to threaten him. "Remember what we talked about, Mr. Campbell."

Deacon took a deep breath, but only nodded. If she'd been in his situation, Lisa knew she would not have been able to hold her tongue. Tom nodded at her tersely and bustled away back to the kitchen, his portly frame rocking from side to side with the exertion.

"Something to drink?"

She ordered a pop and a salad, having no stomach now for the greasy burger and onion rings she'd planned on ordering for lunch. "Thank you."

There was more she wanted to say, but nothing would come out. It didn't seem the place, or the time, to tell him she was sorry for ruining his life. Instead, Lisa sat back in her chair and watched him head toward the kitchen.

The last time she'd seen him, he'd been wearing a black suit, his long hair tied back in a slick ponytail in deference to being in court. It was a far different look from the faded jeans and cotton t-shirts he usually wore, and one that didn't suit him as well.

Three years was a long time. Long enough to forget about him. So why hadn't she?

She had no more time to think about it before a tall blond man slid into the chair next to hers and planted a swift kiss on her cheek. "Hey."

"Terrence, you're late." Lisa spoke a little more abruptly than she'd intended. Seeing Deacon had flustered her.

Terry shrugged and grinned. "Captain O'Neill had me filing again."

Before Lisa could reply, Allegra came back to the table. Her smile for Terry was a lot brighter than it usually was. "Hey, Ter-Bear."

Lisa gritted her teeth. "Al!"

Allegra shrugged, looking innocent. "What? Can't a girl tease her future brother-in-law?"

Terry laughed and squeezed Lisa's shoulder, but Lisa wanted to duct tape Al's mouth closed. "Al, please."

"What?" Al repeated. "Hey, did you order already?"

Deacon came to the table with Lisa's pop and set it down gently in front of her. His eyes took in Allegra, then settled on Terry's blue uniform. When he looked at Lisa, his eyes were faintly amused. His mouth, however, remained in its same straight, grim line.

"Ready to order?"

Terry flipped his menu closed. The men eyed each other. Lisa could practically smell the testosterone in the air.

"Campbell," Terry said coolly. "I heard you were out."

Deacon didn't miss a beat. "Nice to see you, Officer Hewitt. What'll you have?"

Lisa knew what Terry was going to order before he even said it. Smoked turkey on wheat, no mayo, no onions. No chips. Unsweetened iced tea. It ought to have been nice, knowing, but today his predictability annoyed her.

"Well." Allegra smirked at Lisa when Deacon had once more left the table. "What a cozy little reunion."

Lisa stood. "Excuse me. I need to use the restroom."

Her cheeks burning, she left the table. Behind her she heard Allegra murmuring something to Terry, but she didn't care. *Let them think what they wanted.* She needed to splash her face with cold water.

Three years ago, Deacon had asked Lisa out for beer and wings after an adult education class in organic gardening they'd both taken at the Dubois campus of Penn State University. At first put off by Deacon's rough boy exterior and loud motorcycle, Lisa soon discovered he was a man who truly loved working with the earth. He

3

didn't mind getting his hands dirty, and he enjoyed sharing what he knew with others. Deacon Campbell was a paradox, a man whose outward appearance suggested he'd be more likely to belong to the Hell's Angels than the local garden club. Her feelings about him, and about what had happened, were just as tricky.

Three years ago she and Deacon had been on the verge of something special—or at least that's what she'd thought at the time. Her hero from the wrong side of the tracks, her knight in faded denim and shining chrome, her almost-lover.

Below his rough exterior, the earring and long hair and beyond the motorcycle and dirt-stained fingers, Deacon had turned out to be a considerate and generous man. Even—dare she say it?—a gentleman. His kind words and actions had turned out to be just another game he liked to play, as she'd discovered the night he'd robbed The Circle K convenience store while she'd waited innocently in the parking lot.

Lisa left the bathroom and went back to the table. She smiled as naturally as she could at Terry, but he frowned.

"You okay, babe?"

Babe. Lisa restrained herself from reminding him for the thousandth time that she didn't like being called that. "Fine."

"She's not fine." Allegra gave Terry a nudge. "She's embarrassed because her jailbird boyfriend is waiting on us."

"Allegra!" Lisa's voice carried throughout the restaurant, and she forcibly calmed herself. "Terry, don't listen to her."

Terry glared at Allegra, who simpered and shrugged with mock innocence. "Geez, Allegra. You sure know how to put your foot in your mouth."

At Terry's chastising words, Allegra's face turned stormy. Carefully, deliberately, she got up from the table and placed her napkin delicately on the plate. Without another word, she left the restaurant, head held high.

"Your sister... " Terry broke off, shaking his head. "She doesn't like me too much."

Allegra didn't like any of Lisa's boyfriends. Feeling suddenly sympathetic toward Terry, who was always caught in the middle, Lisa leaned over and kissed him.

"Here's your food."

Lisa pulled away to face a stony-faced Deacon, who put their orders on the table and walked away without speaking again. She had no reason to feel guilty she told herself firmly. Anything she and Deacon had was over, ended when he decided to break the law.

Why, then, did she feel like she'd been caught cheating?

* * *

Deacon Campbell smoothed the rumbling Harley Road King up the driveway and parked it. His Mom's car was taking up the most of the space and he had to maneuver a little more than normal to get the heavy motorcycle into its usual resting spot. Sometimes it seemed she forgot he'd moved back in with her.

"I'm home." He crossed the enclosed back porch and into the room that served as a combination living and dining room. "Mom?"

She was in the kitchen, he judged by the delicious smells wafting over to greet his nose. *Homemade meatloaf? Mashed potatoes?* Whatever it was set his stomach to grumbling. Working around food all day usually dampened his appetite, but Mom always knew how to get him to eat.

"Any luck?" Bertha Campbell asked as he crept up behind her to snatch a sample of the cookie dough she was mixing. She slapped his hand away and offered her flour-dusted cheek for a kiss.

"Always get right to the point, don't you?" The sweetness of the dough melted away, leaving behind the bitterness of his answer. He'd spent the morning looking for another job, something a little more challenging and lucrative than waiting tables. "No. Nobody wants to hire a convicted thief."

"So you'll try again tomorrow." Bertha waved him toward the humming yellow refrigerator. "Pour yourself a cup of pop. Your supper'll be ready in about half an hour."

That meant he had time for a shower. Deacon passed up the pop for a bottle of Straub's beer, ignoring his mother's clucking tongue and disapproving eye.

He climbed the stairs he'd been climbing since childhood and headed straight for the tiny, blue-tiled bathroom at the top. In minutes the water from the shower was hot enough to steam up the one small window, and he shed his uncomfortable clothes with a sigh of vast relief.

The water stung his skin, but he endured it, hoping to wash away the stench he knew clung to him even though he couldn't smell anything more offensive than burger grease. It was the phantom smell jail had left on him, and it would take more than just a hot shower to wash it away.

He bent his head to let the scalding water work out the knots in the back of his neck. Lisa Shadd. Her face rose in his mind, making relaxation impossible. He'd known he'd run into her sooner or later. He just hadn't thought seeing her would affect him so much. And seeing her with Officer Hewitt, the man who'd arrested him, made him want to hit something. Hard.

"Deacon! Food's getting cold!"

Mom didn't climb the stairs anymore, not since her back had started hurting her so badly. Her yell startled him back to reality. Deacon shut off the water, which had grown cool, and toweled off.

He swiped away the fog covering the mirror and peered at his reflection. He should shave. Instead he just ran his fingers through his hair and scrubbed his face with the towel. In the harsh fluorescent light over the sink, several silver threads glinted in his black hair and in his beard scruff. *Chalk it up to experience,* he thought with a grim laugh that had little to do with amusement.

"I'm not calling you again!"

"All right, Mom, I'm coming," he shouted down in desperation. Nothing like moving back home to make him feel like a kid again. "Just give me a minute!"

He ducked down the short hallway and into the larger of the two upstairs bedrooms. The room was easily as large as two good-sized bedrooms with a bumped-out dormer and built-in dresser drawers to expand the space even further. A chest-high, t-shaped divider cut the room into three smaller sections for privacy; something he didn't really need since he was the only one using the room now.

For a minute, though he knew his mom would be getting irritated with him, Deacon sat on his bed. When he'd had his own place, the king-sized bed had been a luxury he'd thought he couldn't live without. Now, with the massive bed taking up most of the space on this side of the room, it just felt…big.

And what difference did it really make? He wasn't going to be sharing it with anybody.

Deacon pulled on a pair of faded Levi's and his ratty, gray, hooded sweatshirt without bothering about briefs or socks. Less laundry to do that way. It was a habit he kept, though since he'd moved back home, Mom did his washing for him. He knew she'd scold, but he liked what he had on. He wasn't going anywhere. He didn't have anyplace to go.

As he walked into the kitchen, the meatloaf smelled like Peter had opened the Pearly Gates. "Thanks, Mom."

She flapped her hands at him. "Eat. You're thin as a pile of sticks."

He ran his hand over his flat stomach, feeling the muscles worked for hours to tautness. He hadn't had much else to do for three years. "I'm just fit."

She scoffed. "Women like a man with a little meat on his bones."

He had no more hope for a woman than he had for a job, but at least he wanted a job. The last woman he'd dated had been the one who sent him to the Elk County Correctional Facility. He'd stay clear of women, thank you.

When he didn't answer her none-to-subtle jibe about dating, Bertha tried a different tactic. "The plant's hiring again. I could talk to Bucky Sherman in the personnel department. You could maybe get your old job back."

Deacon thought of the way Bucky Sherman had looked at him that day in court when the jury had delivered its verdict. Bucky's participation as a character witness hadn't helped Deacon's case much—not against the earnest testimony given by Lisa Shadd. She'd been so persuasive she'd even convinced Bucky.

"I don't think so, Mom."

"You won't know unless you try." Bertha plopped another serving of meatloaf onto his plate.

He pushed it away, suddenly not very hungry. "I'm beat. I think I'm just going to go to bed."

As he picked up his plate and moved to carry it to the dishwasher, her hand on his arm stopped him. "Something will come through for you soon, Deacon. This whole town isn't turned against you, honey. It'll just take some time, that's all."

Her words, meant to buoy him up, only made him feel all the more depressed. Deacon forced a smile and kissed her cheek.

"Thanks, Mom."

Time. How much time? And how long could he stand being treated like what everyone, including the woman he'd once thought he might love, believed he was? A criminal.

*   *   *

"Guess who I saw at the supermarket yesterday?"

Lisa's fingers didn't even pause at her keyboard as she answered her sister. "Gumby?"

"Lisa, no!" Allegra slipped into the hard-backed office chair next to Lisa's and used her foot to swing Lisa's much cushier one around until they faced each other. "Your old boyfriend. The crook-turned-waiter? You know—Deacon."

The name, and the thought of the face that went with it, made Lisa's stomach leap into her throat. She faked a casual attitude, forcefully returning her chair to its former position in front of the computer. "Really?"

Allegra was not going to be easily put off. This time she used both hands to twist her sister's chair around. "That's all you're going to say about it? 'Really?'"

"What do you want me to say, Allegra?" Lisa sighed and tossed up her hands.

Her sister looked at her with the sly grin Lisa knew always preceded some sort of mischief. "I thought you might say you were hoping he'd call you. Now that he's back in town and all."

Lisa returned to her work, reaching down with one hand to flick the lock on her chair that would prevent Allegra from doing any more twirling. "Don't be stupid, Al. Deacon and I have nothing together." She tried to lighten her words, though she forced the smile. "Besides, I doubt Terry would like that very much."

"You're no fun," Allegra said grumpily. She unfolded her long, lean frame from the uncomfortable chair and tossed the length of her black hair over her shoulders. "What time will you be home tonight?"

Lisa sighed and forced her attention away from the computer screen. "I'm not sure."

Allegra pouted. "Why not?"

Stay calm. It wasn't worth getting into a fight. "Al, please don't start."

"But you'll be back before it gets dark, right?" Allegra's voice came dangerously close to a whine. She leaned against the filing cabinet, her fingers restlessly playing with the coffee maker on top of it. The glass carafe clattered.

"The lights come on automatically at dusk," Lisa said patiently. "Al, I have to get these proposals done by the end of the week. That means I might have to stay late."

Allegra muttered something under her breath, but didn't explode as Lisa had feared she might. "Okay."

It was as good a time as any to tell Allegra about her other plans. "And when I'm done here, I'm going to the movies."

Allegra sighed heavily and thumped the top of the cabinet. "With him, I suppose?"

"With Terry, yes."

Her sister stalked out of the office without another word, slamming the door behind her. Lisa bent back to the keyboard, trying to concentrate, but it was all too much. First Deacon Campbell had returned to town, and now Allegra was getting worse.

Every family had its own craziness, Lisa's father was fond of saying. In the Shadd family, the craziness was Al. She was dramatic, moody, flamboyant. She could be intensely loyal and incredibly self-centered.

Lisa didn't resent that her sister managed to get away with everything she herself had not. She didn't even mind that Al was tall, thin, and gorgeous whether she spent hours in front of the mirror or just rolled out of bed. What bothered her was Allegra's increasingly irrational behavior.

The sisters had been roommates for four years, since Al had turned eighteen. Back then, it had seemed like a good idea. Neither of them could afford to live on her own and living with family was better than finding a stranger to share space with. Now, however, Lisa's salary was ample enough to pay for her living expenses. The problem was, Al refused to break up the arrangement.

Since childhood, Allegra had been plagued with fears. Fear of the dark, fear of large dogs, fear of open water. Doctors had assured Lisa's parents that Al's fears were normal, and they would go away in time. They had not, and though to the outside world, she functioned as normally as any other young woman, her family knew that Al was…special.

Thanksgiving dinner had to be set on the table at precisely noon or Allegra refused to eat it. Laundry had to be sorted according to a strange, elaborate system that included clipping matching socks together with plastic tags. No room could be entirely dark until she went to bed.

These were the things Lisa had to live with. Now she had to contend with Allegra's jealousy as well. Her sister didn't want her dating. Dates were time away from the house, from Al, who enjoyed dragging Lisa out to bars and clubs, but went into dark rages if more men happened to pay attention to Lisa than to Al.

It hadn't been anything more than annoying until about three months ago when Officer Terrence Hewitt had asked Lisa out to the movies. Though they'd known each other since high school, Lisa hadn't seen much of Terry since the night he'd arrested Deacon in the Circle K parking lot. The night her entire life had changed.

She accepted the date, if only to prove to herself that she could.

They'd had a surprisingly nice time. One nice night had led to another, and Lisa suddenly discovered herself with the first boyfriend she'd had in three years...since she'd dated Deacon Campbell.

Lisa shook herself, focusing again on the words she was typing. Reminiscing about Deacon and her bad luck to get mixed up with him wasn't going to get the marketing plan finished by this afternoon. She curved her fingers back over the keyboard and blinked the blurred screen back into clarity. She'd completely lost her train of thought.

Sighing, she pushed away from the desk, forgetting she'd locked the chair to keep it from twisting. Instead of turning around, she sailed across the room backwards and ran into the row of metal filing cabinets lining the back wall. Luckily, the crash was loud enough to cover her cursing.

"And the new world record for clumsiest dismount goes to...Lisa Shadd!"

"Not funny, Kevin." Lisa got out of the chair and walked it back to the desk. "I was just getting some coffee. Want some?"

Her older brother patted his trim stomach and shook his head. "Nope. Gives me gas."

Despite herself, Lisa began to laugh. Kevin could always make her smile, no matter her mood. "What doesn't?"

He shrugged and stood aside to give her access to the coffeepot perched unsteadily on the filing cabinet. "Not much."

"That's what I thought." She held out a mug to him anyway, and he took it. "Just leave before that gas catches up with you."

Kevin looked around the windowless closet that masqueraded as her office. "C'mon, Lisa. Even I wouldn't do that to you."

Lisa grimaced at the foul brew in her cup, but drank it anyway. "Did you see Allegra?"

Her brother downed his coffee and handed her the empty cup. "Yep. What bug crawled up her—"

"Kevin!" Lisa rolled her eyes. "The usual. She's upset because I have to work late."

"And because you and Terry have a date."

"She told you?" Still wincing at the bitter coffee, Lisa looked for the sugar, but it was gone.

"She muttered something to that affect." Kevin didn't seem concerned.

"Do you think she can go over to your place tonight? Maybe just until I can get home?" She asked the question casually, but Kevin wasn't fooled.

"She's a big girl, Lisa."

Lisa sighed. "You don't have to live with her."

"Thank God!" Kevin laughed.

Her brother's humorous response quelled Lisa from pursuing the subject. Nobody else in the family seemed to see Allegra's problems were escalating, not retreating. It was easy to ignore if they didn't have to witness it first hand, easy to explain away as just more of "Al's silliness." When, Lisa thought, did it stop being silly and become sad?

"Did you know Campbell's back in town?"

"Yes." Lisa sipped the bitter coffee, grimacing. "We saw him yesterday at the Evergreen. He...he's a waiter."

Kevin let out a laugh that ended up in a snort. "Bucky Sherman over at the plant said Campbell's put in an application there. They'll never hire a loser like that."

"He's not a loser," Lisa said and bit down on her tongue. Hard.

Kevin chucked her under the chin, something she loathed, and ducked out of the office. "Face it, Lis. The guy is a loser, he's a waste of space, and you made sure he got what he deserved. Besides, that was a long time ago."

If what she did was so admirable, Lisa thought morosely, then why couldn't she stop feeling so guilty about it?

CHAPTER 2

Deacon turned the water on the hose to a fine mist and gently sprayed his Harley clean of the muck and dirt it had accumulated, along with a generous bunch of soapsuds. Taking a soft cloth, he wiped the now-gleaming paint. Cleaning the bike soothed him. Mindless work.

"You touch that bike like it's a woman."

The voice startled him, and when he looked up, Deacon cursed under his breath. Lisa's sister Allegra tossed her dark hair over her shoulder and smiled at him. The slow, sultry grin left Deacon completely cold. He wiped his hands on the cloth and tossed it into the bucket of soapy water.

"What do you want?"

She pouted and took her hands out of the pockets in her black leather jacket. She wore black from head to toe, and the dark color enhanced her beauty. She looked a lot like Lisa, but without the warmth. Deacon pushed away the thought. He didn't want to think about Lisa.

"Somebody got up on the wrong side of the bed this morning."

"What do you want?" He repeated, bending to gather up his cleaning supplies. "It can't be good."

"Deacon," Allegra said in the I'm-a-naughty-little-girl voice that he hated. "You hurt my feelings."

He paused to raise his eyebrow at her. "Too bad."

"So…is that how you touch a woman?" Allegra walked closer, then trailed a finger along the bike's seat. She tilted her head to look at him, though she was a tall women and they nearly saw eye to eye. "Like that? All…smooth? Or are you rough? I'd expect you to be rough."

Deacon stepped away from her and dumped the bucket of water. Allegra jumped back to avoid getting the chill water on her black leather boots. Her lazy smile turned to a scowl for just a moment, and he saw her visibly struggle to regain the grin.

"That wasn't very nice."

"What are you doing here, Allegra?" Deacon didn't really care very much, as long as she went away.

She must have realized her seductive manner wasn't impressing him, and just like that, it changed. Now she was all cool and haughty indifference. "I like to walk. I walk a lot. I didn't know you lived on Dippold Avenue."

Somehow he doubted that. Her manner and dress suggested she'd taken this route on purpose, and if there was one thing he remembered about Lisa's sister, it was that she didn't do things by accident. If Allegra did something, it was with intent, and usually one that solely benefited her. "So go walk."

"What was it like?" Allegra asked abruptly. All pretense of seduction had vanished. Her eyes glittered with unconcealed interest.

"What was what like?" Deacon spoke against his better judgment. Dealing with Allegra was like picking up snakes. You never knew when one was going to turn around and bite.

"Jail," Allegra cooed. Incredibly, she licked her full mouth, so like her sister's in shape, but cruel instead of kind. Kissing that mouth would be kissing poison.

He turned to go back inside the house without even saying goodbye.

"Deacon!"

He ignored her, and headed for the back porch.

"Don't you walk away from me," Allegra called after him. "Don't you ignore me!"

He couldn't keep the smile from his face at the sound of anger in her voice. Lisa's baby sister had been nothing but a thorn in his side from the first moment they'd met. So now he'd ticked her off? *Good.*

His mother stood in the living room, peering out through the sheer blue curtains to the driveway. "Deacon, who's that girl?"

"Nobody," Deacon said from the back porch door. He stashed his bucket of cleaning supplies under the bench and took his boots off. "Don't worry about it, Mom."

His mom shook her head, still looking. "She looks pretty mad."

Deacon chuckled at that. "I'm sure she is."

"She looks a little bit like that girl you used to go around with. What was her name?" Bertha let the curtain slip shut to turn and look at him.

"Lisa." Any good humor he'd felt at riling Allegra vanished. "That girl out there is her sister."

"Oh." His mom pursed her lips. Deacon could see the questions whirling in her mind, but he had no answers for them.

"I'm going to take a shower," he told her, to fend off the inquisition. "Gotta go to work."

Bertha nodded, still watching him thoughtfully. Deacon kissed her cheek. "Don't worry about it, Mom."

She flapped her hands at him. "Go on. Take your shower."

Not even the steaming water could rinse away the feeling his meeting with Allegra had left with him. There was no way she'd just happened to be walking along his street, not by accident. It wasn't her style. *So why, then?* Why come to see him, and why come dressed to kill?

The phrase, as clichéd as it was, made a sudden chill sweep over him. That's exactly how she'd looked when he walked away. Like she was ready to kill.

*   *   *

The main office at The Garden Shadd was far more lushly appointed than the sad excuse for a workspace Lisa used. It was also a lot busier. Looking around at the bustle and hustle, Lisa was glad for the cramped office she called her own.

"Dad?" She called, winding her way through desks and boxes toward the door at the back that led to her father's private office. "Are you in there?"

"Where else would I be?" her dad asked with an exasperated sigh. "It's month end, Lisa. I'm chained to this desk until the figures work out."

She looked at her father fondly, noting the way his deep blue eyes sparkled even as he complained. "You love month end and you know it."

Doug Shadd leaned back in his chair with a grin and laced his fingers behind his head. Though he'd reached retirement age just the year before, he looked as fit and vigorous as Lisa's older brother Brian, who'd just turned forty. Doug's head of thick blond hair was only just beginning to glint silver in bright sunlight, and the wrinkles around his eyes and bracketing his jaw were clearly laugh lines more than signs of age.

"What's up in the marketing department?" As if he didn't know.

Lisa briefly ran down the list of coupons and promotions The Garden Shadd would be running for the next few months. She ticked off the weekly coupon clipper magazine, the radio spots and the newspaper inserts, then stopped. Dad was still grinning.

"Why are you really here?" he asked finally. He knew her too well.

She decided to get right to the point. "I have a favor to ask."

"Anything, my darling daughter. Name it."

"I'd like you to hire Deacon Campbell."

Doug's grin faded rapidly and he set his chair down on all four legs with a thump. "Why on earth would I do that?"

Lisa moved closer to perch on the edge of his desk. "Just listen to me—"

"The man's a criminal," Doug said in the no-nonsense tone Lisa dreaded. "You, of all people, should know that."

"And I, of all people, helped him get that way!" She slid fingers along the desk's smooth, curved edge.

Her dad sighed. "He made himself what he is. You just helped to see justice served. You saw the surveillance tapes. It was Campbell. You testified to the fact."

"And my testimony sent a man to jail for three years." Lisa didn't mention that her statements had cost her endless sleepless nights fraught with guilt and anxiety.

Yes, she'd seen the video tapes that showed Deacon Campbell entering The Circle K convenience store, and the scenes in which a helmeted man helped himself to the contents of the cash register setting off the alarm. She'd sworn under oath that the man in the tape was the same man she'd ridden with on the back of his motorcycle to the Circle K. Her eyes had told her it was Deacon, but her mind and her heart had never been convinced.

"You want me to hire him?" Doug asked. "After what he put you through? You're lucky you weren't charged as an accessory to the crime!"

Just because she'd been there with him, waiting in the parking lot. Lisa knew she'd gotten off lightly, and that in other circumstances her innocence could have been smeared as easily as a thumb rubbing fresh ink. But she hadn't been charged and hadn't gone to trial. She hadn't gone to jail.

"Dad, please," she said. "Deacon has a wonderful talent. He's got a way with plants and design that would be a great asset to The Garden Shadd. You know if all of that hadn't happened, you'd have been happy to have him on staff."

"But all of that—" Doug waved his hands in perfect mimicry of her gesture. "—did happen. Honey, I know you were sweet on the guy—"

"That has nothing to do with it," Lisa protested hotly.

Her dad frowned. "But I can't hire a man convicted of robbery and assault. What would my customers think?"

"Most of them wouldn't even know," Lisa said. "He'd be in the creative design department. You wouldn't have to send him out on site."

"St. Mary's is a big small town," Doug told her. "Everybody knows everything that goes on around here."

"He's got to get a job somewhere," Lisa said stubbornly, not sure why she was fighting so hard for this. Unless it was a way to assuage her guilt? A way to...to see him again? "Now he's waiting tables down at the Evergreen. Why not have him work here, where we can benefit?"

At that, her dad let out an incredulous laugh. "Benefit from a man who tried to rob The Circle K for two hundred bucks?"

"He's served his time." Lisa rubbed the smooth edge of the desk again, knowing the nervous gesture wasn't helping her case. "Aren't we supposed to help him rehabilitate or something?"

"This is important to you, isn't it?"

She nodded, relieved for once that her dad could read her mind without her having to speak aloud. Doug sighed, louder this time and drummed the desk with his fingers. She could tell by his down-turned mouth that he didn't want to give in to her plea.

"I feel like him going to jail was all my fault," she said quietly. "And I'd like to help him out somehow."

"It's not your fault the man's a crook, Lisa."

Silently, she met her father's gaze without wavering. Doug sighed, still tapping the top of his desk with his fingers. Lisa waited, knowing she had no better argument to give.

Doug groaned, then shook his finger at her. "I'm holding you responsible, Lisa! If anything goes missing..."

"It won't." Lisa slipped off the desk and went around it to give her father a hug. "You won't regret this, Dad. I promise."

"And I want to install a surveillance video in his office. Just to be sure."

"Okay," Lisa said, glad the battle was won.

"I'm just an old pushover."

"Pushover, yes," Lisa teased. "But old? Never!"

"Now you're just trying to flatter me. Get out of here. I'll call Deacon Campbell and tell him you've convinced me to offer him a job."

"No!" The word rang out in the small room, embarrassing her with its unexpected vehemence. "I mean, no, Dad, don't. I'd rather you didn't tell Deacon I had anything to do with you hiring him."

Her dad just looked at her with upraised eyebrows, but he shrugged. "And you think he won't figure it out?" He continued before she could answer. "Okay, I won't say anything about you."

Lisa gave him another squeeze and went back out into the main office again. As she picked her way through the chaos and back toward her tiny but tidy broom closet/office, she thought about the night her life had turned upside down.

Lisa and Deacon had only dated for three months before the decision to stop at The Circle K had changed both of their lives forever. In that short time, she'd thought she'd grown to know the man with the bad boy exterior and talent for making things bloom. Apparently, she'd been wrong. Even now her face flushed hot at the memory of why they'd pulled into the convenience store parking lot instead of heading on back to his place.

"Are you sure?" he'd asked her seriously, twisting around on his motorcycle so he could look at her. The harsh fluorescent light from the store etched his handsome face in shades of black and white. The helmet he now held in his hands had mussed his dark hair.

She'd nodded, not trusting herself to speak. Deacon took her hand in his, brought it to his lips, kissed it. The gesture had sent a white hot bolt of fire down to her belly.

"I can drop you off at the door, give you a peck on the cheek—"

"Stop." She leaned forward swiftly and kissed him hard on the mouth. His tongue dipped between her lips gently, and she sat back on the motorcycle's narrow seat. "Go."

She had not made the decision to make love with him lightly. Nor, she'd thought at the time, had he. Every date had led them to greater intimacy. Their chaste goodnight kisses on her porch had led to passionate embraces on his sofa, and it was only a matter of time before she wouldn't be able to keep from giving in to what her body demanded every time he held her in his arms.

He'd gone inside the mini-mart, helmet in hand, to buy what she didn't normally keep in her purse—condoms. He'd come out in handcuffs. The next time she'd seen him had been in court.

Lisa stopped abruptly, her hand on the door to her office. She couldn't go back to work. *Not today.* Just remembering that last kiss had made her heart start pounding. Her palms felt slick, and a small coil of fire had lit itself in her abdomen again. She shook her head, knowing it was useless to force herself back in front of the computer.

"I'm going to run this copy to the printer and stop at the newspaper," she called into the main office. Nobody would stop her. Running the copy was a chore she did regularly.

Once behind the wheel of her car, she stopped the trembling of her hands by gripping the steering wheel. She caught sight of her eyes in the rearview mirror, and didn't like their wild look. She took a moment to breath deeply, then smoothed her hair and moistened her lips with the stick of balm in her purse. Another few deep breaths and she was fine.

Fine except that no matter how she tried, she couldn't forget about Deacon Campbell's kisses.

*   *   *

What stupid, masochistic inclination had prompted him to take Doug Shadd's offer to work at The Garden Shadd? Deacon asked himself the question one more time as he parked the Road King in an employee spot and lifted off his helmet. He knew Lisa's family owned the nursery. He'd been pretty sure he'd never be hired there because of his past with her. That was why he hadn't bothered applying there, even though he had the credentials. When Doug Shadd called him last night after dinner and offered him a job, Deacon had been too surprised to say anything but yes.

Deacon needed a job. He wanted to work with the ground, growing things and helping people realize their dreams of the perfect yard or garden. Working at The Garden Shadd would let him do that. It was the largest nursery and garden shop in the area. Why should he turn down an offer of work, just because the owner's daughter had sent him to jail for a crime he hadn't committed?

Deacon secured his saddlebags, tightened his belt, and hooked his fingers through the helmet. He might see Lisa today or he might not. He'd better prepare himself. If he had one consolation, it was that his presence at the nursery would be as uncomfortable for her as it would be for him. Like some weird sort of revenge.

Except that now, with one work boot poised on the edge of the concrete steps leading to the greenhouse, Deacon knew he didn't want to get back at her. He just wanted to see her. He wanted to ask her why she hadn't had enough faith in him to see beneath the helmet on the man robbing The Circle K. Why she hadn't returned his letters. Why she'd never, not once, visited him.

"You must be Deacon," said the short plump woman potting marigolds at the long trestle table just inside the greenhouse door. She held out her hand, streaked orange and lined with dirt. He took it. "I'm Jamie. Doug told me to look for you today."

He looked over the pots of flowers. "Do you want me to start here?"

Jamie laughed, her double chin jiggling. "This is stuff anyone can do. No, you're going to be in the design department today. They're having the monthly meeting to go over the client list and stuff."

He'd expected to be put to work doing the most menial jobs, and now they were waiting for him to join their meeting? He looked down at his faded and torn jeans and flannel shirt, the scuffed work boots. "I should've dressed up."

Jamie laughed again. "You'd have been the only one. It's through that door there, down the hall and make your first left. They've taken over the lunch room today."

"Thanks." Deacon already liked Jamie, whose plump cheeks seemed made for smiling.

He followed her directions past a row of office doors. One opened just as he passed, and he nearly collided with the woman coming out.

"You!" Allegra's handful of papers fluttered to the ground.

"Hello, Allegra," Deacon said in resignation. He'd anticipated running into Lisa here. It hadn't occurred to him that Allegra might also have started working at the family business.

Her pretty mouth curled in a sneer. "You're heading the wrong way. The safe is in the main office. But you probably know that already, don't you?"

It took all his willpower to not react, but it was worth it to see how his lack of reaction antagonized her. Allegra jerked her head toward the papers on the floor. "Pick those up."

Deacon did not like being told what to do. He stepped over the papers and continued down the hall. Behind him, he heard Allegra mumbling. He expected his quick glance back to show her fumbling with the papers and sending him black looks. What he saw instead made him pause.

Lisa's sister knelt in front of the scattered pile, fists clenched. She rocked slowly as she muttered, then touched one of the papers with one finger. She jerked back as if burned. Still muttering, she touched another paper, then another, faster and faster until finally she'd touched every paper in quick succession.

He must have made some soft sound of surprise at her actions because her head flew up. Her eyes, bright but unfocused, cleared rapidly and turned to a glare so fierce it made him physically take a step back. Allegra scooped the papers into her arms, crumpling them, and went back into her office. She slammed the door.

Deacon had no time to wonder what all that had been about. The scene left him uneasy, though, and as he walked toward the lunchroom door, he recalled what Lisa used to say about her sister.

"A little nuts," he said under his breath. "Yeah, that's a good description."

He stopped just outside the lunchroom door to brace himself for what awaited him.

"...late," Deacon heard a man say.

"What do you expect?" Said another, and though he didn't finish the statement, Deacon knew what he meant. *What do you expect...from a criminal?*

For a moment, Deacon seriously considered just turning around and walking away. He'd find work someplace else. He didn't have to work here, where at any moment he could come face to face with Lisa. Where every day he'd be working with people who'd already written him off before they even bothered to give him a chance.

Bertha Campbell hadn't raised any quitters. Deacon might be considered the black sheep of the family because of his supposed wild ways and the trouble he'd gotten into, but he wasn't a quitter. Doug Shadd had offered him this job for a reason, and Deacon was going to make certain he proved he was worth hiring.

He stepped through the door, clearing his throat. He already knew Doug, but the man sitting next to him at the long lunch table looked enough like him Deacon guessed it must be a son. He knew Lisa had three brothers and two sisters, and he knew only two of the brothers worked at The Garden Shadd. One of them was still in high school, which left only one choice. If only he could remember the guy's name...

"Good morning, Doug...Kevin," Deacon said, making a guess. The faint look of surprise on Kevin's face proved he'd guessed right.

Deacon held out his hand and both men stood to shake it.

"Have a seat," Doug offered. "We're just about to get started."

Deacon pulled out one of the hard plastic chairs and sat down, wondering if he should have brought a pen and some paper. Both men had thick date books and pages of notes in front of them. They stared at him, equal expressions of assessment on their faces.

"I'd like to thank you for hiring me." Deacon figured it couldn't hurt to be honest. He was at a disadvantage with them, and he knew it, but it didn't sour his mouth to say nice things with it.

"Don't thank me." Doug waved his hand. "Thank…"

"Sorry I'm late!"

And there she was. Lisa, her honey-colored hair swept back today in a sleek roll at the nape of her neck. When he'd known her, she'd always worn it loose around her shoulders. Instinctively, Deacon got to his feet just as Lisa turned and saw he was there.

Her face paled instantly. She dropped the handful of papers she'd been holding, and they scattered on the floor. She bent to retrieve them, the serviceable gray skirt she wore riding up her thighs in a way Deacon fought not to notice.

Kevin bent down to help her, laughing at her clumsiness. "I swear, Lis, you're all thumbs."

The brotherly teasing sent red circles flaring in her pale cheeks. Lisa scowled at him, yanking the papers from his hands and slapping them on the table. Kevin, still chuckling, raised his hands as if to ward off her blows, and took his seat again.

When Deacon was able to tear his eyes away from her, he saw Doug watching him. The man didn't look pleased, and could Deacon blame him? If he had a daughter, and some man was looking at her the way Deacon had been… Yeah, he guessed he could see why the old man might be mad.

"Sorry," Lisa said a little breathlessly. "I wasn't expecting… I mean…" She stopped to clear her throat, awkward silence hanging in the air like the unpleasant odor of burnt bread.

"It's all right." This was probably a mistake. Obviously nobody had told Lisa he was going to be working here. From the nervous way she plucked at her papers and avoided his eyes, he could tell she wasn't too thrilled with the surprise either. "Maybe I should just go."

"No," Lisa cried at the same time her father said the same word.

With a bemused look at his frazzled daughter, Doug said it again. "No, Deacon. You're part of the team now. I took the opportunity to look over your resume and portfolio yesterday afternoon, and I'm really impressed. I think you're going to bring a lot to this meeting today. We have some new clients I think you're going to be perfect for."

Deacon sat again. So did Lisa. Now her papers were straight, he thought she might risk a glance at him. Still nothing. She was acting like he was going to leap across the table and bite her, for crying out loud!

"Let's get started," Doug said.

As they discussed the regular clients' needs and went over the list of potential new business, Deacon warmed to the work. Self-confident by nature, he jumped right in with his opinions and ideas for many of the land plots shown in the photographs Doug and Kevin presented. It occurred to him at first that he might be expected to sit back and listen, but after both of the other men nodded and agreed with his thoughts, Deacon relaxed. Doug had said he was impressed with Deacon's work, despite it being three years out of date. Maybe working here wouldn't be so bad after all.

Except for Lisa. Throughout the entire meeting she'd spoken in a monotone and studiously avoided looking at him while passing around the sheets of upcoming promotions. When his hand had accidentally brushed against hers, she'd jerked away so suddenly it was like he'd burned her.

The meeting ended and Lisa excused herself quickly. Kevin followed her, his backward glance at Deacon just short of hostile. Deacon waited stiffly as Doug gathered his reports, not sure what he was supposed to do next.

"Let me show you your workspace," Doug offered. "Since neither Kevin nor Lisa seems to be available."

Deacon followed the older man through a series of short hallways and out into the greenhouse again, then among the rows of lush foliage to another door. It led to a spacious potting shed, well-lit and comfortable, with an architect's table in one corner. One set of shelves held office supplies and another gardening gloves and tools.

"Nice," Deacon commented, looking around.

Doug handed him the pictures and notes from the meeting. "I'll leave you to get started. If you need anything, just ask someone."

Just like that, the older man left. Deacon stood in amazed silence, then shook his head with a grin. He hated having someone hanging over his shoulder, watching his every move, telling him what to do. This freedom was an unexpected bonus, and one he wasn't sure what to think of.

It felt good to not be under suspicion. He'd had enough of that to last a lifetime. He actually felt like whistling as he flipped through his first assignment, landscaping for a fried chicken and ice cream joint on the far side of town. It wasn't until he got up to sharpen his pencil at the wall sharpener that he noticed the small glass covered opening in the wall. Hidden as it was behind the shelves, and completely nondescript, most people wouldn't have even noticed it. For Deacon, though, who'd spent the past three years under the watchful glare of dozens of such glass eyes, he knew right away what it was.

A surveillance camera. Apparently they didn't trust him after all.

CHAPTER 3

Lisa bent to scratch behind Tabby's ears and let the fat orange cat rub against her legs. The cat loved when Lisa wore nylons, and would rub itself all over the slippery fabric until its fur stood up in great, bushy spikes. Usually Lisa tried to keep Tabby from underfoot, but tonight the animal's simple affection was just what she needed.

"Oh, Tabby," Lisa sighed aloud. "What have I done?"

How could she have forgotten Deacon would be at the meeting? Dad told her he'd called and offered Deacon the job, and that he'd be starting today. But when she'd walked into the lunch room for the design meeting and seen him... Well, they were all just lucky she hadn't lost her lunch in the lunch room.

He hadn't changed much. Some silver threads had woven themselves into the thick darkness of his hair, which he now wore trimmed short instead of in silky lengths to his shoulders. The lines around his eyes had deepened, but the deep brown eyes themselves and the black brows, smooth and shaped liked crow's wings, were still the same. He was thinner than she'd remembered beneath the bulky flannel shirt and blue jeans.

But he was still Deacon.

At last Lisa nudged the cat away and shucked the pantyhose, now covered in cat fur, from her legs. "Yuck!" She tossed them directly into the kitchen trash, pulled a can of tomato juice from the refrigerator, and headed upstairs for a hot bath.

Before she could even start the water, the phone rang. With a groan,

Lisa flopped down on her bed and yanked the hand set from the cradle. "Hello?"

"So?" Allegra's voice trilled through the phone line. "No movie tonight?"

"I got a message from Terry on the machine," Lisa said dryly, knowing her sister would already have listened. "He had to work late. Where are you?"

The background shrieking told Lisa the answer before Allegra spoke. "Kevin's."

Lisa made a mental note to thank her brother. "Watching the kids?"

Allegra snorted into the phone. "As if. I'm getting ready to come home."

Lisa groaned silently. After coming home to the empty house, she'd been looking forward to an evening curled up on the sofa watching an old movie on TV. "Great."

"Kevin said you looked like you were going to puke today at the meeting."

Lisa gritted her teeth. "Kevin doesn't know everything."

"Dad said he liked Deacon's ideas, but that he still wouldn't trust him with the cashbox."

Now Lisa let out a garbled sound of aggravation. "Let's not talk about it, okay?"

"Don't get your panties in a twist," Allegra said. "I'll be home in an hour. Get dressed. We're going out."

Lisa sighed, rubbing her eyes. The bed was so soft, the covers thick and inviting. She had just put on fresh sheets, and her favorite pajamas were clean and scented from the dryer this morning. She had the remote control all ready.

"No."

Allegra snorted. "I'll be home by seven-thirty."

"I said no," Lisa cried into the phone.

"Wear something sexy," Allegra said blithely.

The buzz of the dial tone came next, and Lisa slammed the phone back into the cradle in frustration. *Something sexy?* That meant Allegra wanted to go over to Dubois and hit one of the bigger bars. Lisa was not in the mood for a thirty-minute drive just to sit around listening to throbbing dance music and fending off drunken college guys' advances.

She just wouldn't go, that was all. She looked at the alarm clock. Six-thirty. She'd take her bath, then maybe order a hoagie from Vito's for dinner.

Even as she ran the water, she knew it was no use. Allegra would show up at seven-thirty, always prompt when it was something she wanted to do and invariably always late when it was something she didn't. Though three years younger than Lisa, Allegra knew how to bully her older sister into doing what she wanted. Unless Lisa just wasn't home when Allegra showed up, they'd both be going to Dubois.

That was it! Lisa sat up in the slippery claw foot bathtub, bubbles and water sloshing over the side. She wouldn't be here! Allegra wouldn't hang around to wait for her, and she could be home by nine p.m. But where to go to wait out her little sister's arrival?

Instead of a hoagie from Vito's, she thought she might treat herself to a better dinner. The Evergreen had good specials on Friday nights, with live music that didn't make her head pound. She'd be able to get a nice, quiet table and eat her dinner, then head home in time to slip into her fresh, clean jammies under her fresh, clean covers, and go to sleep.

That eating dinner alone and going to bed early sounded like a lonely and sad way to spend a Friday evening did not escape her. Lisa sank back beneath the scented bubbles, trying not to frown. If Terry hadn't called off their date, they'd have spent the night like they usually did. Dinner and a movie, followed by a passionless kiss at the doorstep.

It also did not escape her that the three months she'd spent with Deacon had been more intense, more exciting, than the past three months she'd had with Terrence. Just the thought of Deacon made her stomach tighten in the hot water. Her eyes flew open, but it was too late. His face had already filled her mind. Lisa groaned and slapped at the water.

"Damn," she said aloud, in a tone that made fat Tabby turn her tufted ears in Lisa's direction. "What was I thinking?"

Urging her father to hire Deacon had seemed like such a good idea yesterday. The Garden Shadd would benefit from Deacon's expertise, and she would have expiated some of her guilt by helping him get a job. Her guilt. The problem was, she could barely look at the man without remembering their last night together, and the promise of lovemaking never fulfilled.

She groaned again and slipped completely beneath the water. It was quieter under there, so quiet she could hear the pounding of her own heart in her ears. Too bad she just couldn't stay under there forever, like returning to the womb.

The water caressed her everywhere, its touch as gentle as a lover's.

Gentle as Deacon's hands would have been had they made love that night three years ago. Sputtering, Lisa shot out of the water. Wouldn't anything keep her from thinking about it?

She toweled off quickly, grateful for the chilly breeze sweeping in the open window. She needed some cooling down, all right. What on earth was wrong with her? She was acting like a jittery old maid.

Which wasn't so far off the mark, she thought morosely. She slipped into a comfortable denim skirt and her favorite cotton pullover. Lisa finished dressing and ran a comb through her wet hair, glad she'd been letting it grow so it was easier to put up. A swipe of pressed powder and a slick of lipstick and she was ready to go, but she still stared at her reflection critically.

She'd turn twenty-six in a few months, and what did she have to show for it? She still worked in her family's business, lived just a few blocks away from her parents, and wasn't married. Her boyfriend was more friend than lover, and the one man she'd thought she loved was back in town after getting out of jail.

Damn. She was thinking about him again.

*   *   *

Deacon's white shirt was too tight at the neck, and the black string tie strangled him even further. Even his black pants hugged his waist too snugly for comfort, but it wasn't worth complaining about. Tom Lee would just tell him to go out and buy his own uniform instead of using the one The Evergreen provided. Since Deacon wanted to keep his job at The Evergreen until he was sure The Garden Shadd was going to work out, he'd make do.

It was a whole different world on the other side of the bar, he reflected as he watched Danny the bartender mix his drink order. Deacon had spent plenty of evenings down at the Evergreen, but always as a patron. Now that he was the one in the monkey suit dealing with slow kitchen staff and impatient customers, he had greater sympathy for wait staff everywhere.

"Kitchen backed up again?" Danny topped off the mug of Straub's and handed it to Deacon.

"All night." Deacon took the glass and put it on the ridiculously tiny tray Tom insisted they use instead of just carrying the glasses like normal human beings. "We're out of stuffed mushrooms and the lobster special is almost gone, too. It's only seven-thirty."

Danny laughed. "Gonna be a long night. Glad I'm behind the bar tonight and not waiting tables."

There were lots of dissatisfied customers, and all of them seemed to be in Deacon's section. He'd only been waiting tables for a week, and was still getting used to the elaborate system Tom Lee insisted his wait staff use. Lee thought flourishes and furbelows would add class to his kitchen's adequate but not outstanding food.

Didn't he know The Evergreen was pretty much the only game in town? Unless you wanted to take your date to The Golden Corral or Fred's Chicken and Cream, the only other choices were fast food places and a couple of pizza and hoagie joints. The Evergreen was considered a "nice" restaurant only because it had white tablecloths and matching china on the tables.

"Waiter, excuse me." A portly man waved his fork at Deacon. "My fork is dirty."

"I'll get you another one right away." Deacon thought about adding a bow and a scrape, but decided the man and his equally rotund wife wouldn't appreciate his attempt at humor.

With that potential disaster thwarted, he headed back to the kitchen to see what was holding up the rest of his orders. Before he could get there, the Evergreen's hostess, Nancy, stopped him.

"I had to put another one in your section," she said apologetically. "She's in number 23."

Deacon didn't complain. It wasn't Nancy's fault. "I'll take care of it right away."

The Evergreen's huge, multi-page menu hid everything about the woman sitting at the table except for her hands. Deacon got out his notepad and pen, pausing just long enough to smooth back his hair. "Can I start you off with something to drink?"

"Yes, I'd like a—" The woman stopped when she dropped her menu, clearly as stunned to see him as he was her. It was Lisa. "What are you doing here?"

Her question was pretty silly since she'd seen him there before. "I work here."

"But I thought you worked at—" She stopped again, as though at a loss for words.

He'd help her out a little. "I work there, too."

She nodded quickly, switching her eyes away from his. The creamy skin at the base of her throat began to flush a dull crimson visible even in The Evergreen's dim lighting.

"A drink?" Deacon asked coldly. Her reaction to him was irritating and embarrassing. What did she think he was going to do to her? She was the one who'd effectively sent him behind bars. If anyone should be upset, it should be him.

"Coke, please," she whispered.

He left the table and headed back toward the bar to get the drink. When he returned, she looked a little calmer. Then he noticed the shredded remains of a paper napkin scattered on the table. He'd had enough.

"Lisa."

She jumped. She actually jumped. Deacon frowned, looking around the restaurant to make sure nobody else was paying attention to them.

"Maybe I should switch tables with Rhonda," he said.

"No." Lisa ventured a look at him. "I'm all right."

"Do you know what you'd like to have?" He asked formally. She told him quickly, and he wrote it all down. "All right. I'll go put your order in."

"Thank you," she called after him.

She'd spoken a little too loudly, making most of the heads in that section of the dining room turn to stare at her. Then at him, which he wouldn't have minded except for the whispering that followed it. So much for anonymity. Not in this small town.

The kitchen seemed to be catching up on things, which meant Lisa's salad was ready in just a few minutes. Steeling himself for another round of awkward silence interspersed with stammering and blushing, he took it over to her table. She surprised him by speaking to him calmly.

"Deacon," she began hesitantly. "I'm sorry."

The salad bowl clattered to the table, making heads turn again. "For what?"

"For acting like such an idiot," she said. "Today in the meeting, and just now… I was being stupid. I'm sorry."

It had been too much to expect she'd apologize here, now, for being the reason he'd spent the past three years as part of a jail work crew. Did she think that just saying sorry would make things all right? Three years didn't erase so easily.

"Is there anything else I can bring you?" He asked as though she had said nothing.

She said his name again, lower this time. For the first time she met his gaze steadfastly, without twitching or turning away. "I *am* sorry."

The words hung in the air between them like smoke. "Can I get you anything else?"

She looked down at the salad without much interest in her eyes. "No, thanks."

Her apology rang in his ears as he checked his other tables. Extra napkins, refills on beverages, scraping crumbs off the tables between the entrée and dessert. All these things took up his actions, but not his attention.

She was sorry? That was it? She announced to him in the middle of a public place, while he was working, no less, that she was sorry? What was he supposed to do? Just…forgive her?

That's exactly what she expected, he thought, pouring coffee as bitter as his feelings. *That would make it a lot easier for her, wouldn't it?* Especially since her father had decided to hire him at the family business—something he was sure she didn't like.

He'd had three years to think about seeing her again, to think about what he'd say and do. How he'd demand answers to all the questions he had about them and the time they'd spent together. Three years was a long time to dwell on things like that. Too long to let it all go just from hearing two little words.

*   *   *

The dinner she'd looked forward to as a treat sat in her stomach like a pile of rocks. Lisa pushed away the slice of pumpkin pie—her favorite—that Deacon had brought her. She hadn't been able to enjoy it. Tonight, the sweet orange pie tasted sour.

"If you're finished, I can take the check." Deacon's voice was cold, his manner stiff. Now he was the one who wouldn't meet her eyes.

"Sure, yes." She fumbled in her purse for her wallet, and pulled out her credit card. She offered it to him without thinking, then realized she had enough cash in her wallet to cover the bill. "No, wait. I don't want you to take the card."

His lips thinned and his fingers tightened on the bill, crumpling it. She suddenly realized how she'd sounded. Afraid to let him take her credit card like he was some sort of thief who couldn't be trusted. That wasn't what she'd meant at all, but it was too late to change. Explaining would only make things worse.

She took the thin plastic card and handed him two twenty-dollar bills. "I don't need any change."

Again, the way his mouth turned down and his eyes sparked, she knew she'd made another mistake.

"That's nearly a forty percent tip," Deacon said.

"I want you to have it."

Without another word, he turned, and took the money and the check. Lisa sat back, wanting to kick herself. The young couple at the table next to hers was staring again. She smiled at them and nodded, and they whispered to each other. She knew they were talking about Deacon, and probably her, too.

She made a quick visit to the women's room to wash her hands from the sticky pumpkin pie. When she got back to the table, she saw her money sitting there. Nearly thirty dollars of it which meant he hadn't taken any tip at all. Lisa sighed. Had she thought she could bribe him into forgiving her?

"Excuse me," she said to Nancy, who'd been in Lisa's graduating class from ECC High School. "Can you tell me where Deacon Campbell went?"

Nancy gave her a quick look of curiosity as she ran one lacquered nail down a list at the hostess' podium. "Um...well, it says here he had the early shift tonight. He's probably gone by now."

"Darn," Lisa muttered. "Thanks, Nance."

"Sure," Nancy said. "Have a good night!"

Lisa doubted that would be possible. She tucked her purse under her arm and pulled on her light jacket, then headed out in to the chill, dark parking lot. The revving sound of a motorcycle caught her attention immediately, and she searched the lot for what she hoped would be Deacon and his Harley.

The man on the big motorcycle was just pulling onto the street. She called Deacon's name, waved her purse and ran a few foolish steps toward him. It was too late. He pulled out of the lot, the bike roaring like an animal, then she saw nothing but the red blink of his taillight as he stopped at the intersection's stop sign.

"Shite and double shite," Lisa said, using the Irish obscenity as an afterthought. She'd picked it up during her summer internship on the Emerald Isle, and nothing else seemed to quite fit the situation.

She looked at her watch, noting the time was later than she'd planned to be out. There was nothing more to do but go home. She certainly wasn't going to run after him, even though the bike was still within shouting distance. *No.* Whatever she had to say to him, and she wasn't quite sure what that was, would have to wait for a better time.

She was just stepping up to her car when the masked man stepped out of the shadows and demanded her purse. "Don't move!"

Lisa wasn't about to. Her heart had frozen in her chest mid-thump. She held out the bag, a fifty-cent throwaway she'd picked up at The

Resale Shop. Whatever she had in it wasn't worth dying for.

The man, face covered by a rubber mask that looked like Bill Clinton, took a step toward her. "Drop it!"

She did as she was told, not wanting to antagonize him. His height marked him as an adult, but his voice was little more than that of a scared kid. A teenager. He stepped closer to the bag, nudging it with his toe. She'd supposed her attacker would pick up the purse and run, but he reached out and grabbed her wrist.

"Take..." His voice squeaked and broke. "Take off your panties!"

"What?" The demand shocked her into protesting. "No way!"

He shot his head from side to side nervously. Lisa had parked along the back edge of the lot near the row of evergreen trees that gave the restaurant its name. From the rustling among them, she thought the young man in front of her wasn't alone.

Now her heart unfroze, pounding a desperate rhythm of fear in her chest. A few red spots danced in her vision, and she realized she was holding her breath. *Don't faint! Don't panic!*

"I need your panties," Bill-Clinton-mask said with another quick jerk of his head toward the tree row. His fingers twisted on her wrist, and she yelped. He might be young, but he was stronger than she was. "Right now or else!"

She didn't want to ask or else what. Lisa craned her head to see if by some miracle someone, anyone, was leaving the restaurant. There was no help there. Through the windows, she could see a set of diners enjoying their meals, but it was light inside and dark out here. None of them, even if they happened to look, would see what was happening.

"Okay," she said slowly, leaning away from him as far as she could with his hold still on her wrist. At least it didn't appear he had any sort of weapon. "Just a minute."

"I don't have a minute," cried Bill-Clinton-mask in a high, strangled voice.

To Lisa, he sounded like he was on the verge of fainting himself. The trees rustled again and three black-garbed figures, faces covered with similar rubber masks, emerged.

Whatever sense of calm relief she'd felt at noticing he was unarmed fled immediately at the sight of the three dark bodies surrounding her. Bill-Clinton-mask still held her in his vise-like grip, and though she felt the chill clamminess of his fingers sliding on her skin, he was still holding too tightly for her to hope she could slip free.

"Hurry up, bro," spoke the figure in a Jimmy Carter mask. His voice was lower and his body thicker, but Lisa sensed he was no more a man than Bill-Clinton-mask. None of them were. She was going to be attacked and raped by a bunch of high school boys!

"Give him your panties," said Richard-Nixon-mask. "Hurry up!"

"Ah, dude, this is going all wrong!" Ronald Reagan, mask askew, barked. "He was just supposed to grab the purse and ask for the panties…"

"I'm not giving up now." Clinton-mask ground his fingers tighter around her wrist, pulling her off balance. "Give me your panties before I take them myself!"

"Dude," chastised Reagan-mask. His eyes through the holes in the mask were wide and rolling. "That's not the way we said it should go down!"

"I don't care!" Clinton-mask shook her, dragging Lisa forward a stumbling step. "Give 'em!"

"Okay, all right," Lisa said soothingly. She recognized the sound of panic in the young man's voice. If she gave him what he wanted, maybe they'd all just go away. It sounded like none of them really wanted to hurt her. "You can have them."

Clinton-mask let out a shrill, hysterical giggle. If he dropped her wrist, Lisa was prepared to run as fast as she could to The Evergreen's safety, but he didn't let go. Awkwardly, she lifted the edge of her skirt with her free hand, and hooked her thumb around the waistband of her underwear.

"Oh, man," cried Clinton-mask in unmistakable excitement.

The other president-masks all shifted on their feet, watching the restaurant and urging Clinton-mask to hurry. Lisa wriggled the underpants down to one thigh, but could go no further with her hand still imprisoned by Clinton's grasp.

"I can't get them any further," she said, hoping they'd just run away and leave her alone.

Clinton-mask shoved her to the ground. The fall knocked the breath out of her, making it impossible to see what the other three president-masks were doing. She could only pray they weren't preparing to jump on top of her. Clinton-mask grappled with her long denim skirt, tearing at the plain white cotton briefs she wore.

Beneath the mask, his breath came in harsh, whistling gasps. His eyes, when they met hers through the eye holes, were staring and wild. His fingers were cold on her skin.

"Bro, let's get outta here!" Carter-mask this time.

Nixon-mask grabbed Clinton-mask by the shoulders and tried to pull him off. "Dude, you're out of control! C'mon!"

"She said to get a purse and panties, and I'm gonna get 'em," grunted Clinton-mask, still struggling to pull Lisa's panties down. With a final yank that left her bare bottom crunching gravel, he tore the white undergarment completely off her.

She was thankful for the darkness and the length of her skirt that shielded her from his view. As it was, he held up the torn piece material like a knight holding up the Holy Grail. His laughter was what finally set her off. Robbing her and assaulting her was one thing, but finding amusement in her distress was unthinkable.

Lisa kicked him as hard as she could in the groin. The blow vibrated all the way up her leg, and she could only imagine how it felt to Clinton-mask. The young man let out a garbled wheeze and what would have been a scream, if the pain had let him make any noise at all.

Clinton-mask fell onto into the gravel, his buddies making commiserating sounds of pain as they tried to help him up. Lisa rolled to her feet, ready to run. A roaring growl filled the night, close to her face, and she fell back.

Deacon's Harley spun the grit and stones, spattering her face. Lisa threw up her hands to shield her face and stood. The heavy folds of her skirt fell back down around her ankles.

Clinton-mask was still writhing on the ground, but the other president-masks were no longer trying to help him up. Deacon punched the kick stand down on his bike and leapt off it. His red helmet glinted like fire in the orange parking lot lights. With the face shield down and his leather-gloved fists raised menacingly, he didn't look human. He looked like some sort of alien warlord, a cyborg. An avenging angel.

The president-masks fled before him like fluff blown from a dandelion. Clinton-mask, spying the threatening form bearing down on him, somehow managed to find the strength to fight the pain from his bruised groin. He got to his feet in a flash, tripped and went down to his knees in the gravel. Yelping, he pushed to his feet again and flew into the tree row. The sounds of branches slapping flesh and cries of pain and terror echoed through the night.

"Are you all right?" Deacon knelt beside her, his arm around her. He yanked the helmet from his head. He smelled like pumpkin pie.

Lisa caught sight of her watch, stunned to realize that less than ten minutes had passed since she'd stepped out into the parking lot. She nodded, not trusting herself to speak. Deacon's arm on her shoulder was blessedly warm. Suddenly she felt chilled.

"Hey, what's going on out here?"

Lisa saw a tall, strongly built man racing toward them. His face in the orange light was grimly focused. His fists were clenched.

"Get your hands off her," he commanded Deacon.

"Hey, man, no problem," Deacon said smoothly, squeezing Lisa's shoulder. "I was just trying to help."

"Step away from her, mister, unless you want trouble," Lisa's would-be protector said. "I saw what was going on! You were trying to rape this woman!"

Deacon sighed heavily, but he dropped his arm away from her. "You've got it wrong."

"Back off!" The man turned to her. "Are you all right, miss?"

"I'm fine." Her voice didn't sound as shaky as she'd feared it might. She looked toward Deacon. "And he was trying to help me. A bunch of high school boys attacked me, not Deacon."

"You know him?" The man still looked suspiciously at Deacon.

Seeing Deacon's rumpled dark hair, his leather chaps over faded jeans, and the denim vest bespangled with the Harley-Davidson logo, Lisa guessed how a stranger might mistake him for someone who might be up to no good. Hadn't she, who thought she knew him, discovered his bad-boy exterior matched his internal character all too well? But not in this case. This time, he'd come to her rescue.

"Yes, I know him," Lisa said firmly. "But thanks for your concern."

"I saw a scuffle out here," the man said doubtfully, still giving Deacon an evil look. "I heard some screams as I was coming out of the vestibule. I saw this man grabbing you...."

"It's all right, really," Lisa assured him. "They ran off into the trees."

She looked down at the ground. "They didn't even get my purse." She didn't mention the other object Clinton-mask had demanded. The mortification was too much.

"My wife's called the police," the man said.

"Great," Deacon muttered.

"Great," Lisa echoed. Now that everything was passed, the last thing she wanted to do was spend the evening telling the local cops how an adolescent boy had tried to steal her purse and her underwear.

"If you're sure you're all right," offered the man hesitantly. He looked back and forth from her to Deacon, his brow creased in concern. "My wife's waiting for me over there."

"Sure, go on," Lisa said. "And thank you so much."

The man didn't seem to want to go, but he did, casting a hard look over his shoulder at Deacon. Then they were alone, the two of them, and his stare made a different sort of chill run down her spine.

"Thank you," she said. "If you hadn't come back —"

"You looked like you were handling it pretty good on your own."

"Why did you come back?"

His gaze pierced her and made her knees week. "I heard you call after me. I was going to keep driving home. Then I changed my mind."

He'd been coming back to talk to her. Lisa's heart thudded a little, but pleasantly. He'd actually turned around to come back for her. Now he opened his mouth as if to speak, and she wanted him to. It didn't matter what the words might be—accusation, confession, or explanation. All that mattered was that he was going to talk to her.

All at once the red-blue, red-blue of the police car lights lit up the parking lot and turned the orange from the overhead lights to alternating bands of fire and sickly purple. Deacon bit back whatever he'd been about to say, his full mouth closing abruptly. A pang of disappointment filled her stomach.

Deacon bent down and picked up two things from the ground. "You might want these."

He pressed her purse and the shredded remains of her white cotton panties into her hand.

CHAPTER 4

"So let's go over this one more time," said Officer Hewitt. Though he spoke to Lisa, his sharp gaze didn't waver from Deacon's face. "You were attacked by four men wearing rubber masks."

"Reagan, Nixon, Clinton and Carter masks," Lisa replied. "Terry, I told you all this already."

Deacon knew the cop was up to something. He just didn't know what. They'd been at the station for hours, far longer than should have been necessary for Lisa to tell her story and sign the essential papers. He didn't like the way the other officers milled around the desk, looking at him. Like he'd committed a crime.

"And they took your purse and your…" Deacon was pleased to see Hewitt falter. "Your underwear."

"They tried to." Lisa was beginning to sound aggravated, and no wonder. Hewitt was questioning her like she'd pushed herself down in the gravel. "I told you before. Only one of them actually assaulted me. The others just watched. I got the feeling they'd been put up to it somehow."

Hewitt cast another piercing glance at Deacon. "Uh-huh."

Lisa sighed impatiently. "Terry, I think they were just kids. They didn't hurt me really."

The cop was looking at her with raised eyebrows. "Honey, they pushed you down in the parking lot! Your hands are all scraped up. What do you mean they didn't hurt you?"

Lisa's cheeks flushed. In a low voice, she answered, "I mean they didn't hurt me, Terry. I'm okay."

"Are you saying you don't want us to pursue this?" Hewitt sat back in his seat, frowning.

"No," Lisa said hastily. "I just... I think they were just doing it for a dare or something."

"Robbery and assault isn't something to be taken lightly," Hewitt told her sternly. Lisa looked chastened. "If we find these young men, you can be sure they'll be facing criminal charges."

"And jail time?" she asked weakly, with another quick look at Deacon.

So that was what this was about? She was worried about sending somebody else to jail? Deacon frowned at her, aware that every move he made was under the scrutiny of half a dozen officers. She hadn't seemed to care so much when it had been him up on the stand, even when he'd protested his innocence. She hadn't believed him.

"Yes, Lisa." Hewitt looked at Deacon.

Right then, Deacon knew something was up. They were going to try and pin something on him, just because he had a record. He watched the cop's eyes flicker behind him, giving some sort of silent signal to his co-workers.

Hewitt's smile didn't meet his eyes. "You can go now. We'll let you know."

Lisa got to her feet and clutched the beaded handbag. It was a little worse for the wear after landing in the dirt. She leaned awkwardly across the desk, allowing Hewitt to kiss her cheek.

"Call me later," she said quietly.

Deacon got up from his seat when she did, knowing even as he did so what would come next.

"Not you, Campbell," said Hewitt. "We still need to talk to you."

Deacon glared at the cop, but there wasn't much he could do about it. They were going to grill him like a burger on the Fourth of July. Lisa, however, looked confused.

"Why are you keeping him?" She asked. "I told you everything about what happened already. Deacon was helping me."

"This doesn't concern you, babe," Hewitt said. "Go on along home."

If he thought Lisa was one to be put off with a patronizing comment, Deacon thought with real pleasure, the cop had sorely misjudged her. Lisa didn't move. She stared down the cop, bringing a flush to his face.

"Please don't call me babe," she said coldly. "And don't patronize me, Terry. This certainly does involve me."

"But... Lisa, just go on home. I'll call you later. Let me do my job." Hewitt seemed shaken by her resolve.

Lisa raised her eyebrow at him and put her hands on her hips. "And does your job include harassing innocent people?"

Hewitt sneered. "Innocent? I guess we'll see, won't we?"

"Terry—" Lisa began, a warning in her voice, but Deacon cut her off.

"You can go," Deacon told her, returning to his seat. He didn't really want her to see him get laid out on the platter. Not again.

"No." She shook her head, the stubborn woman. "If this involves what happened to me tonight, I have a right to know about it."

"Once a thief, always a thief." Hewitt said to Lisa, but again looked at Deacon.

"I was convicted of robbing a convenience store." There was no use in Deacon proclaiming his innocence again. "You want to tell me how that translates into stealing ladies' purses and their scanties in dark parking lots?"

"And I already told you, it wasn't Deacon at all," Lisa cried, her voice frustrated. "There were four people. Deacon came up on his motorcycle. He wasn't one of them, I'd swear to it."

"We're not suggesting that Mr. Campbell here actually was one of the offenders," Officer Hewitt said smoothly. "But he is a suspect."

"Why?" Lisa cried indignantly.

Deacon was as surprised at her vehement defense of him as the cop was. In fact, Lisa seemed surprised herself. She glared across the desk at Hewitt, then flicked Deacon an expression he couldn't identify.

"Your testimony sent Campbell to jail three years ago."

"Yes." Lisa lifted her chin but didn't look at Deacon. "So?"

"He has a prior record," Hewitt pointed out. "And a motive."

"Motive?" Now Lisa was on her feet, leaning over the desk and waving her finger right in the cop's face. "A motive to steal my underwear, for God's sake? Terry, what the hell's the matter with you?"

Her outburst had the whole station looking in at them. Hewitt's thinned lips and set jaw showed he didn't like that—not one bit. Didn't like the little woman acting up, Deacon thought, with a flash of insight into Hewitt's character. This pointing of fingers had more to do with Deacon's romantic past than with his criminal record. Hewitt was jealous, and Deacon smiled at the thought.

"He thinks that because your account at the trial was what put me in jail, I might have a reason to want revenge." Deacon met Hewitt's angry glare steadily, his smile never wavering. Let the cop say what he wanted, he couldn't pin this on Deacon.

And if Terry he kept insisting, it seemed he was going to find himself driving a wedge between himself and Lisa, which would be quite all right with Deacon.

"That's ridiculous," Lisa snapped, but a moment later he saw by her look that though the thought hadn't occurred to her, it made sense.

Officer Hewitt sat back in his chair with a smug grin. "Mr. Campbell is exactly right. How astute."

"But Deacon came back to help me," Lisa said softly.

"What better way to prove my innocence?" Deacon said. The game was on. Hewitt liked to play apparently.

"Right again."

Lisa sighed, looking very tired all of a sudden. Brown smudges shadowed her gray eyes. She rolled her neck on her shoulders as though to get the kinks out.

"You have no proof," she said finally.

"We still have some questions we'd like him to answer," said the cop.

"Then I retract my statement."

Deacon and Hewitt both spoke at the same time. "What?"

"I'm withdrawing my statement," Lisa said. "I don't want this investigation to go any farther. I won't press charges."

"Are you insane?" Deacon sputtered. The woman had gone crazy.

Hewitt might have wanted to ask her the same thing, but he'd managed to restrain himself. "We can't do that, babe."

Lisa's reply was a growl. "Watch me. Babe." The last word was a snarl, not an endearment. It seemed to sting Hewitt.

Deacon had almost forgotten how hard-headed Lisa could be when she wanted something. Lisa slung the strap of her handbag over her shoulder. She flapped the papers Hewitt had given her and tore them in half quickly, then dumped the scraps in the trash.

"You're nuts," Deacon told her, even as something stirred inside him. Was this her crazy way of assuaging her guilt? What had changed her mind about his character that she'd be so willing to take this stand for him?

Hewitt frowned. "You're being unreasonable."

"Deacon didn't have anything to do with what happened tonight," Lisa said firmly.

"You of all people shouldn't be so certain of this man's innocence in anything." Hewitt scowled and crossed his arms.

"Frankly, I'm tired of being told what I should or should not be certain about." Lisa slipped her arms into her lightweight black jacket and slung her purse back over her shoulder. "I'm retracting my statement. You have no reason to keep Deacon here. I'm leaving now. Good night."

"Wait," Hewitt called after her, and she turned. "Lisa, don't go off mad."

"You haven't left me much choice, Terry," Lisa said, and swept out of the office.

Now the two men stared each other down from across the desk. Deacon stood, expecting Hewitt to tell him to sit back down. The cop didn't say anything, though, just watched him.

"You can't tell her what to do," Deacon told Hewitt almost apologetically. The guy was a self-righteous blow-hard with an ax to grind, but Deacon still felt a little sorry for him. He'd been on the receiving end of Lisa's will once or twice, and he knew how hard she could hit.

"Don't tell me how to treat my girlfriend," Hewitt retorted, his mouth twisting.

Okay, so they'd never be friends. Deacon shrugged. "Just some advice, man. Lisa doesn't like being told what to do."

"And you're an expert on Lisa?" Hewitt said in a low voice.

"No." He'd never claim that.

"Get out of here," Hewitt said, dismissing him.

Deacon was all too happy to leave. After the close air of the station, the fresh night breeze was a sweet perfume. He gulped it greedily, then headed over to his motorcycle. As he unbuckled his helmet and prepared to pull it on his head, her voice stopped him. She called his name, then appeared from the dark. She'd been waiting for him.

"Didn't you learn your lesson about hanging around dark parking lots?" he asked gruffly, not sure he wanted to hear her reasons for waiting.

She laughed, a sound he'd imagined often in the past three years. "I think a police station parking lot would be pretty safe, don't you?"

"What do you want, Lisa?"

The bluntness of his question seemed to shock her. Her smile faltered, the good-humored laughter fading away until the night air was once more silent around them. Finally, she cleared her throat and held out her hands to him.

"I wanted to thank you again."

"You're welcome," Deacon said. "I'll see you at work on Monday."

"Yes." But she didn't go, just stood there staring at him with those damned lovely eyes.

"Do you want me to wait while you get in your car?"

She shook her head. "Deacon, what were you coming back for?"

"To talk to you," he said. "To hear why you were calling after me."

She nodded as though his simple explanation made sense. "What would you have said?"

"I would've asked you," Deacon said, "why you did what you did."

She had the grace to look away, and the sense not to ask him what he meant. "I'd have asked you the same thing."

"The questions might have been the same, but the answers wouldn't have." He slid the helmet on and flipped up the dark face shield.

"You know I had to tell the truth," she countered.

"So did I." He swung his leg over the bike.

"But we both said different things!"

"Then one of us," he replied as he started the engine, "was wrong."

*   *   *

Every light in the house blazed as Lisa pulled into the driveway. She rested her head on the steering wheel, mentally gathering her strength before going into the house. Allegra was home, and by the looks of things, she wasn't happy.

Sighing, Lisa got out of the car and went to the kitchen door. It was almost too much. She was bone weary, and her palms and rear ached from her tumble into the gravel. Did she have the strength to deal with Al now? And did she have a choice?

The answer to became clear as she stepped into the tiny kitchen. Allegra waited at the kitchen table, a burning cigarette in her hand and an ashtray full of dead butts on the table. Lisa hung her jacket on the coat tree, waiting for the tirade.

"Where...have...you...been?" Each word, sharp as a knife, was punctuated by the clicking of Allegra's jaw as she bit them out.

"At the police station," Lisa said.

"With him."

"Terry was there, yes." For some reason, Lisa was reluctant to tell Allegra the truth about her evening.

"Ter-Bear." Allegra sneered. "So, what'd you two do? File? Eat donuts?"

"I'm going to bed." Lisa got up from the table and headed for the door to the hallway. Allegra reached out as she passed, snagging Lisa's arm.

"I waited for you all night."

Lisa pulled out of her sister's grasp. "You shouldn't have."

Allegra's laugh was harsh. She stubbed out the cigarette and bent to the plate of pie in front of her. Without another word, she shoveled the dessert into her mouth, spilling fruit and pastry out of her mouth and down the front of her shirt. Pie wasn't the first stain on her clothes. Ice cream from the empty gallon container on the table also marked the fabric, and ketchup, and some other things Lisa didn't recognize.

"Al, stop it right now," Lisa snapped. She jerked the pie plate away from her sister and tossed it in the sink, not caring if it broke. "I'm not in the mood!"

"I came home and you weren't here," Allegra cried through her mouthful of food.

Lisa pointed to the notepad by the yellow wall phone. "I left you a note."

Her sister swiped her mouth with the back of her hand and got up from the table. As she pulled open the refrigerator door, Lisa saw Allegra wore a short, leather skirt. No stockings. Her feet were bare with expertly painted crimson toenails. Allegra yanked the carton of milk from the door and began gulping the contents. Milk splattered on her and on the floor.

"Enough!" As Lisa snatched the carton from her sister, she slid a little in the puddle. She shoved the carton back in the fridge. "Go to bed, Allegra!"

"You weren't here when I got home," Allegra said. "And...the...house...was...dark!"

Lisa felt like crying. She took her sister by the arm and pushed her down into her chair. "I left the light on in here for you. I left you a note. And don't tell me you waited for me here, Allegra, because I can tell by the way you're dressed that you went out anyway."

A sly smile painted itself across Allegra's face. "You missed a really great time, Lisa."

"Clean yourself up, and clean this place up," Lisa said coldly. "I mean it, Allegra."

Allegra whined, a nasty, creeping noise that rose the hair on Lisa's neck. "Why didn't you wait for me, Lisa?"

"I didn't want to go out to some bar and watch you get drunk and flirt," Lisa said bluntly.

Allegra frowned. "You could've asked me out to dinner, too. You just didn't want to be with me."

That was true, but Lisa knew better than to say so. "Go to bed."

Allegra surveyed the mess in front of her. "Oh, God, I ate all this? I ate all this? I ate all this?"

Lisa watched her sister's throat work, and disgust rose in her. "Dammit, Allegra, if you're going to puke, do it in the bathroom!"

Allegra slammed the table with her hand, making the ashtray jump. "Why are you always so mean to me?"

Lisa began to count to ten inside her head. She could have turned and walked away up the stairs to her bedroom, but that would not have stopped Allegra's outburst. Now she counted. She continued on to twenty before she felt calm enough to reply.

"You are my sister and I love you," she said. "But we've been over this and over this, Allegra. I have a life. I have to have a life, Al!"

Allegra's look of scorn cut Lisa so deeply she felt like she might be the one to get sick. "With Terry? Oh, please. I've seen you get more excited about a new pair of shoes."

Her sister hit close to the mark, but Lisa wasn't about to admit it. "What do you have against Terry?"

"You deserve better," Allegra muttered. She lit another cigarette, but as usual, didn't smoke it. Allegra never smoked them, just burned them.

Lisa had heard that before. "That's for me to decide."

"I'm going to bed," Allegra said, as though Lisa's comment wasn't worth answering.

Even though that was all Lisa wanted—to sink into her bed and go to sleep—Allegra's casual response infuriated her. "I'm not cleaning up your mess this time. You made it. You clean it."

Allegra looked stunned. Then her eyes narrowed. "I'll do it tomorrow."

Lisa knew her sister well enough to know that wouldn't happen. The mess on the table and sink would begin to draw flies before Allegra would take care of it. "Do it now."

"You can't tell me what to do," Allegra said.

Lisa squared her shoulders. "You spoiled, little brat. I'm tired of cleaning up after you! When you moved in here, we agreed you'd do your share. I expect you to start doing it!"

It was like watching a movie in fast forward. One minute Allegra was scowling, her face dark with fury, and in the next second she was wreathed in smiles. "Sure. Okay. You're right."

Lisa, who'd been prepared to go to battle, felt herself deflate in the face of Allegra's sudden good humor. "Thank you."

"Boy," Allegra joked as she began clearing the trash from the table. "Getting knocked on your ass really put you in a bad mood."

It wasn't until she was slipping into her cozy sheets that Lisa realized something strange. How had Allegra known about the mugging? Lisa hadn't told her.

*   *   *

Deacon had every intention of quitting Monday morning. He went to Doug Shadd's office, knocked on the door, and went inside when Doug invited him to. He even opened his mouth to explain he appreciated the job offer, but he'd be unable to continue.

Twenty minutes later, he left Doug's office with a thick file of notes, site photos and budget requirements for a new town project. As he walked down the hall toward the doors leading outside to the greenhouse, he couldn't help smiling ruefully. Now he knew where Lisa got her stubborn will.

Doug hadn't given him a minute to list his reasons for quitting. In a way, Deacon was glad for the older man's take-charge attitude. Without this job, he'd never be able to move back out on his own. He didn't want to work at the Evergreen forever.

Leaving St. Mary's wouldn't be the worst thing in the world. He'd done it before during his brief stint in college and for internships at some of the larger horticultural facilities in the state. Hershey, with its chocolate-scented air and bushes shaped to spell the name of the factory, had been nice. So had working in Lancaster for Longwood Gardens. He'd particularly enjoyed the water gardens there.

But nothing beat coming back home to the mountains.

Allegra waited for him outside his office door. Today, instead of black leather, she wore a blue-and-white checked dress that looked like it came straight out of a 1950's tv sitcom. She even had a string of pearls looped around her neck. The dress might be a vintage resale shop find, but those pearls weren't costume jewelry. Allegra toyed with the strand as though enticing him to comment on the necklace's beauty. Deacon didn't.

"Good morning, Allegra," he said politely, and tried to brush past her into the office.

"So, you and Lisa are going to be working on the new Memorial Park children's garden. Should be fun." Allegra leaned back against the doorframe, blocking his entrance.

Lisa? Deacon's smile turned to a frown as he thought of Doug's good-natured insistence he take this particular project. He hadn't mentioned Lisa when giving it to Deacon.

As if sensing his distress, Allegra gave him a commiserating smile. "It won't be that bad."

She was up to something. He just didn't know what. "Why would it be bad?"

Allegra's look was knowing. "Don't play dumb with me, Deacon. Or maybe you're not playing."

He ignored her jibe about his intelligence. "I need to get into my office."

"I'm just surprised you can stand to look at her after what she did to you," Allegra said blithely, as though she hadn't heard him. "I'd never send my boyfriend to jail. My sister's just too honest for her own good. She always has to do what she thinks is...right."

"I know."

What should have been a compliment became an insult with Allegra's sneer. She shook her head, as though she just couldn't believe Lisa's stupidity. Deacon physically pushed past her, and Allegra laughed as she stepped out of his way.

After he shut the door, Deacon thought about Allegra's words. Lisa had to do what she thought was right. It was something he admired about her, something he liked. Until, of course, her honest nature had sent him to jail.

But could he blame her? He'd seen the surveillance tapes. If he hadn't known he was in the bathroom while the real criminal stole his helmet and committed the crime, Deacon would have thought himself guilty, too. There was no denying the similarity in build, dress and demeanor between him and the real perp—not to mention the guy was wearing his cycle helmet. Deacon knew Lisa really believed him to be the man on the tapes who helped himself to the cash register. What he didn't understand was how she could have believed her eyes and not her heart?

There was no use dwelling on the past. Their relationship was long over and cold in the ground. He should just let it stay dead.

Deacon nonchalantly hung his denim work shirt over the camera lens. *Let them try and see through that!* Then he spread out the file's contents carefully.

The project, an expansion of the already spacious Memorial Park recreation area, called for a special children's garden. Kid-friendly plantings like sunflowers, marigolds, corn and pumpkins were to be interspersed with a series of flowers chosen specifically to bloom all season long. The city council had also outlined plans for a water garden section. Deacon's job was to choose the sorts of plants that would work in the setting, design a pond and waterfall, the paths, benches and specialty areas. He settled into his chair and lost himself in the work.

*   *   *

A knock on the door coincided with his growling stomach and he realized it was lunch time. "Come in."

"Looks like we'll be working together." Lisa paused in the doorway, looking fresh in white slacks and a light denim shirt. Again, she had her hair pulled up. He wondered what she'd do if he reached out and tugged it down to tumble around her shoulders.

"Yeah." There was more he could say, but small talk didn't appeal to him.

"I wanted to make sure you were okay with that."

"Why wouldn't I be?" He got up from his desk, stiff from the hours of sitting. His back crackled and popped as he stretched, and so did his neck. "I'm just about ready to head out for lunch."

"May I join you?"

He hadn't expected that. Deacon gave Lisa a hard look. "Why?"

"Because I'm hungry, too."

He shrugged. "All right."

He didn't ask her where she wanted to go, but she followed him out through the greenhouse and into the back parking lot.

"Do you want to follow me?" He asked pointing at his bike.

"Let's ride together."

For a moment, he thought she meant on the Harley. In a flash, his mind recalled the way she felt straddling the cycle behind him, her arms tucked firmly around his waist, her cheek pressed against his back. She'd always laughed when riding, saying the wind tickled her.

Then he saw she meant for him to go in her car, and he realized she was waiting for an answer. He wanted nothing more than to be on his motorcycle in the warm summer sunshine, feeling the wind on his face, but he nodded instead. Something about Lisa always had him saying yes.

"What are you hungry for?" Lisa was a careful driver, eyes on the road, hands planted firmly on the wheel. It occurred to him suddenly that he'd never driven with her before. They'd always gone on his bike.

"Fried chicken," he said, because all at once that was all he could think about. "Biscuits, slaw, the works."

She laughed lightly, but her humor sounded strained. "Okay." She hesitated. "I thought we'd go over to the park and check out the site. We can eat there."

For a minute he'd thought she wanted to talk to him about the things that had happened. "Sounds good."

She swung through the drive-thru window at Fred's Chicken and Cream and picked up a bucket of the fresh, delicious fried chicken and all the sides. Deacon's stomach rumbled as he held the grease-spotted paper bucket. In the past three months since he'd been home, it seemed that he craved spicy, flavorful food. Jail food had provided his body's basic needs, but nothing more.

In just a few minutes, they arrived at Memorial Park. Today, with the sun shining, the playground teemed with hordes of children running and jumping along the huge castle play structure. Lisa parked in the lot and helped him gather up the bags of food.

"It's going to be over here." She pointed past the pool and beyond one of the baseball diamonds. "It's going to replace that old field, which will be rebuilt on the other side of the park."

Some trees shaded one of the benches away from the hustle and bustle of the playground. Deacon sat down on one end and Lisa at the other. They spread the food between them, opened paper napkins, popped the tabs on soft drinks. The cole slaw and potato salad were perfectly tangy and the biscuits as flaky and buttery as he'd dreamed. The chicken, under its crispy exterior, practically melted in his mouth. The food was so good it wiped nearly every other thought from his mind.

"I didn't bring you here just to see the site," Lisa said quietly. She hadn't even taken a bite. "I wanted to talk to you about what happened that night."

Here it was—his chance to ask her why. Deacon looked at her clear gray eyes, at her honey hair, at the way her full mouth pursed with trepidation. All at once, he wasn't sure he wanted to ask her anything at all.

CHAPTER 5

Lisa came straight to the point. "Why did you do it?"

Deacon carefully set down the handful of biscuit and chicken, then wiped his fingers on his jeans. "I didn't."

Had she really expected a different answer? "I saw you," Lisa said in a low voice.

"You saw someone." Deacon began wrapping the food. "If that's all you have to say, I think I'm done."

Lisa didn't want it to be done. She reached out her hand, desperate to talk to him, to figure out why he'd done what he did. To learn why, even now, he continued to lie.

"Deacon, if it wasn't you, who was it?"

He didn't pull his hand away—not at first. Then he removed his fingers from her grip and wiped them again on his jeans. Like her touch had made him dirty. The action made her want to cry.

"I don't know. Someone who lifted my helmet while I was in the bathroom."

"The police didn't find anyone else, and they were there within ten minutes," Lisa said. "They searched the whole place. They found the money in your pocket...."

"I wasn't wearing the jacket," Deacon said. "Or the helmet. I was washing my hands in the bathroom when they busted in and grabbed me. I know what you saw on the video, Lisa, and I can't explain it any more than you can. But it wasn't me."

"Why won't you stop lying?" she cried.

"Why won't you trust me?" he countered.

"Because I know what I saw," Lisa told him. She slurped at a soda to quench her dry throat, thought the sweet beverage made her feel slightly nauseous.

"I'm done," Deacon said, dismissing her. He stood, tossing a crumpled napkin onto the remains of his half-eaten lunch. "I'll meet you back at the office."

His story hadn't changed. He looked at her with a gaze gone stormy, but Lisa did not look away. She had to know.

"Was it all a lie then?" she asked quietly.

Her question stopped him from going. Deacon stood over her, fists clenched. She watched him physically force himself to relax. He flexed his fingers, and she saw he'd pressed half-moons into his palms from the strength of his grip.

"I can't say I've never lied in my life," Deacon said. His gaze pinned her like a bug on a piece of collector's velvet. "But I've never lied to you, Lisa. Not about that night. Not about anything."

Now she did cry, the tears hot and stinging in her throat. Burning drops slid down her cheeks, and she was helpless to stop them. His response was what she'd waited three years to hear, but even now, she couldn't believe him.

"You know what hurt the worst?" he asked her, almost hypothetically. "That you never even tried to find out why I'd do such a damn stupid thing. That you just took what you saw at face value without asking yourself if you really believed it could be me."

"I had no choice," she cried. "They asked me to make a statement, Deacon. I couldn't lie!"

"You never spoke to me after that night. You never called. You never came to see me. You never even wrote," Deacon told her. A casual observer might have missed the tremor in his voice, but to Lisa it was entirely too clear. "You just wrote me off like a bad investment."

His words stunned her. Lisa wiped her cheeks, shaking her head. "But...but I did! I did write you!"

His mouth twisted. "Now who's the liar? I never got any letters!"

"I sent you one letter," she said. "You didn't answer. I thought that was the end of things."

"I never got it."

"I sent it," she insisted. She could see he didn't believe her.

"Catch-22," Deacon said. "Seems neither one of us can trust the other."

"We had something once," Lisa said. "We almost had something wonderful."

"You think so?" Deacon raised his eyebrow at her. "Something so wonderful you were willing to send me to jail?"

"I wasn't willing!" Furiously, she began bundling the food into the containers. It gave her hands something to do to keep them from slapping his face. "For God's sake, Deacon, it tore me apart to do that to you!"

"Did it?" he asked so softly she almost missed it.

Lisa stopped fooling with the lunch and met his gaze. "Yes. It did."

"Sure it did," Deacon said. "Tore you up so much you ran right into the comforting arms of Officer Friendly. Tell me, Lisa, did he ask you out that night, or did he at least wait until they sent me away?"

"Terry and I have only been dating for three months," Lisa replied stiffly. "Not that it's any of your business."

"Not unless your boyfriend keeps trying to make me responsible for every crime that happens in St. Mary's," Deacon said.

"Terry is just doing his job." Lisa gathered the containers and shoved them haphazardly back inside the large paper sack. "It has nothing to do with me."

"No?" Deacon scoffed. "You don't think Officer Hewitt might be a little jealous? That might be why he's always breathing down my neck."

"Terry is a professional. And he doesn't have any reason to be jealous."

Deacon reached out, startling her, and grabbed her hand. Lisa dropped the sack of food. Deacon stepped closer to her as he tugged her toward him. They ended up nearly touching, her face tilted up to see his.

"Doesn't he?" Deacon whispered.

Lisa watched the slow, lazy flick of his tongue across his lips and shivered. "Terry doesn't know," she whispered.

"Doesn't know what?" Deacon's grip wasn't painful, but it was tight. If she tugged, he might let her go, but Lisa stayed where she was. "That we dated? Or that we were going back to my house to make love for the first time that night?"

"He doesn't know that." She could smell him, the light scent of soap and musk. Of sexual attraction. She felt her own tongue sweep her lips and was rewarded by the sight of his gaze riveted on her mouth. "I never told him. He knows we dated, yes, but he thinks it was just casual. That we only went out a few times. That...that I didn't like you very much."

"And is that true?" Deacon asked.

"No," Lisa replied.

"No?"

She wanted to answer him. Wanted to tell him the truth. She had never told him that she loved him. To tell him now, three years after her love had been snuffed out like a flame in the wind, would be foolish. More than foolish, idiotic. If she hadn't told him when she'd been willing to give him her body, why on earth would she do so now?

So, instead, she just repeated her answer. "No."

"And now?"

Thinking of Terry had broken the spell. Lisa pulled away and Deacon let her go. She bent to the soggy paper bag and tossed it into the trash pail.

"There is no now," she said. "Whatever we had ended three years ago. I need to get back to the office."

Without waiting to see if he'd join her, Lisa turned and went back to her car.

*   *   *

Having Lisa avoid him was worse than having her jump when he spoke to her, but having to watch her get pawed by that blue-suited monkey made Deacon want to puke. If turning around and walking the other way wouldn't have been so obvious, he'd have done it. Instead, he was stuck trying to squeeze past them into the tiny lunch room.

"Hey, Campbell," Hewitt said, with a grin the size of Montana. He draped his arm across Lisa's shoulders, rubbing the bare skin with his fingers.

"Terry," Deacon said with a nod. He headed for the pop machine, jingling the coins in his pocket. With any luck, they'd be gone by the time he finished microwaving his leftover meatloaf.

He heard the scrape of chairs on the linoleum floor. So much for them leaving. Deacon grabbed the can of pop out of the machine and popped the button on the microwave. He could put his plastic food container inside and manipulate all the buttons without turning around, but he couldn't stay facing the wall forever.

Since their last conversation at the park, the only communication he'd had with Lisa was through inter-office memo, email and an occasional voice mail message which she was always certain to leave after she knew he'd gone for the day. Three weeks was a long time for partners on a project to go without physically seeing each other, especially in a work area as close as The Garden Shadd. In fact, he wasn't quite certain how Lisa had managed it, except with perseverance and dogged stubbornness. She was deliberately avoiding him without compromising the project.

"Here, babe," he heard Hewitt say. Lisa murmured something in reply, and Terry laughed. "So? We'll ask him to join us."

Bastard. Deacon gritted his teeth, knowing Hewitt had it in for him. The microwave dinged and he pulled out the steaming meatloaf, then slipped in the small container of mashed potatoes. One more task to keep him busy while they talked about him behind his back. Of course, he could turn around and they could talk about him to his face, but that wasn't an attractive option.

For the past three weeks, he'd had a lot of time to think. Knowing Lisa was in the same building, even if he never saw her, meant a lot of his thinking was about her. It was a waste of time. She'd made her feelings, or lack of them, clear enough. Surprisingly, Deacon found accepting what they'd had was in the past also left him with one other feeling toward her–forgiveness.

"So, Campbell," Hewitt said, loudly enough Deacon couldn't pretend not to hear him even over the noisy microwave. "What's for lunch today?"

"Meatloaf," Deacon said, turning just enough to show the other man the container. "And mashed potatoes."

"Sounds great," Lisa's boyfriend said with false heartiness. "You must be quite a cook."

Deacon could see where this was going, all right. "My mom made it."

"Your mom?" Hewitt's voice sounded like he was trying not to laugh. "Oh, that's right. You still live at home."

Like he was some adolescent boy, Deacon thought, his annoyance growing. "Yeah. For now. Mom likes the company."

"Sure," Hewitt said.

At last the food was hot, and Deacon had no more excuses for not facing them. He gathered his lunch and headed for the door. Hewitt stopped him with an invitation.

"There's plenty of room here," Hewitt said, indicating the table. "I'm sure Lisa wouldn't mind sharing."

Lisa gave Hewitt a glare of such heat and magnitude Deacon was glad he wasn't on the receiving end of it. Hewitt, though, seemed too dense to know when he was treading on thin ice with her. Deacon hoped the man found the games he was playing with Deacon worth the price he'd have to pay with Lisa.

"Not at all," Lisa said, her eyes flashing. "Deacon, sit down."

It wasn't a request. It was a command. Deacon sat, bemused, his anger toward Hewitt turning into pity. The man had no clue. It didn't make watching him touch Lisa any easier to stomach, but at least Deacon might have the chance to see her cut the other man down. If she got angry enough, and if Terry kept picking at her, she was going to blow up.

Hewitt popped open a clear container of strawberries and laid them out on a paper plate. He picked one up and offered it to Lisa, who reached to take it. Hewitt shook his head and popped it into her mouth for her.

Lisa's cheeks turned nearly the same color as the fruit. "Thank you," she said in a strangled voice.

"How's the new project coming along?" Hewitt asked. "Lisa tells me the children's garden is going to be great. She says your designs are perfect."

Ah. So Hewitt is jealous. Deacon gave Lisa a glance, but she was concentrating on her salad. She'd said his designs were perfect? "Without Lisa's input, the garden wouldn't be half as good."

She looked up at him. "But it's Deacon's idea for the water garden and interactive fountain that'll really make it something spectacular."

Now Hewitt was looking from Deacon to Lisa and he didn't look happy. Apparently, Officer Friendly didn't like not being in control of the situation. "Yeah?"

"It's pretty amazing how much you can accomplish on paper," Deacon said. "Lisa's great about leaving a paper trail. Heck, I don't think I've actually seen her in three weeks, but she keeps coming up with fantastic ideas."

She had the good grace to blush again. "Sometimes it's easier for partners to work together if they're not breathing down each other's necks."

Deacon sat back in his chair. "Eventually what's on the paper has to go in the ground."

She forked her salad, but didn't bite it. "Then the project will be over, and we can put it in the past. We'll never have to think about it again."

"Are you kidding?" Deacon asked her. "We'll think about it every time we see it. It'll never be in the past."

"Once something is over, it's over," Lisa said firmly, stabbing at her lunch again.

Her boyfriend kept looking at her, then Deacon. He might not be the brightest crayon in the box when it came to Lisa's moods, Deacon thought, but he was smart enough to see the conversation was about more than just the children's garden. Terry's face darkened into a scowl.

"Just because something ended," Deacon said quietly, "doesn't mean you can't ever think about it again."

Her fork clattered against the side of her bowl. This time Lisa managed to get the food into her mouth. She chewed furiously.

"Sometimes thinking too much about the past means you don't spend enough time thinking about the future." Hewitt was good at sounding menacing, but Deacon wasn't scared.

Was the man talking to him or to Lisa? Lisa seemed to think the words were directed at her because she swallowed heavily. She took a drink before answering, a tactic even Deacon could see was meant to delay her reply.

"And sometimes," she said darkly, "people get so caught up with worrying about the future, they don't bother to appreciate the present!"

It was like being in an episode of *The Twilight Zone* or some French farce. Nobody was saying what they really meant, yet they were all talking about the same thing. The weirdness of it all made Deacon want to laugh.

"Yeah," he said around a mouthful of meatloaf. "Sometimes you have one of those projects that just feels right, you know? And other times, no matter how much you work at it, the damn thing won't come together."

Now Lisa and Hewitt both glared at him. The temperature in the lunch room seemed to rise a few degrees. Deacon just grinned.

"Sometimes you appreciate things more if you have to work harder at them," Hewitt's voice was ice.

Deacon couldn't stop the cocky grin from spreading across his face. "Sometimes. Myself, I prefer the easier way." He pinned Lisa with his gaze. "I like spreading the butter when it's already soft. Hard chunks of butter just tear up the bread. How about you, Lisa? Which way do you like it better?"

She put her fork down and wiped her mouth. "I don't use butter."

"Oh." Deacon shrugged. Then he clapped his hands against his knees. "Well, I guess I'd better get back to work. I'll look for your next email, Lisa. See you later, Terry."

He really did feel badly for the guy who obviously was in love with Lisa. Deacon knew that feeling. It made a man do crazy things. Like their entire conversation just now.

"Do...do you think you'll be working on a lot of projects when you're done with this one?" Hewitt asked, trying to sound casual and failing.

Deacon shrugged. "We make a good team."

His statement hung in the air like smoke. At least, the words made Hewitt cough like he'd inhaled a lungful of something foul. Deacon ignored him, watching Lisa. She set down her fork and nodded.

"Yes," she said. "We do."

Now Hewitt looked panicked and annoyed all at the same time. The game was slipping out of his hands. "Can't wait to see it finished," he said lamely.

"We should meet after lunch," Deacon told her. "To go over the rest of the plans."

Lisa nodded again. Her cheeks were still pink, but she smiled at him. "Yes. My office?"

Deacon gathered his food and drink and got up from the table. "I'll see you then."

He winked at Hewitt as he left.

*   *   *

Allegra twirled around on Lisa's chair. "Have a nice lunch?"

"It was fine, thank you." Even now, Lisa wasn't quite sure what had happened. One minute she was furious with Deacon for his underhanded, out-of-thin-air conversation; the next she was actually forgiving him. After adding Terry's none too subtle comments to the mix, and she felt a lot like she'd just been wacked on the head with a big piece of wood.

"How's Ter-Bear?"

"His name's Terry," Lisa said, in no mood for Allegra's cute games. "Or Terrence. Or Officer Hewitt."

"Is that what you call him when you're doing it?" Allegra asked with a snort that indicated she already knew the answer. "Does he whip out his handcuffs? Does he strip search you?"

"Do you have any sense of decency at all?" Lisa cried. "For God's sake, Allegra, that's none of your business! What is the matter with you?"

Allegra got out of Lisa's chair and minced over to the filing cabinet. "He's that bad in the sack, huh?"

"Allegra!" Lisa tossed her purse on top of the printer table and slid into her chair. Then she started to laugh. The chuckle turned into a full-out guffaw that had tears streaming from her eyes.

The truth was, she'd never been "in the sack" with Terry. The farthest they'd gone was a few listless kisses and some hand-holding. Terry was always a complete gentleman and that was something Lisa appreciated. Thus far, she'd found it easy to ignore the look he had sometimes at the end of their dates. The look that meant he was willing to go further if she was. She wasn't.

"You're a freak," Allegra said, though not unkindly. "A sex-starved freak."

"Oh, Al." Lisa wiped her eyes.

"I knew it!" Allegra banged her hand on the filing cabinet. "You and him are scrogging like monkeys! Admit it, Lisa. You and the Termeister have been getting it on. I can't believe you wouldn't tell me, your only sister!"

Lisa was laughing so hard she couldn't speak. Did Al really believe she and Terry were involved in a mad, passionate affair? On the rare occasions they were at Lisa's house, Allegra was invariably underfoot. When did she think they had time?

"I can't believe you," Allegra muttered, and Lisa saw her younger sister was truly upset.

"Oh, Al," she repeated, but the sound of a throat clearing from the doorway stopped her from saying more.

Deacon. She'd forgotten all about him. *How much of the conversation had he heard?* By the stony look on his face, Lisa guessed he'd heard enough. She quickly sobered. Now they both thought she and Terry were a pair of sex-crazed weasels. Why did Allegra thinking that make Lisa laugh, but Deacon thinking it made her want to deny it out loud?

"C'mon in." Incredibly, Allegra walked over to the door and kissed the air by both his cheeks. She made a face at Lisa over her shoulder, then left.

Deacon peered after her. "That was weird."

"My sister is weird," Lisa said.

Now they were back to being uncomfortable. It wouldn't help to tell him she and Terry weren't even having sex, much less doing it with handcuffs. And it wasn't any of his business anyway.

"I brought the latest design sketches and the plant suggestions," Deacon said finally. He set down a pile of papers on top of the printer table. "And I have them on disk."

Lisa pushed the smaller office chair toward him and he sat next to her in front of the computer. She could smell him. Not cologne. Her face heated as she thought about sex. Not with Terry. With Deacon.

"Let's take a look." She barely recognized her own voice.

"Should I just slip it in?"

Lisa nearly groaned. The disk, she told herself. He meant the damn disk! "Sure."

He did, and a few brief clicks of the mouse brought up the plans. She'd seen them before, but with Deacon sitting so close to her and thoughts of bodies intertwining filling her mind, Lisa couldn't concentrate on the project at all.

"I thought sunflowers would be great right here." Deacon leaned across her to point at the screen.

His elbow grazed the side of her breast and Lisa shivered. "Delicious! I mean, delightful."

He pulled away to look at her. "Are you all right?"

She could not go on like this. Lisa decided to plunge into the truth. "Not really."

His look of concern was incredibly genuine. "What's wrong?"

"Deacon," she began and couldn't continue. She sighed. "I'm not really sure what to say."

"Uh-huh." He sat back, looking suddenly and impossibly huge in the tiny chair.

"About lunch today," she said.

"Uh-huh?"

He wasn't making things any easier. Lisa took a deep, deep breath and blew it out making her bangs wave. "Were we talking about the same thing?"

"I don't know," Deacon said with a lazy grin that made her heart pound. "What were you talking about?"

As much as his flirting made her palms sweat, Lisa couldn't afford to keep getting swept away by unexpected erotic feelings. It was interfering with her job and her relationship, such as it was, with Terry. She and Deacon had to clear the air between them. Right now.

"Us," she answered him firmly.

Maybe he'd been expecting some more double talk because her frank answer seemed to set him back. "I thought there wasn't any us."

"There isn't any us," she corrected his tense. "But there was. And we can't keep pretending it didn't matter."

Deacon crossed his arms over his chest and fixed her with a look so stern it almost made her change her mind. "Did it?"

"Yes." Admitting it finally was like having an entire circus' worth of elephants lifted from her chest. "It meant very much to me."

Deacon glanced at the open office door and swung it most of the way closed. "Are you sure you want to talk about this, Lisa?"

She pushed her chair slowly back so it rolled farther away from him. She needed a clear head. "I have to talk about this. It's been eating away at me for three years."

He nodded slowly as though he understood. But he didn't speak. Lisa nearly froze again beneath the weight of his gaze, but she forced herself to continue.

"That night changed my entire life."

"No kidding," Deacon said wryly. "Mine, too."

She was relieved that instead of anger he was choosing to react with humor. "I wanted it to change my life. I was expecting it to change my life. I just thought, given the circumstances, it would be a change for the better and not for the worse."

"Your life seems pretty good," Deacon told her.

Lisa pinned him with a heavy gaze of her own. "I'm not complaining about my life. But I want you to know that the decisions I made three years ago were not made lightly. Not the decision to make love to you, and not the one to testify as I did either."

"I know." Deacon ran his hands through his hair, rumpling it.

"I can't take back that second choice," she continued. "I can't change the past three years. But I had to tell you that in all this time, I've never stopped wondering what that night would've been like."

"Me neither."

The admission hovered between them. Where would it go from here? The possibilities seemed endless.

"There's something else I've always wondered," Deacon said. "If you trusted me enough to go to bed with me, why couldn't you trust me enough to believe me when I said I wasn't the thief?"

She didn't know how to answer that. His question was valid. It was a question she'd asked herself a thousand times since that night. And she still had no answer.

"My eyes told me it was you," she said.

"And what about your heart?" he asked softly. He reached out and pressed his palm flat against her chest. The gesture was sexual in only the faintest and most distant of ways.

She started to protest, and he took his hand from her heart to place his fingers across her lips. "What about your heart, Lisa?" he asked her again.

Lisa stopped trying to think. She closed her eyes and just let herself feel. Three years ago, Deacon Campbell had been her first thought upon waking and her last upon going to bed at night.

What had happened that night at The Circle K?

"Maybe," she said, in a voice that sounded dreamy and far away. "Maybe it could have been someone else...."

The door to her office flew open with a bang. Startled, Lisa opened her eyes as violently as the door. Allegra fell into the room clutching at the doorknob.

"Were you eavesdropping?" Lisa got up from her chair. "Allegra, were you listening to us?"

It was a rare occasion when Al couldn't think of anything to say, but now all she did was open and close her mouth and stammer feeble excuses. Equally as rare were times when Al seemed to actually feel guilt for her outrageous behavior, but now thankfully seemed one of those times. Lisa was irate.

"What on earth is wrong with you?" she cried. "I've had enough, Al, I really have! Are you crazy?"

"Don't you call me that," Allegra said, finally pulling herself together.

"I think I'd better go." Deacon gathered his papers and files and moved past Allegra out the door. "Lisa, I'll talk to you later."

Damn. "Allegra Shadd, I could smack you right in the face," Lisa snapped when he'd gone.

Allegra set her jaw. "Go ahead!"

This was worthless and suddenly all too much. "I've got to get out of here," Lisa muttered, pushing Allegra aside. She grabbed for her purse atop the printer table, but it was gone. "Where's my purse?"

"Why don't you ask your jailbird boyfriend?" Allegra asked slyly.

"Don't be an idiot," Lisa said, but suspicion made her pause.

"Go on," Allegra urged. "Ask him. He was right there."

"Deacon didn't take my purse." A quick search of the office showed the bag was gone.

"Terry says once a thief always a thief," Allegra said in a sing-song voice.

"Since when do you care so much about what Terry says?" Lisa snapped. "Fine. I'll go down to Deacon's office. He doesn't have my purse."

The walk to Deacon's office didn't take more than three minutes, but Lisa found herself dragging her feet. The door was closed and she hesitated after raising her hand to knock. She would be insulting him just by asking if he had her purse. She couldn't do it.

Allegra didn't let her sister falter. She stepped up to the door and rapped soundly on it. Deacon's voice, muffled, came from inside.

"Come in!"

"Go on." Allegra shoved Lisa on the shoulder.

Lisa opened the door. She didn't want to do this. Allegra didn't bother letting Lisa speak either.

"We're looking for Lisa's purse," Allegra said boldly. "Did you take it?"

The wounded look Deacon gave Lisa was enough to make her turn around. "He doesn't have it, Al. Let's go."

"Wait," Allegra said. "Don't you even want to check? Just to be sure?"

"No," Lisa said.

"Go ahead," Deacon told her. "Check."

She shook her head. "No."

"Are you sure?" Deacon asked her. The answer she gave would mean more than just whether or not she wanted to check his office.

Lisa didn't hesitate this time. "Yes. I'm sure."

Allegra made a sound of disgust. "You're an idiot."

Lisa didn't care. Deacon's smile was warm enough to turn her insides to melted butter. Maybe, Lisa thought, she'd start eating butter, after all.

CHAPTER 6

What a difference a week could make. Deacon and Lisa had gone from being wary adversaries to laughing together over stupid jokes. Even now, he watched as she chuckled with one of their student interns about the antics of a popular television cartoon duo. Deacon lifted his face to the bright spring sun squinting against the glare. The heat felt good on his skin. He'd been feeling a lot of heat lately, and only some of it from the warmer weather.

He could fall in love with a woman who wasn't afraid to get her hands dirty. *More than dirty actually. Downright filthy.* He watched Lisa wipe her skin on the faded denim jeans she wore, admiring the way the action pulled the light blue cloth so tight against her....

"Rear?" Lisa asked.

Deacon snapped to attention, feeling like a little boy with his hand in the cookie jar. "What?"

Lisa gave him an odd look. "I asked if you wanted to start working on the rear."

Hell, yeah is what Deacon wanted to say, but he knew she meant the rear of the garden plot. Not hers. "Sure. Just let me grab a drink."

"It's roasting out here today." She met him at the truck and took the chilled bottle of water he handed her. "I can't believe it's only April."

Lisa raised the bottle to her forehead and rubbed it along her skin, then dropped the cold plastic down to the base of her throat. Deacon felt his own throat constrict at the sight. He'd been around plenty of women whose every action was planned to push a man's buttons.

Women like Allegra, for example. But Lisa did nothing more than breathe and he felt like a teenage boy again. A horny teenage boy.

"It's really coming together." Lisa nodded toward the work crew setting rows of perennial grasses along the brick path. "How's the pond?"

Deacon watched the movement of her throat as she swallowed, wanting to put his mouth on the tender skin there. "Almost ready for the fish."

Lisa smiled at him, completely oblivious to the affect she had on him. "We'll have this put to bed way before deadline."

Put to bed. The picture that phrase called to Deacon's mind was one he'd have to shove away, and quickly, if he wasn't going to embarrass himself. "Want to walk over and check it out with me?"

Lisa tilted her wrist, then scowled. "Damn, I keep forgetting I lost my watch. I'm meeting Terry at noon for lunch."

Would it be stupid and childish to lie to her about the time just so he could steal some of her time away from Terry? Of course. Was Deacon above being stupid and childish? When it came to Lisa, he didn't think so.

"You've got plenty of time," he said, though noon was only about ten minutes away. "C'mon. You can tell me which fountain head you like better."

The pond was only a short distance from the rest of the garden. Eventually, a stone path would connect the two spaces, but for now they trudged through dirt and clods of grass. The rough ground made walking tricky, and Deacon reached out a hand to steady Lisa when she kicked a rock out of the way.

"Oh, Deacon," she said, looking at the quietly churning expanse of water. "The kids are going to love this!"

He hoped so. It was his best work so far and Deacon was proud of it. He showed her the two types of heads for the pump—one would create a bell of water and one would make the water spurt up in a traditional fountain spray. "Which one?"

Lisa touched the bell fitting. "That one."

Installing it meant wading into the knee-high water. "I'll do it later."

Lisa tilted her wrist again, letting out another frustrated exclamation. "Damn!"

Even when he'd known her three years ago, she'd never been without a watch. Constantly checking the time was a habit of Lisa's, one that was almost obsessive and nearly unconscious. She'd check her watch in the middle of a sentence and continue without missing a beat. It used to bother him, like she always had someplace else to be, but seeing her without the familiar timepiece on her arm seemed strange.

"What happened to your watch?" He tried to lure her into conversation that would make her forget about meeting Terry. At least for a few more minutes.

She shrugged and looked annoyed. "I don't know. I always, always leave it on my dresser next to my birthstone ring. A few days ago, it was gone."

Over Lisa's shoulder he could see the Memorial Park parking lot. A shiny blue cruiser had just pulled in alongside The Garden Shadd truck, and a tall blond figure was stepping out. Terry. Deacon kept talking.

"Maybe you took it off someplace else."

Lisa shook her head. "I don't think so." She laughed a little uneasily. "Then again, I seem to be misplacing a lot of things lately. If I didn't know any better, I'd say someone was sneaking into my house and stealing...."

Her voice trailed off and she met his eyes. There it was again, that damned invisible wall he'd thought they'd torn down. Deacon smiled to show he didn't take offense even though the thought did get under his skin. Would the subject of theft forever be associated with him?

"I'm sure I'm just getting absent-minded in my old age." Lisa tried to joke. "I mean, the stuff that's missing doesn't have any value to it."

Deacon flicked his glance over her shoulder again. Hewitt hadn't yet spotted them, but it would only be a matter of time. "What kind of stuff?"

Lisa ducked her head with an embarrassed smile. "Oh, just...things. Some laundry. A hairbrush. My favorite lipstick. I'm sure they'll turn up."

"Sure," Deacon agreed, still watching Hewitt.

Lisa turned and saw Terry who still hadn't seen them. "Oh, shoot, I think I'm late. I've got to go."

"I'll walk back with you."

It must be a real thorn in Terry's side to know how much time they were spending with each other, Deacon thought with a nasty smile as he followed her. Not that any of the time he spent with Lisa was anything more than business, of course, but as the project got further underway, they had been spending more time on the job. He wasn't complaining.

Lisa's foot caught a clump of earth and she started to trip. Instantly, Deacon's arm flew out to catch her before she could fall. Instead, Lisa stumbled against him with a soft, startled, "oh!" He could smell the lush fragrance of her hair and the perfume he knew—just knew—she dabbed at the base of her throat and behind her ears. It was intoxicating.

For one eternal moment Lisa didn't pull away from his grasp. Her hands rested lightly on his forearms and her knees tapped his shins, so close had she stumbled. She stared up at him, lips slightly parted. He'd seen that look in her eyes before. It was how she'd looked when she wanted him to kiss her.

"Lisa!" Terry's voice broke the spell, and Lisa stepped quickly out of Deacon's grasp.

"Right here," she called. She looked back at Deacon. "I'll see you back at the office, okay?"

He didn't have any choice in the matter, so Deacon nodded. He turned and headed back toward the pond. He might not be able to keep Terry from taking her to lunch, but he sure as hell didn't have to watch the two of them making kissy faces with each other.

*   *   *

All Lisa wanted was a cool shower, an icy drink, and some air conditioning. The day had been unseasonably warm, and working on the children's garden project for most of the day had left her filthy. She hung her keys on their hook and went immediately to the refrigerator.

She fought back a wave of annoyance when her search for a cold pop came up dry. Allegra didn't drink sodas. She claimed the caffeine gave her headaches. Lisa could always count on the case of soda she ordered biweekly lasting her the entire two weeks. She still had a week to go, but where was her pop?

She settled for a glass of iced tea instead. As she squirted a splash of lemon juice and a generous spoon of sugar into the drink, Lisa tried to think if she'd really drank more than twenty cans of pop in less than seven days.

Had Terry helped himself to a few? But Terry hadn't been over to the house since last week.

It was just one more mystery to add to the growing list. Things misplaced or missing entirely. Light bulbs burning out, and not just one or two, but four or five in one evening. And now the disappearing beverage.

This project with Deacon had really started distracting her, Lisa thought as she took her tea and went into the living room. It was a wonder she got any work done at all. Being near him meant she could hardly think straight, and being away from him wasn't much better.

The living room was a disaster she could no longer ignore. "Al!"

No answer. Lisa knew her sister was home, though, because she could hear her sister's music playing from her room. Lisa looked around the room at the scattered fashion magazines, dirty plates and discarded articles of clothing. Her sister was a slob. Not news by any stretch, but seeing the level of mess in the room was more proof Lisa had been too caught up in erotic fantasies lately to pay attention to the necessary details of life.

"Al," she cried again, not expecting an answer. When Al was listening to her music, nothing short of a nuclear explosion could rouse her.

Lisa finished her tea and debated just leaving the mess for one more day. A cold shower. Soft sheets. Dreams of Deacon...

"Al!"

She took the back stairs from the kitchen since they led directly to Al's room. The music grew louder as she got closer to the room at the top of the stairs, and Lisa got angrier. Her sister wasn't a teenager any more! She was an adult with adult responsibilities.

"Allegra!" Lisa pounded on the door. Still no answer—and no wonder. Lisa would have been surprised if her sister could hear anything over the throbbing dance music blasting from behind the door.

She threw open the door, ready to yell. What she saw instead made her stop, stunned and speechless.

Allegra stood in front of her full length mirror, naked except for her bra and underwear. In one hand she held what appeared to be an eyeliner pencil, though one which had been used to little more than a nub. Her face, expertly made up, bore no expression even as she mouthed the words to the song.

Writing covered her entire body.

"Al?" Lisa went over to the portable stereo on Allegra's dresser and turned the music off with a snap. "Are you all right?"

Her sister blinked and stopped singing. Her eyes swam into focus. Her hands came up to cover herself briefly, then she was the old Allegra. She laughed. Tossed her hair. Grabbed her robe from the back of the chair and slipped it on.

"Don't you know how to knock?"

"What did you do to yourself?" Lisa asked uneasily.

Al shrugged. "I'm deciding if I want a tattoo. I thought I'd see how it would look."

Lisa crossed to her sister and grabbed her arm. Yanking up the sleeve of the robe, she began reading some of the words written on Al's arm. "Garter belt. Lipstick. Gallon of Milk. That's what you want to get tattooed on yourself?"

Al jerked her arm away and slid the robe down to cover herself. "Maybe. Like I said, I'm just trying some things out."

Something was not right. This went way beyond Allegra's normal idiosyncrasies. The first slow pang of fear uncoiled itself in Lisa's gut.

She spoke calmly, watching her sister for any reaction. "Allegra, that is not normal."

Allegra sighed, long suffering. "Lisa, you worry too much. You've been working too hard. By the way, I found your sunglasses."

"You did?" Lisa paused. She'd been looking for them for three days, and had finally bought a new pair. "Where were they?"

Allegra fixed her sister with a look of pity. "In the microwave."

"What were they doing there?"

Allegra just shook her head. "Don't know. But the frozen burrito was on the counter next to your keys."

All at once, Lisa felt like she had to sit down. Allegra clucked sympathetically as Lisa sank onto the perfectly made bed. Lisa repressed a shiver.

"The microwave?" she repeated in a small voice.

"What's been on your mind lately?" Allegra asked.

Was that concern, actual concern, in Allegra's voice? That seemed hard to believe. Lisa watched her sister pull on a pair of jeans, ironed and crisp, from a hanger in the closet. Al slipped on the jeans, then the shirt with movements smooth but so swift Lisa barely got another glimpse of the weird writing all over her body.

"You've been putting in awfully long hours on that children's garden thing," Allegra continued when Lisa didn't answer. "And spending nearly every night out with Terry. Let's face it, Lisa, you haven't been yourself lately."

No, she hadn't. "I guess I'm just tired."

Allegra snorted, smoothing the red material of her shirt over her perfect, flat stomach and turning sideways to look in the mirror. Apparently satisfied with what she saw, she sat next to Lisa and put her arm around her. "It's probably a good thing you're not going out tonight."

Terry wouldn't agree, but how did Allegra know Lisa had already called off her date with him? "What makes you think I'm not going out?"

Allegra shrugged. "You're not dressed for it."

Something about the answer rang false, but Lisa wasn't quite sure why. "What are you doing to do?"

"Go to Mom and Dad's," Allegra said. "They rented a bunch of movies. Kevin and Andrea are going out and dropping off the kids. I said I'd help. Besides, me and Troy have to finish our air hockey tournament."

"Sounds like a real party," Lisa said more stiffly than she meant. Nobody had invited her. Even her younger brother Troy was staying home to join in—a rare occasion for the teen who usually had high school sports practices or other activities to keep him occupied.

"It should be," Allegra said lightly. She smoothed the shirt again three times. She paused, then three times more. After another pause, she ran her fingers over the material as if to start another succession of smooths, but stopped herself. Her fingers hooked into claws, but they remained still. She turned to Lisa with a bright smile. "Like my shirt?"

"Is it new?" She'd never seen it before.

"No," Allegra said, suddenly turning away. "I've had it forever."

The lie was so blatant Lisa couldn't even comment. The beginnings of a headache tapped at her temples. "I think I'll just go to bed."

"You do that," Allegra said. "Sweet dreams."

The small, empty bedroom that connected Allegra's room to the front hallway was dark, even when Lisa flicked the light switch.

Another burnt-out bulb?

At least the room was bare and she wouldn't trip on anything. Lisa felt her way to the door on the opposite side and burst out into the light of the hallway. Her room, directly across from the spare room, had never looked so good.

At least one thing was good about all this freakiness. She'd stopped thinking about Deacon for awhile. Sweet dreams? Lisa thought after she'd showered and slipped between her cool linen sheets. She'd prefer no dreams at all.

*   *   *

"You look tired." Deacon knew the way to win a woman's heart usually meant not telling her she looked tired. But Lisa did. Gray circles shadowed her sexy gray eyes, and her cheeks were pale.

She paused while flipping through the pad of designs they were going over. She sighed, seemed about to speak, then stopped. She worried her lower lip between her teeth.

"Lisa?" he asked, really concerned now. For the past week, she'd been subdued. At first, he'd thought it was because she was feeling awkward around him again, but now he saw something had to be bothering her. "What's wrong?"

To his surprise, tears glistened in her eyes. Her fingers trembled as they flipped through the pages on her lap so fast he knew she couldn't possibly be really seeing them. He reached out and put his hand on hers.

"Talk to me," he said softly.

She looked up at him, still biting at her lower lip. Soon she would draw blood. Lisa's mouth opened, then closed. She struggled to speak. Finally, whatever had been holding her back let go, and a torrent of words poured out.

"It started with my watch," she said. "Then my glasses. And they were in the microwave! But the burrito was on the counter. And my stuff went missing from the laundry, but I just thought maybe Allegra had borrowed it. But she says she hasn't, and she has a closet full of new clothes I've never seen, but where's my stuff? And—"

"Slow down," Deacon said. Her rapid-fire, slightly hysterical response alarmed him. He'd never seen her so distraught. "Take a deep breath and start over."

A few deep breaths seemed to calm her. She even managed a weak smile as she looked at him. "Sorry."

"It's okay."

They sat like that in Lisa's tiny office just staring at each other. With anybody else, it might have quickly become uncomfortable, but Deacon didn't mind just looking at her. Lisa flashed a weak smile at him.

"A lot of strange things have been happening, that's all." She sighed. "Terry seems to think I'm working too hard."

Deacon knew Terry's real problem with Lisa's recent work assignment and it wasn't the long hours. "It's too bad he isn't more understanding."

Lisa nodded, and for just one second, Deacon felt a flash of guilt. It wasn't right to take advantage of her mood like this. Then he thought of Terry Hewitt's arms around Lisa and the guilt vanished.

Lisa peered up at him with wet eyes. Then she smiled. "You are a dog."

"What?"

"You," she repeated slowly, "are a dog! Deacon Campbell, are you trying to cause trouble for Terry?"

She'd caught him out. *Damn.* Why did he always forget how smart Lisa was? The best response seemed unrepentant honesty.

"Sure am," he said with a grin.

Lisa laughed. The sound was a welcome relief from her earlier worried tone. She punched him lightly on the shoulder.

"He should be more understanding,'" she mocked, putting a lot prissier tone into the statement than he had. "More like you maybe?"

Now his defense was up. "Well, yeah, like me."

"Why?" Lisa asked him. "Why are you trying to cause trouble?"

Deacon, who usually had a ready answer for any question, remained silent. He couldn't tell her it was because he was jealous. He couldn't tell her the truth that he wanted her in his arms again and he wanted a second chance to prove to her he was the kind of man she could fall in love with.

Instead, he shrugged. "I guess I'm just a troublemaker."

"I guess you are," she said, and seemed to be waiting for more.

All at once, the tiny office seemed even tinier. Had their knees been touching this entire time and he only now noticed? Deacon realized he could smell her perfume, a mouth-watering scent like vanilla. He swallowed hard to keep the drool from dripping out of his mouth. Three years ago, he would've kissed her and damn the consequences.

"It's getting late," he said. "We'd better finish up these designs."

Did she look disappointed? He wouldn't let himself think so. Deacon turned his attention back to the pile of papers they were looking at.

"Yes, we should. I have a date tonight with Terry and I promised him I wouldn't be late this time." Lisa paused and he felt the weight of her gaze burning a hole in the side of his cheek.

Deacon pretended to be engrossed in the designs. She was testing him. The only problem was he didn't know which response would make him pass, and which would make him fail.

"Let me just check my email," she said. "The funds officer from Bank of St. Mary's said she'd send me the details about the draws for payment. Dad's been asking me about the money for all the supplies we've used so far."

Deacon grabbed a pen and his binder and began labeling some updated items they'd been discussing. He wasn't paying attention to Lisa's monitor until her gasp made him look up. Images flashed on the screen—and they weren't from any bank.

"How do I make it stop?" Lisa clicked frantically with her mouse.

It appeared to be some sort of automatic slide show program that opened from an email attachment. No matter what keys she hit or how much she moved the mouse, nothing stopped the pictures from coming. Deacon hadn't seen the first few, but the ones showing up now grew increasingly more lurid and pornographic with each one.

Images of every sort of aberrant sexual practice replaced shots that might have come from a men's adult magazine. Pictures of violence and death began replacing the sex shots, and when a close up photo of a gunshot victim filled the screen, Deacon reached over and simply turned off the monitor.

"What was that?" Lisa cried, shaking. Her cheeks had paled again. "How did that get on my computer?"

"Maybe it was some sort of joke," he said, helpless to explain to her. "A sick joke."

"Who would send something like that to me?" Lisa pushed her chair away from the computer as though it might contaminate her.

Deacon took her hands in his, concerned to find them icy cold. He rubbed them between his own trying to calm her. Truthfully, the pictures had made him sick to his stomach, too. There'd been nothing funny about any of them, and if it was a joke, it had come from someone with the Marquis de Sade's sense of humor.

"Lisa?" Doug Shadd stood in the doorway, holding a file. "What's going on?"

"Dad," Lisa cried. "There was something terrible on my computer!"

Doug eased his way past Deacon's chair and stood beside his daughter. "One of those chain letters? Or a virus?"

Lisa shook her head. "I don't think so."

"It looked like some sort of slide show," Deacon said.

"Dad, the pictures were really horrendous." Lisa seemed a little calmer now, though her cheeks were still pale. "Porn and dead people..." She trailed off shuddering.

"Let's take a look," Doug said, and pushed the monitor's on button. "Ha, ha," he read aloud. "Like what you see?"

Doug clicked the mouse and the message vanished, replaced by the normal Inbox screen of Lisa's email. "It's gone now."

"Which message did it come in?" Deacon asked. "Who sent it to her?"

Doug barely glanced at him and fiddled with the mouse. "How can you tell? I don't know how to work email."

Deacon had spent hours in front of the computer during his sentence. Good behavior had earned him limited internet access and visits to the library where he'd read every computer book he could get his hands on. He'd never be a programmer, but he knew how to work almost any system.

"Let me see." He pushed his chair over and looked at the messages, scanning the headers. "That one."

"Pix 4 U," Lisa read.

"Do you recognize the sender?" Deacon asked. "It's sxxygrrrl@badtimes.net."

Lisa shook her head. "Doesn't sound familiar."

"Could it be a mistake?" Doug asked, still rubbing Lisa's shoulder comfortingly. "A what do you call it—a ham?"

"Spam," Deacon corrected, looking at the message. He clicked the mouse a few times to bring up the message's properties. "I don't think so. See? The message was sent here to Lisa's Garden Shadd internal mail address, not the one she usually uses for outside correspondence. And it was directly addressed to her with her full name and the address."

"It was sent from inside our system?" Dismay colored Lisa's voice.

"No," Deacon said, trying to reassure her. "But it did come from someone who knows your internal address. So it's someone who knows you."

"It's not a funny joke," she said vehemently with another shudder.

"I can try to find out more," Deacon said. "But I'll have to open it up again."

Lisa nodded, her mouth thinned in a grim line. "Okay, but I'm not going to look."

With a click of his mouse, the screen filled again with the lewd and increasingly disgusting photos. Deacon tried several commands before finally hitting one that shut down the program before it reached the end. "Ha, ha. Like what you see?" He hit another few keys, hoping to pull up more information. "Sounds like a virus header, but I don't think it's a virus. Or a joke."

Doug came around the other side of Lisa's chair to better watch what Deacon was doing. "You seem to know an awful lot about computers, Deacon."

At first, Deacon took the man's comment as a compliment. "Thanks."

The silence that greeted his reply made him turn to look at Lisa's father. A grimace of suspicion tugged at his mouth. His eyes were hard.

"You seem to know a lot about that message, too," Doug continued. "Like I said, I don't know too much about email. Can you really tell all that from just a few clicks on the keyboard?"

Or did he know from some other way, Deacon knew the man meant. Like being the sender himself. "You can tell a lot about computers by just hitting a few keys, Doug."

"Too bad you can't do the same for people," Doug Shadd said. "Come on, honey. Let's get you out of here."

Lisa followed him willingly enough, with nothing more than a see-you-tomorrow for Deacon, left to stare at the mocking screen of her computer. His fingers poised over the keys, waiting while his mind struggled with how to react to Doug's silent accusation. He could try to learn more about who sent the message, but what would he do with the answer? Bring it to Lisa on a platter like some sort of offering? Cast himself further under suspicion?

Deacon didn't hesitate any longer. Maybe the message was a fluke. Maybe it was a joke. But whatever it was, it wasn't his problem.

A click of the mouse, a tap of some keys, and the message disappeared into the far reaches of cyberspace. Just like his hopes of putting the past behind him.

CHAPTER 7

"I wish you'd reconsider," said Marcia Shadd quietly. She reached out to touch Lisa's arm. "Your old room is still here, you know. Any time you want it."

"I'm not Allegra," Lisa meant the comment to sound light. It came out harsher than she'd intended and she winced when she saw her mother's hurt look. "I'm sorry, Mom. I just meant that I'm okay. I'll be fine."

"Alone in that house all by yourself? You two girls worry me," Marcia fretted. She turned back to the kitchen counter and toyed with the several plastic bowls lined up along its edge. "Why you had to move all the way across town is beyond me."

Lisa sighed mentally. "Mom, I'm a big girl. And I like living where I live."

Marcia nodded. "I know, honey. I just wish you and Terry would finally settle down—"

"Mom!" Thankfully, they were the only two in the kitchen, so she didn't have to listen to any comments on her mother's admission. "Terry and I... We... What makes you think I'm going to marry Terry?"

"Well, aren't you?" Her mother looked surprised. Pursing her lips, she bent to pull a paper grocery sack from a drawer and began putting the containers in it. "Allegra says you two spend every evening together. She says you and Terry are getting serious."

"Allegra should mind her own business." Lisa grabbed a glass and got some cold water from the faucet. "Mom, I don't need all that food."

"What?" Her mother often pretended deafness when she didn't want to hear what was being said. Lisa didn't bother repeating it. "A mother can't send some leftovers home with her daughters?"

"It's a ten-minute drive from here." Lisa slipped onto one of the worn, red vinyl kitchen chairs. "And we both cook. You act like we're starving to death."

"It's not for you anyway," Lisa's mom answered in a bit of a huff. "Your sister will appreciate it, if you won't."

That could be because her sister didn't know how to do a damn thing for herself, Lisa thought resentfully watching her mom pack the bag. She thought about letting her mother in on a little secret—the food she sent would grow green hair and start to ooze before Al even noticed it was in the fridge, and it would stay in there until Lisa couldn't stand it any more and threw it all away.

"I swear," Marcia said fondly, tapping the top container which had once held non-dairy whipped topping. "I send over these containers and I never get any of them back. What do you do, eat them?"

Great. Now Lisa would have to make sure she washed the containers and sent them back home. "Not exactly."

"Honey, is that thing about your email still bothering you?" Marcia poured herself a cup of coffee from the ever-present supply and sat down across from Lisa. "Dad said it was pretty graphic."

It was more than the email. It was all the strange things happening to her lately. It was Allegra's selfishness, and it was Terry's recent insistence on taking their relationship further than she was prepared to go. In short, it was just about everything in her life.

"Dad said he thinks Deacon Campbell had something to do with it. Not that he can prove it, of course, but you can bet he'll be keeping an eye on him."

"Deacon had nothing to do with it," Lisa said. Didn't that sound familiar? It seemed she'd been saying the same phrase over and over quite a bit lately.

From the other room came a burst of raucous laughter and Allegra's outraged squeal. "You're cheating!"

Family Fun Night. A tradition since Lisa's childhood, somewhat changed since most of the kids were grown and moved out of the house. The addition of spouses and grandchildren added to the fun, but also to the frenzy.

Allegra burst through the swinging doors and into the kitchen, breathing hard. "Troy sucks!"

"Allegra," Marcia admonished. "Your brother does no such thing."

Lisa bit back a laugh at her mother's unintentionally funny comment. "I thought you were playing Monopoly."

Allegra whirled to the fridge and whipped out a bottle of water. Gulping half the contents, she flung herself into the chair next to Lisa's. "They can play by themselves."

"Troy bought Park Place and Boardwalk again?" Lisa asked, knowing it was her youngest brother's favorite ploy, and Allegra's biggest pet peeve.

"That's just not fair," Allegra said. "I'm barely halfway around the board! Where's the cake?"

"I swear, how do you girls keep so thin?" Marcia gave Allegra a fond look that made Lisa want to choke.

"Nerves," Lisa said.

Allegra's eyes narrowed, but she didn't comment. "Are you staying over tonight?"

"No," Lisa said. "I'm meeting Terry in about an hour."

"Don't you think it's time you brought Ter-Bear over to the house for Family Fun Night?" Allegra asked coyly. "He is practically part of the family."

"That would be so nice," Marcia enthused. "We'd love for Terry to come. Why don't you invite him, Lisa?"

Lisa felt like slamming her head onto the table. Repeatedly. At least then the headache she felt pinching above the eyes would make sense.

"Maybe next time," she answered instead, knowing the answer might be enough to put off her mother, but wouldn't satisfy Allegra. A warning look might do that, and she gave her sister one of those.

Allegra switched tactics. "What are you two doing tonight? Just thought I'd ask, since I'm going to crash here tonight. You know, in case you two want to get busy."

Lisa growled. The sound hurt her throat, but she was powerless to stop it. Marcia looked startled, and Lisa could see her mother's mind slowly processing the exact nature of what Allegra had said.

"Oh, Allegra," Marcia scolded. "Such talk!"

Al shrugged. "She's an adult, Mother. She's entitled to a sexual relationship. Not that I agree, of course," she added with a moue of false saintliness.

That's rich. Allegra had slept with more guys in the past two months than Lisa had in her entire life. But she could see her mother smiling dotingly at Allegra. The look she gave Lisa was slightly scandalized. Telling the truth as she knew it about her sister wouldn't win her any points and would only cause problems.

"On that note," Lisa said stiffly, pushing away from the table. "I'll be going now."

"Oh, honey, don't run off like that," Marcia protested. "Al was just teasing."

Lisa forced a smile to her mouth and bent to kiss her mother's cheek. "Great meal, Mom. Allegra, don't forget to take that stuff home with you. 'Bye. I'll call you later."

Allegra squeaked as she looked at the food on the counter. "Can't you...?"

"Nope, sorry," Lisa said blithely. "Gotta run. 'Night!"

And she was free. She slipped out the back door and stood in the summer night air, gulping it in like it was water and she was in the desert. From the back porch, she could see inside to the living room and her family gathered around the table. She loved them, she really did. But sometimes it was easier to love them from afar.

She hadn't bothered driving from home since the walk was only about twenty minutes. She'd never been afraid to walk by herself before, but now as she stepped out onto the cracked and bumpy sidewalk, Lisa couldn't stop a small shiver from tickling her spine. She told herself not to be ridiculous. The incident in The Evergreen's parking lot had been a fluke thing. She hadn't been hurt, had she?

Still, as the dusk made the automatic street lamps begin to turn on, she walked a little faster. The night was cooler than the day had been, but the goosebumps rising on her bare arms did not come from the night air. Lisa rubbed her arms briskly once, then forced herself to act nonchalant.

She had already made the left onto Russ Street and was heading toward Ida, meaning to take it all the way to Depot Street, then down to her house on Curry Avenue. Suddenly, walking through the dark, residential streets became incredibly unappealing. She'd walked that route a hundred times since moving out of her parents' home, and those streets a thousand times in the years she'd lived in Saint Mary's.

Even the fact her planned route took her right by the police station wasn't enough to make her go on. Well-lit and more heavily traveled Saint Mary's Avenue seemed a better choice, even though it meant dragging out her walk by another fifteen minutes.

I could always go back to Mom and Dad's and beg a ride, she thought, to chastise herself for being such a fool. She wasn't desperate enough to do that though. She didn't want to admit to them that the attack still affected her.

Instead of continuing on Ida, Lisa made a quick right onto Dippold Avenue. The steep hill ahead would do her thighs good, and in a few minutes, she'd be on the main street. From there, she could easily make it to the police station and wait for Terry there. No need to tell him she was afraid, Lisa thought. He'd just think she was eager to see him.

A win/win situation.

"Fancy meeting you here."

The words, curling out of the dark, made her gasp in surprise. She knew that voice. *Deacon.*

"What're you doing there?" She asked.

"I could ask you the same thing," he drawled, unfolding the length of himself from the concrete front porch.

"I was at my parents' house," Lisa said. "I'm walking home."

"Really?" He asked.

The light from the street lamp didn't quite reach his face. So why did she know he was smiling? Deacon's white shirt glimmered as he walked toward her.

Lisa's heart pounded, and she wasn't sure if it was from anticipation or fear. "Really."

"And you just happened to turn down my street."

"I didn't know this was your street."

He nodded, now a clear picture in the street lamp's glow. He looked tense and Lisa couldn't figure out why. "Allegra didn't tell you?"

Now she was beginning to be annoyed. "No. Why would she? How would she know?"

"Because a couple weeks ago she came walking down here herself," Deacon said.

"When my sister does something, she usually has a reason," Lisa said. "Whatever it may be. This is just chance."

"Lucky chance, I guess." Deacon seemed to relax. "You live down on Curry Ave."

He'd remembered. Of course he had. "My folks live up on Edward."

"That's a long walk," Deacon said. "Especially at night."

She could tell he was thinking about the night in the Evergreen parking lot, too. "I decided to take the main road."

"Nice night for walking anyway," Deacon said.

The conversation, for all intents and purposes, was over. She should keep walking. Lisa's feet didn't move. She and Deacon stared at each other. The harsh light cast his face into slashes of black and white, and she found herself wondering if the light was as unkind to her. And why should that matter?

"What're you doing?" she blurted.

Deacon looked around as though surprised she'd asked. "Sitting outside. Mom's down playing bingo, and my brother Steve is bringing her home later."

"So you're just...sitting."

He smiled, his teeth like ivory. "Yup."

Lisa didn't know why that struck her as funny, but it did. She began to laugh. Deacon joined her, and they laughed together, the sound ringing through the night and chasing away her fears.

"Sounds fun," Lisa said through her chuckles.

"It is. You should try it sometime," Deacon answered, as though daring her.

"Maybe I will," she said. "Right over there?"

He gestured broadly. "Best spot for it."

Lisa crossed the small hump of grass that passed for a lawn and sat down on the bumpy concrete. The porch was just large enough for two people to sit comfortably side by side. A large and fragrant rose bush spilled its perfume into the air from beneath the house's windows, and Lisa sniffed it.

"That's my favorite smell in the whole world," she said, as Deacon sat down next to her. "Too bad roses are such a pain to take care of. I'd have dozens."

"A pain?" Deacon said. "Don't let your dad hear you say that. Heiresses to The Garden Shadd shouldn't be talking bad about roses."

They sat in silence for a few moments, breathing in the scent and enjoying the night air. Lisa didn't feel chilly any more. If anything, sitting so close to Deacon made her cheeks feel flushed.

"So this is sitting," she murmured.

"Yup."

"Nice."

"Yup."

It had been a night much like this one three years before. A lazy summer night fraught with possibilities. If she turned to him now, he'd kiss her. And did she want that?

Lisa thought that yes, she probably did. But could she do it? Could she really throw away the past three years and pretend they'd never happened? Forget about Terry who certainly deserved better?

She was saved from deciding when Deacon spoke. "That day in my office when you were looking for your purse? Why didn't you search for it?"

Now she could look at him. With words between them, it would be easier to stop herself from giving in to the crazy desires flashing through her head.

"Because I knew you didn't take it," she said seriously.

She knew his eyes were deep and dark, but in the scanty light from the street lamp they could have been any color. Deacon blinked, watching her. Lisa thought again of kissing him, and knew if he tried, she wouldn't stop him. Not now. Not with the night whispering to her like this.

"What would it have been like, do you think?"

She knew what he meant and what he was thinking about. It was all either one of them had been thinking about since he first spoke to her from the darkness, she was certain.

"It would've been magic." She didn't care if she sounded giddy. That's the way she felt.

Deacon reached out to touch her cheek. Lisa leaned into the touch, afraid to close her eyes and afraid to meet his gaze. His hand, warm on her skin, was rough from work. Should she turn her head a little to the left, she'd be able to press her lips to the throbbing pulse at his wrist.

"Lisa," Deacon whispered.

If she answered him, all would be lost. She would let him pull her against him. She'd open her mouth beneath his and let him kiss her like he used to. She'd let him touch her with the caresses that had been haunting her dreams for three years, and she would not stop to think about the consequences.

"Why?" he asked.

It was enough to pull her out of her sensual reverie. "Why what?"

"Why did you know I didn't take your purse?"

There was such a thing as too much talk, she thought sourly. "Did you?"

"Of course I didn't," he answered.

"Then why are you worried about it?" she snapped.

He dropped his hand from her face and she was glad of it. Glad, too, for the darkness that hid the fierceness of her blush.

"I'm just never sure if the past is really behind us," he said. "I never know if you're going to look at me in that way again."

His words hurt, but she knew what he meant. Still, she had to ask, to clarify. "What way?"

"Like I'm going to bite you," he said. "Like you're afraid of me."

She was afraid of him, of the way he still made her feel, even after all this time. "No, Deacon."

"I like working at The Garden Shadd," he said. "And I like working with you."

"I like working with you, too. We're really making progress."

"We used to be real good friends."

She thought of them tangled together on the couch in his old apartment, hands and mouths on each other. Not the way she acted with her friends. But she knew what he meant, and his words pleased her.

"Yes."

Deacon took her hand. "Do you think we could be friends again?"

"That's it?" she said, startled.

She'd been thinking about him kissing her, and he'd been thinking about being buddies?

"I like hanging out with you," he said with a light punch to her shoulder. "I remember you can throw a mean game of darts."

Oh, did she feel like an idiot. Of course he hadn't been thinking the same things she had. How could he? She'd made it perfectly clear things had changed, and they could never go back to what they'd had before.

She moved imperceptibly away from him on the porch. "I always could beat your butt at darts. And in pool."

"Hey," Deacon protested. "Let's not go there."

"Friends would be good," she said, forcing herself to shove away any other thoughts she'd had.

"It just makes sense," Deacon told her. "We have to spend a lot of time together and everything. And after that day in my office, I thought that maybe... Well...it seemed like we had a good chance at starting over. It seemed like you were ready to anyway. I just wanted to make sure."

"Starting over," she said in a low voice. He didn't mean it the way she would have. Starting over to be buddies. Really, though, wasn't that better? Didn't it make much more sense? And really, wasn't it the only option? "Okay."

"Friends?" Deacon said.

"Friends," Lisa answered. "You want to shake on it?"

Deacon held his arms out wide. "Friends can do better than that, can't they?"

Of course they could. Chuckling a little at herself for getting so foolishly worked up earlier, Lisa opened her arms to. They hugged.

For the first second, the hug was nondescript and nonchalant. Immediately after that, it became something else. Deacon's hug was firm and strong, his arms around her didn't waver and didn't squeeze too hard. The broad, muscled plane of his chest felt good beneath her cheek, the point of his chin pressed not too tightly to the top of her head. His hands, fingers spread, drifted lightly on her back.

She felt cocooned, but far from safe. Her heart began to beat a triple-time rhythm. She should pull away. She had to pull away or do something foolish.

But she didn't pull away. It felt too good to be in Deacon's arms again. This was no friendship hug. They'd be fooling themselves if either of them thought it was. Yet, she'd been wrong before, thinking he was going to kiss her and he didn't. Could be she was wrong now? Were the emotions sweeping through her of her own making and Deacon wasn't feeling the same?

The hug had to end sometime. Already it had stretched out longer than was conceivably appropriate. And still they both held on as though neither one wanted to break contact. She could float in Deacon's arms forever.

The moment passed, as it finally had to do, and Lisa felt a twinge of sadness. There'd be no going back. They'd sealed the unspoken agreement. Friends they would be. And wasn't that better than nothing at all?

They pulled slowly apart, their cheeks touching as she lifted her head. Then, in that incredibly brief moment when their mouths were nearly touching, Deacon did the unthinkable.

He kissed her.

CHAPTER 8

It was better than she remembered. His mouth was hot and sweet. He tasted of peppermint. She breathed in, and he breathed out, and he filled her.

Lisa felt her head tip back as Deacon kissed her harder. His tongue swept hers, just once, as though testing. She put her hand to the back of his head and that gave him the answer he needed.

When his hand slipped up to cup her breast through her thin tee-shirt, however, Lisa had to pull away. Even the sweetness of his kisses couldn't make her forget they were sitting on his front porch in front of the neighborhood's eyes. It might look like nobody was watching, but in a small town, there was always someone looking.

"I'm sorry." Deacon dropped his hand from her chest, but didn't move away. His breath whispered on her cheeks.

"We don't need to give everyone a free show," she whispered back, embarrassed. Without his mouth on her, it was easier to think.

"No, I guess not." He smiled, leaning forward until his forehead bumped hers. "And I'm not really sorry."

Lisa sighed. "Oh, Deacon, why did you do that?"

He pulled back, his eyes surprised. "You're mad?"

She took his hand and pressed it to her lips. "No. Just...not sure what to think."

"You think too to much," he told her. "Don't think about it, Lisa. Just let it happen."

"Let what happen?" she demanded in a low voice, still aware of how public their private interlude really was. "Making out on your front porch like a couple of teenagers?"

"I shouldn't have kissed you."

"No," she cried. "I mean, I don't know. I'm so confused."

He scooted back from her the fraction of an inch he could before he'd fall off the porch. The space between them didn't do much except emphasize the heat still lingering from the amazing kiss they'd just shared. Deacon crossed his arms over his chest and stared at her.

"I thought we'd settled all this," Lisa said helplessly.

"I guess we didn't," Deacon countered.

She let out a low moan of frustration. "I thought we were going to be friends."

"That seemed pretty friendly to me."

Damn him, he was still joking. Lisa frowned. "I don't make out with my friends."

He must have sensed her lack of humor about the situation because he sobered up quickly. "You think I don't know that? I know you, Lisa. I know what kind of woman you are. And all that tells me is kissing you was not a mistake."

She rubbed her temples. "Deacon, three years ago…"

His back stiffened and his jaw set. "Three years ago, what?"

"Do you really think we can just pick up where we left off?" she asked him almost angrily.

He didn't say anything for a minute and she was glad. She wasn't really sure what she wanted him to answer. Then he let out a breath of air between pursed lips and spoke. "Yes, I think we can. I think we want to. I know I want to."

She shook her head. "How can you? After what happened? After what I did?"

He put his hand on hers to stop her from talking more. "If I can forget and forgive, Lisa, can't you?"

Could she? Lisa tugged her hand from his and stood. The small, bumpy lawn didn't offer much room for pacing, so instead she just shifted slowly from foot to foot. Then, realizing it looked like she had to use the bathroom, she put one foot on the porch's concrete step and leaned on her knee.

"You asked me to believe you didn't do it," she finally said. "And I want to. I really do."

His voice was flat. "But you don't."

Her answer surprised her. "Deacon, you're a good man. With a good heart. I don't know what happened at The Circle K, but I don't believe you're a liar."

The light from the street lamp slanted across her shoulder and lit up his eyes. "I told you, Lisa, I never lied to you."

"I believe you," she said. And she did. Probably she always had. "And if you say you didn't rob that store…then I believe you."

He reached out a hand to her and she went to him. She put her knee on the porch just between his thighs and leaned in to kiss him. His arms slipped around her waist, his fingers splaying over her hips. Lisa put her hands on his shoulders feeling the muscles grown harder and more pronounced since the last time she'd felt them.

His shoulders weren't all that had gotten harder. Her knee nudged something she definitely wasn't sure she was ready for. And yet, didn't the thought thrill her that she could so affect him, even with the simplest of kisses?

"What are you going to tell Terrence?" he murmured in her ear, and Lisa pushed away from him so hard she nearly fell.

"Terry!" Damn, she'd forgotten all about Terry. Lisa twisted her wrist, forgetting again she'd lost her watch. "Damn!"

"Lisa?" Deacon questioned.

"I was supposed to meet him at ten o'clock when he got off work," she said. "What time is it?"

Deacon's watch had a nice green light on it. "It's ten-thirty."

Lisa muttered a garbled expletive. "This is not good."

"Whoa, slow down," Deacon said, reaching for her even as she danced out of his grasp. "I'm getting the feeling you're having second thoughts."

"Second thoughts, third thoughts," Lisa said. "He's not exactly going to be thrilled!"

"Nobody likes getting dumped," Deacon said.

If he was trying to be commiserating, he failed. Lisa spun to face him. "Who said I'm dumping him?"

"The past twenty minutes says," Deacon told her. His voice had no smile in it now.

Lisa's head spun. "I don't know what to do," she said, not meaning to speak aloud.

"It's pretty easy," Deacon said. "Dump Terry—"

"Will you quit saying that?" she hissed. "I'm not dumping anyone!"

"I see." Deacon sounded angry. "I thought I knew what kind of woman you are. I guess I was wrong."

He got to his feet. His hand was on the screen door. Lisa stopped him.

"Please," she said. "I'm just confused. This is all a little sudden. You said earlier that Terry ought to be more understanding. I guess I'm asking for the same from you."

He snorted. "You like him that much?"

"He's a good man," Lisa said, and it wasn't a lie. That Terry didn't make her heart beat faster wasn't his fault and it never had been. "He doesn't deserve to just be…dumped."

"You have to tell him." Deacon leaned against the front of the house. "He'll find out even if you don't."

Whether Deacon meant Terry would find out because he was a police officer or because the town was so small, Lisa didn't know. But she did know he was right. She had to tell Terry. It wouldn't be fair to him if she didn't.

"Then what?"

"We pick up where we left off," Deacon said.

Lisa sat on the porch hugging her knees. "No. Not exactly."

With an exasperated sigh, Deacon sat next to her. "Then what?"

"We start over," she said. "I like you, Deacon…."

"Really?" he asked jokingly, and she stuck out her tongue at him.

"…but I'm not ready to just plunge back into what we had before," she said. Her heart felt lighter for the admission.

Deacon nodded and took her hand. "Okay."

"Okay?" She'd been half afraid he'd refuse. Then where would she be?

He kissed her swiftly and lightly on the cheek. "Absolutely. I'll take you on dates, buy you flowers, the works."

"Really," she said in speculation, thinking about it. "You never bought me flowers before."

"I didn't work in a greenhouse before," he reminded her.

"Oh, yeah," Lisa said with a laugh, thinking about where he'd worked while taking the gardening classes. "You used to bring me light bulbs from the Sylvania plant."

"You light up my life," he told her, repeating the corny joke he'd said way back then.

The sick feeling in Lisa's stomach had begun to subside, but only a little. "I have to go meet Terry. He's probably worried."

"I'll give you a ride home," Deacon told her. "C'mon."

She protested, but he insisted. "I'm not letting you walk home in the dark. Even if you hadn't been attacked already, I wouldn't. Now be quiet and put on the helmet."

She hadn't been on the back of a motorcycle since the night at The Circle K. Now, riding behind Deacon as the powerful machine vibrated her entire body, Lisa couldn't help think about the promises of the kisses they'd shared. *Starting over,* she thought as Deacon leaned into a curve. She could handle that.

Only the single porch light glowed when they got to her house. Allegra must really have stayed at their parents. Lisa couldn't pretend she wasn't relieved. The last thing she needed tonight was a confrontation with her sister.

"Good night and thanks for the ride," she said, suddenly shy.

Deacon grinned under helmet. "Any time, lady."

"See you on Monday," she told him, hoping he'd disagree.

"I'll call you tomorrow," he said. "We'll talk."

She watched him ride away and couldn't stop the silly, stupid grin from stretching her mouth. It was like being twelve years old again. She didn't mind. It had been a long time since she'd felt this giddy and lighthearted. Lisa fit her key into the lock and entered the dark kitchen, still grinning.

"Have a good time?" The question wriggled out of the blackness.

Lisa screamed and stepped back even as she fumbled with the light switch. Instantly, harsh light flooded the kitchen. She blinked against it, but could still see the figure sitting at her kitchen table.

"Terry! You scared me!"

It was an understatement. He'd terrified her. Lisa's hands shook and her knees felt so weak she had to sit in the chair across from his.

"You were late," Terry said flatly. "I called your parents' house and they said you'd left. I got worried. I came here to wait for you."

He still wore his uniform. The dark blue color set off his rich blue eyes. Terry was a handsome man. Why didn't she love him?

"I was walking," Lisa said. "And I decided to take a different way home. And…I ran past Deacon's house."

"Huh." The short burst of sound wasn't quite a word, not quite an answer.

Lisa continued, knowing there was no sense in putting off the inevitable. "He was outside. We started talking."

"Yes?" Terry waited as though he knew she had something more to tell him.

She couldn't do it. She couldn't tell Terry she'd let Deacon kiss her.

He would be angry, but more than that, he'd be incredibly hurt. She didn't want to hurt Terry who'd been nothing but sweet to her in their time together.

Lisa suddenly felt like the biggest jerk on the planet. She hung her head, knowing she looked guilty. "Time got away from us. I lost my watch."

"You lost your watch." Terry repeated the words as though trying to mine a different truth from them. As though the excuse was too lame to even consider as truth.

"And I lost track of time," Lisa said. "I just forgot, Terry."

"You forgot our date?" Terry asked, a twist of humor on his mouth. "It must've been some conversation."

Tell him. But she couldn't. Not like this. She had to break things off with him, yes, but not that way.

"I'm sorry," was all she could say.

Terry tapped the table top with his fingers. Lisa sighed, twisting her hands in her lap. She couldn't meet his eyes.

"And he drove you home on his—" Terry paused in distaste. "—His motorcycle."

"He didn't want me to walk alone."

"You could've called me. I'd have picked you up."

"I didn't think about it." It was the truth.

"No, you didn't think about me, did you?" Terry yelled.

Lisa jumped at the shout. "Terry, I'm sorry—"

"You should be!" He shoved back from the table with a gesture so sudden it tipped his chair over. The chair crashed to the floor, skidding across the vinyl flooring and coming to a stop just under the sink. Terry didn't seem to notice the damage which was more frightening than his anger. "You should be, Lisa!"

"What else do you want me to say?"

He whirled to face her, her expression a twisted mask of anger. "I want you to say you won't see him any more."

"I can't say that," she answered quietly. "We work together."

"You can change that, if you want," Terry said.

"I can't do that, and you know it." Lisa's headache, which had ebbed during the time she'd been with Deacon, was coming back.

"You can if you want to." Terry leaned against the counter, his nightstick thumping the cabinets underneath. "But I guess the question is, Lisa, do you want to?"

She didn't say anything, knowing he didn't really want to hear the truth. Terry cracked his knuckles in rapid succession. Lisa waited.

"I guess that's my answer." Terry pushed off from the counter and started toward the door.

"Wait," she felt compelled to say, even though there wasn't any reason for him to.

Terry paused, his back stiff and straight like he'd been kicked someplace tender. "Just tell me one thing, Lisa."

"What?" She dreaded the question.

Without turning, he said, "Did you ever like being with me better? Ever?"

At this point a lie would only hurt worse than the truth. "No." Saying it made her sick and relieved at the same time.

His shoulders slumped, but only briefly. Terry touched the door with his fingertips, pausing before pushing it open. "He's a thief, Lisa. A no-good, lying thief. He's not good enough for you."

"Terry, it's not what you think," she said, though she wasn't sure what Terry thought, or even what was going on with Deacon and herself.

"No?" he asked quietly. "Then…then I can call you tomorrow?"

"Sure," she said with so much false heartiness the room rang with it. "Of course, you can."

"Okay," he said with a sigh all at once so sad it made Lisa want to cry herself. "Tomorrow. Good night, Lisa."

She answered his farewell and watched him shut the door behind him. A clean break would have been better, but she couldn't do it. Why'd he have to ask her? Why couldn't he have just gathered up his wounded pride and stormed out of her kitchen, telling her to go to hell?

Because that wasn't Terry, Lisa thought, letting her head sink into her hands. He was good and kind, and he was also very, very stubborn when he wanted his own way. She should have just told him no, but she hadn't, and what further mess had she gotten into because of it?

The answering machine blinked rapidly, its red light like a malevolent eye. Lisa needed a drink, a cold one. No pop in the fridge, though she knew she'd bought a six-pack just two days ago. She popped the top on a can of tomato juice instead and pushed the answering machine's button for playback.

The hiss of silence, only lightly broken by some muffled breathing. The click of a hang up. Wrong number. Their phone numbers was only one digit off from the local pharmacy, and they got a lot of wrong number calls. Another hang up. Then another.

Lisa began to feel uneasy. The silence seemed more menacing, the heavy breathing less like the sound of a confused dialer and more like someone deliberately not speaking. Someone...angry.

Terry. Of course, he'd have called here first—and maybe several times—before coming over to wait for her. He wouldn't have left a message, not if he expected to see her soon.

Yet, the messages didn't sound like Terry. Not his breathing, if she could even tell by something as subtle as that. Not his style, either, no matter how worried he might have been. Terry was brisk and business-like. These hang ups sounded almost sly.

Then the phone jangled, startling her so she splashed tomato juice across the front of her sleeveless blouse. "Damn!"

Lisa grabbed the phone. She expected Deacon, or maybe Terry, but the voice on the other end wasn't either of theirs. She recognized the breathing, though. It was the same muffled sound as on the hang ups.

"Hello?" She demanded into the phone. "Who is this?"

A laugh...a low, raspy laugh. A rough, slurred voice she couldn't determine to be male or female. The phone began to slip in her suddenly-slick hand at the sound of it.

"Where've you been, Pretty Lady? I've been calling all night."

"Who is this?" she demanded with less strength this time.

"I'm not your hunky dory boyfriend, I'll tell you that," the voice mocked. "If I was, I'd be pretty pissed off at you for standing me up."

"Don't call me again," Lisa snapped into the mouthpiece.

"Don't hang up," the voice commanded. "Or I won't tell you where your underpants are."

"What?" Lisa took the phone away from her ear long enough to look at it.

"Those young boys down at the laundromat," the voice continued. "Such a shame. What perverts! Taking your underwear like that."

"How do you know about that, if you didn't do it?" Lisa demanded.

"I didn't say I didn't do it," the voice hissed. The light undertone of humor had vanished. "But I don't have it now. They do."

"What do you want?" Lisa asked, somewhat calmer now. Something about the voice snagged at her mind, but she couldn't figure out why. "Why are you harassing me like this? Were you behind what happened at The Evergreen?"

"Maybe," came the reply. "But you'll never know. And neither will Officer Friendly, no matter how much he tries to butt in. He'll never figure it out. Not that one."

Lisa glanced, finally, at the small box which normally showed the number of the person calling. Now it only said "unavailable." They got a lot of those numbers, too.

"What do you want?" Lisa repeated.

"I know everything you do," the voice whispered.

Click. It was gone. With shaking hands, Lisa put the phone back in its cradle.

"What was that all about?"

Lisa screamed, a shriek so loud and strident it embarrassed her even as it left her lips. The tomato juice flew out of her hands and splattered all over the floor. Lisa, turning with arms held up protectively, fell against the doorway to the living room.

She knew it was Terry, of course. She'd recognized his voice before she even screamed. His sudden reappearance after the frightening phone call had simply pushed her into the freak-out zone.

For once, she thanked the fates for Terry's take-charge attitude. Silently, he put his arms around her and propelled her into the living room and onto the sofa. Then he sat beside her, chafing her cold hands in his.

"What's going on?" he asked her finally.

"I just got a prank phone call, that's all." She tried to speak lightly, but Terry wasn't fooled.

"It was more than just a prank, wasn't it?" He sat back on the couch, reaching over to turn on the light.

In the lamp's golden glow and with a uniformed officer beside her, the phone call didn't seem so threatening. "Apparently someone down at the Spin and Suds likes my underpants."

"What's that mean?" Terry asked suspiciously.

"Things have been going missing," she told him.

"Like your watch," he said. She could see him mentally taking notes. Just like a good police officer.

"And other things. My underwear. My favorite tee shirt. Things I thought Allegra might have borrowed, but she didn't."

"And the caller just said they stole them from the laundry?" Terry frowned.

"If not him, then somebody involved with him," Lisa said.

"It was a him?" Terry questioned.

Actually, the voice had been hard to categorize. "I just assumed so. I've never had a dirty phone call from a woman."

"It was dirty, too?" Terry asked.

It hadn't been—not exactly. Not in the traditional sense anyway. "It made me feel dirty," Lisa whispered, looking down at her hands to stop herself from bursting into tears.

He does smell good, she thought, as Terry pulled her into his familiar embrace. His hands stroked her hair gently. Soothing. He was very soothing.

"You should've told me all this earlier," he scolded.

She'd thought of the times she'd tried to tell him, and of how he'd dismissed her. Lisa sat up. "I did try. You didn't want to listen."

"That's not true," Terry said.

She wasn't going to argue with him about it. Something occurred to her. "What're you doing here anyway?"

He looked surprised. "I got your beep. I thought you were paging me to come back. I thought you might want to talk."

"I didn't beep you," Lisa said.

He pulled his pager from his waistband and tilted the screen to show her the number. It was hers, all right. Lisa shook her head in confusion.

"I didn't page you, Terry," she said.

"Are you sure?"

A simple question, but one that set her teeth on edge. "Of course, I'm sure! I think I'd have remembered, don't you?"

Terry stared at her. "You're overwrought. Maybe you forgot."

"I did not page you," Lisa gritted out. "When did I have time? I was on the phone with that prank call, remember?"

Terry's look of concern became a scowl. "If you don't want to try and talk about this, Lisa, just say so. I'll go."

Lisa leaned back into the cushions and propped her feet on the large ottoman. She closed her eyes, feeling suddenly exhausted. "Terry, at this point, I'm not sure what I want you to do."

She couldn't have been more shocked to feel his mouth on hers. Lisa's eyes flew open and her hands came up against his broad, blue chest. Terry kissed her with more passion and skill than he ever had before.

Lisa was too surprised by both the abruptness and quality of the kiss to stop him at first. Terry seemed to take her lack of protest as consent because the kiss grew deeper. He pushed her down further on the couch until he half-covered her with his body. His hands began roaming.

He was much bigger than she and heavier. With his tongue in her mouth, it was hard to tell him to get off. Lisa pushed, but Terry, so caught up in the moment, didn't seem to notice.

It wasn't until he came up for a breath of air that Lisa had the chance to snap, "What the hell do you think you're doing?"

She expected him to look contrite. There was an expression in his eyes, but it wasn't contrition. Smugness, maybe, mixed with some anger. She'd never seen him look that way before and it scared her.

In a flash, whatever it was had gone, and he was the Terry she expected. "I thought you might want me to."

"After what I just told you? After what happened tonight?" Lisa rubbed her bare arms with her still-chilly fingers.

"You were so upset," he told her. "I thought I could make you feel better."

"By mauling me?"

His mouth thinned. "It was just a kiss, Lisa."

A kiss unlike any others they'd shared before, she wanted to point out. "It's been a long night. I'd really just like to go to bed."

"I could stay," he said softly, reaching out a hand to touch her hair. "Let me stay tonight, Lisa."

For one brief, insane moment, she thought about saying yes. Not from any desire to take Terry to bed with her, but just so she wouldn't have to be alone. Saying yes, though, meant complications she did not want to pursue.

"No," she replied firmly. "You'd better go."

Terry sighed, letting his hand drop. "You won't even give me a chance, will you?"

"A chance for what?" She asked. "Sex? Terry, for God's sake, this is not the time."

"It's never been the time with you, has it?" He asked. "Not for me. Maybe for that greaseball loser...."

"You leave Deacon out of this," she said.

Terry laughed meanly. "It's a little late for that, isn't it?"

He was hurting, and she didn't blame him for his cruel words. She would not, however, get into an argument with him right now. Both of them were ready to say things they would later regret.

"Just go," Lisa told him. "Please."

"Damn it, Lisa," Terry said. It was the first time she'd ever heard him swear. "You're driving me crazy."

"Let's be adults about this, okay? It's late. We're both tired. We can talk about this tomorrow."

"You'd let him stay," Terry said bitterly.

That he was probably right didn't make it any easier for her to reply. "That's none of your business."

"Did you think that maybe he's behind this all?" Terry asked her.

"Don't start." Lisa pushed further away from him into the cushions. "Just don't."

"Your dad told me about the email you got at work," Terry said. "And now the phone calls. He's got a reason to hurt you, Lisa. Can't you see that?"

Unless she told him about the conversation she'd had with Deacon tonight, she could not explain to him why he was wrong. Instead, Lisa just shook her head. "I told you before he has nothing to do with this."

"No? He could've dropped you off, then called from a cell phone."

"And you could've done the same thing," Lisa snapped. "The call didn't come until after you left. You came back after it was over. It could've been you, Terry!"

She'd only meant to counterpoint his argument against Deacon, but her suggestion clearly infuriated him. Terry got up from the sofa and straightened his barely creased uniform. He even took the time to resettle his hat.

"I'm a police officer," he said. "My job is to catch the scum bags who do stuff like that."

He wanted an apology she wasn't ready to give. When he didn't get it, Terry went to the house's front door across the living room. He rattled the lock and slid the safety bolt into place.

"I'm checking all the locks before I leave here," he said sternly. "And on the windows. Campbell might be content to just drop you off and ride away, but I'm not."

She couldn't protest, not when she was glad to have him secure the house. "Thank you."

He nodded. "It's my job. And I love you."

It was the first time he'd said it. Thankfully, he didn't wait for her to reply. Terry checked the entire house with his swift and purposeful manner, and pronounced it secure.

"I'll call you tomorrow." He left her sitting on the couch.

Tomorrow. She'd have to deal with everything tomorrow. Lisa looked at the clock, and realized with a groan, that midnight had come and gone. She no longer had until tomorrow; tomorrow had become today.

With aching head and whirling thoughts, she went to bed and fell instantly into a deep and blessedly dreamless sleep.

CHAPTER 9

Lisa was working in a forge. Clang. Clang. Clang. She struck the metal bar with her hammer over and over, but it wouldn't bend. Wouldn't shape itself into anything useful. She tried to toss it aside, but it clung to her hand like it had been glued.

Clang. She struck it again, frustrated. Clang. Clang....

With a gasp, she woke. She'd been dreaming after all. The clanging she heard was real, and coming from downstairs.

Bright sunlight flooded through her window, casting dappled patterns from the tree outside onto her lavender comforter. The clang came again, but this time she recognized it. Somebody was trying to get in.

Allegra! Terry had insisted Lisa bolt the door after him last night, and Allegra was locked out. Lisa flipped off the light summer covers and ran down the stairs to the kitchen.

"It's about time," Allegra groused when Lisa finally opened the door. "Why is this locked?"

"Terry made me do it."

Allegra winked. "Ah... Didn't want to be interrupted?"

"I got a prank phone call last night," Lisa said.

Allegra pushed past her and into the kitchen. She pulled open the fridge and scrambled around inside, pulling out a jug of orange juice. Without bothering with a glass, she glugged the juice and wiped her mouth with the back of her hand.

"Heavy breather? Kids asking if your refrigerator's running?"

Lisa shook her head, watching in distaste as Allegra put the juice back in the fridge and pulled out a jelly jar. She stuck her finger in and licked off the glob of jelly, then stuck her finger back in.

"Allegra!"

Allegra stopped, her finger in her mouth. "What?"

"Use a knife!" Lisa's entire body wanted to tense, and she forced herself to relax. "You're not the only person who lives here, you know."

"Duh." Allegra rolled her eyes and put the jelly back in the fridge. She looked at her sister, pausing to really pay attention for once. "You okay?"

"No, I'm not." Lisa went to the coffee maker and began preparing a strong brew. She felt like she needed it this morning. "I'm freaked out."

"Really?"

Allegra's speculative tone made Lisa turn. She caught a glimpse of sly mischief in her sister's eyes, then Allegra bent back into the fridge, hiding her face. Her shoulders shook briefly as though she might be laughing.

"It's not funny, Al," Lisa said. To her dismay, tears coated her voice.

Allegra's head popped up from behind the fridge door. Now the look in her eyes was concern. Seemingly real, but Lisa could never be sure. "You really are freaked out."

"Yes." The coffee pot burped behind her. "That's what I've been trying to tell you!"

Allegra took Lisa's hand and pulled her to sit at the kitchen table. "So why'd you stay here all alone last night? I thought Terry'd stay with you. He likes doing that sort of thing, doesn't he? Being all protective and stuff?"

"Terry and I broke up last night."

Allegra seemed shocked. "What?"

Lisa met her sister's eyes. "Despite what you've been telling Mom, Terry and I were not that serious. At least I wasn't."

"It's that jail geek loser, isn't it?" Allegra said grimly. She rapidly peeled an orange and popped a piece into her mouth. "Campbell."

Lisa sighed. "That's only part of it. Coffee's ready. You want some?"

Allegra glanced at the coffee pot and waved her sister to stay sitting. She got two mugs and the sugar bowl and rapidly fixed two cups of heavily sweetened coffee. She plunked one down in front of

Lisa.

"You're an idiot," she said flatly. "Deacon will only mess with your head and get you in trouble. He's a criminal!"

Lisa held up her hand. "Don't start with me today. My love life is my business."

Allegra looked hurt. "Fine."

Lisa winced at the too-sweet drink and pushed it aside. "I'm going back to bed for a while."

"It's nearly noon," Allegra said, stunned. "You never sleep in like this!"

"I had a rough night, okay?" Lisa snapped. Seeing her sister's pout should have made her feel contrite.

Allegra sniffed. "Go back to bed if you're going to be such a grouch."

She got up from the table, leaving her used mug where it was. Of course. She flounced from the kitchen and headed up the back stairs to her room. Lisa heard the door slam.

She looked at the clock, then at the phone squatting on the counter like a toad. When would it ring and who would be on the other end? Deacon? Terry?

Or somebody worse—the person who saw everything she did?

*   *   *

Deacon fiddled with the air conditioning knobs in his mother's car. The tiny vehicle was already sweltering, even though it wasn't quite noon. At last a blast of cooler air sputtered out of the vents. *I'll have to do some work on the car for Mom,* he thought, still fiddling. Even though she could no longer drive herself anywhere, it didn't make sense for her car to go to junk.

Bertha opened the passenger door and slipped inside. "Sorry," she puffed, wrestling with her purse and a large plastic shopping bag. "Had to get some more things."

"Mom," Deacon said in exasperation. "Paula can go to the grocery store for herself."

Bertha snorted. "This is stuff for the kids, Mr. Smarty Pants."

Deacon's sister's two boys and two girls looked forward to Grandma's visits because she always brought cookies and sweets. Deacon smiled, shaking his head. For Bertha to go someplace without taking along something she'd baked would be sacrilege.

He shifted the bag onto the back seat. "Let me put it in the back for you.Ready to roll?"

Bertha nodded. "Thank you for driving me to Johnsonburg, honey. I know you have other things you'd rather do."

Deacon glanced at the dashboard clock. "It's early, Mom. I'll be back in plenty of time."

To call Lisa, he thought. He hadn't wanted to do it earlier with his mother puttering around in the kitchen. If he could get Paula to agree to drive Mom back home later this afternoon, he could leave right after lunch and have the whole house to himself.

He wasn't quite sure what he was going to say to her. Last night still seemed like some sort of dream. Had he really kissed her? And had they really talked about starting over?

"Your mind's in the clouds today," Bertha remarked.

Deacon grinned. "I guess so."

"You gonna tell me why?"

"Nope."

Bertha laughed. "It's just good to see you smiling again, honey."

It feels good to be smiling again, Deacon thought. He wasn't smiling two hours later, though, with a quartet of kids screaming in his ear and Paula telling him she couldn't drive Mom home after all.

"Joey has soccer practice later," Paula said. She and Deacon huddled in the kitchen, not wanting Bertha to overhear. "And the kids have plans with friends tonight. Bob's out of town until Wednesday. I just can't be running back to St. Mary's today, Deacon. I thought you were going to take her! That was the plan."

Deacon scowled, watching his sister fuss with the platter of cold ham she was serving for lunch. "C'mon, Paula. I have some things I need to do."

Paula pulled a tray of warm buns from the oven. She set the platter on the stove top and brushed her hair from her sweating forehead. Her expression was not pleasant.

"I can't," she said in the warning tone he recognized. "And don't push me on it. Those kids are already driving me bonkers and this heat is just plain nasty. I'm about ready to lose my temper, so please don't...."

"Okay," Deacon said, resigned. He patted Paula's shoulder. "Chill."

She flashed him a grateful smile. "Thanks, Deacon."

She pushed past him with the platter, indicating with a nod that he should take the rolls. Deacon put the bread in bowl and followed her into the dining room, but he didn't have much appetite.

He'd just have to call Lisa later.

*   *   *

Lisa had gone back to bed, but she didn't get much sleep. She just kept waiting for the phone to ring. Finally, just to pass the time, she decided to shower and get dressed.

She was glad again, that when she and Allegra had moved in together, she had snagged the only bedroom with its own bathroom. Allegra had to use the hall bath, and they didn't need to share. Lisa relished the privacy of having her own bathtub, especially with her sister's less- than-stellar cleaning habits.

She ran the water cool, since even with the fans on, the house was warm. The pounding spray felt good on the back of her neck and shoulders, almost like a massage. She closed her eyes, trying to let the tension drain away.

She nudged the water a little warmer and squeezed handful of her favorite shampoo into her palm. The bottle was nearly empty, and she frowned, trying to remember. Hadn't she just bought a new bottle? She lathered up her hair, scrubbing her scalp and letting the water rinse her clean. Her conditioner was the same—nearly empty. Now Lisa began to be annoyed. She was positive she'd replaced the expensive brand of conditioner just last week. She didn't use that much of it.

One disadvantage of having a shower connected to the claw foot tub was lack of wall storage. Because of the way the showerhead connected to the wall, she couldn't even hang one of those wire shelving units from it. Consequently, she kept all her bath products in a plastic crate that fit precariously between the edge of the tub and the wall.

Now Lisa searched the whole crate finding that nearly all the bottles were missing their contents. *Allegra,* she thought angrily. Her sister must be borrowing her things without asking.

The shower's soothing properties were useless now. Lisa rinsed and turned off the water. She bent to retrieve a towel from the small bookcase she'd set up between the door and the tub. Her questing fingers found only one.

"What is going on?" she said in frustration. She'd done laundry only a few days ago, including a load of towels.

Now she pulled out the worn yellow towel she'd had since living at home. Where were her purple-and-green striped towels? She wrapped the threadbare towel around her hair and stood naked in the breeze from the window. Her eyes scanned the bathroom finding the pile of towels heaped in the corner next to the toilet.

She muttered a curse and bent to pick up the first towel. It felt heavier than normal as though saturated with something. And it smelled, too, like her shampoo. Cautiously, Lisa pulled the heavy cloth away from the others and gasped out loud. Her entire supply of towels, all four of them, lay soaking in a glutinous mess of shampoo, conditioner and body wash.

She dropped the top towel back onto the pile and washed her hands frantically at the sink. Her eyes kept finding the pile even as she scrubbed. Lisa forced herself to look away, but catching sight of her face in the mirror was no more reassuring. She looked terrified.

Had Allegra done this? But Lisa could not imagine her sister doing such a vengeful thing. Using her things, certainly, especially since she considered anything Lisa had to be up for grabs. But wasting it like that? No, Lisa thought, trying and failing to calm herself. Somebody else had been in her bathroom.

With shaking hands, she opened the medicine cabinet and found something else to frighten her inside. Her carefully lined up bottles of medicine and beauty products had been moved around. The changes were subtle. At first glance, nothing seemed out of place. Upon closer inspection, though, the pain reliever she usually kept on the top shelf had been moved to the lower shelf. Several other bottles had been shifted, too. It was possible she'd done it herself without thinking about it, but she didn't think so.

She shut the cabinet with a click. Someone had been in her house. Someone had been in her bathroom.

She felt violated. Lisa pulled on some clothes and went out into the hall. "Allegra!"

She heard the music from her sister's room, so she knew she was in there. Lisa went through the empty bedroom and knocked on Allegra's door. The music became softer.

"Yeah?"

"Let me in," Lisa said.

"Door's open."

Lisa pushed through, ready to tell her sister everything. What she saw stunned her to silence. Allegra's room was blanketed in clothing.

Allegra stood in front of the mirror wearing a cocktail dress. She twirled around, admiring her reflection from all sides. Lisa saw two more nearly identical dresses hanging from the closet door. Shoes lay piled in mismatched pairs all over the floor. Jeans and shirts fought each other for space on Allegra's bed, and piles of lingerie lingered on doorknobs and dangled from dresser drawers. It looked like a suitcase had exploded in the room.

"Where'd you get all this stuff?" Lisa cried, her bathroom experience forgotten for the moment.

Allegra stopped twirling, the dreamy look on her face turning hard. "Around."

"Around where?" Lisa picked up a brand new jacket. She glanced at the price tag and sticker shock hit her. "And with what?"

Allegra grabbed the jacket out of Lisa's hands. "I deserve some new things once in awhile, Lisa."

"Once in awhile, sure," Lisa said. "But this…this is a lot of new things, Allegra. Where'd you get the money to pay for this stuff?"

Allegra's pretty face turned dark. She unzipped the cocktail dress, letting the pretty gown fall unnoticed to the floor. She didn't even bother stepping over it to pick up the next one. She tugged that one on over her head, wrinkling it.

"That's my business," she answered Lisa.

"What do you even need four black cocktail dresses for?"

Allegra was busy staring at her reflection again. "This one makes me look fat, doesn't it?"

Allegra wouldn't look fat in a sumo suit. Lisa watched her sister pull off the second dress leaving it crumpled in a pile, too. Allegra didn't bother with the other dresses. She held up a pair of jeans to her waist. She slipped on leg in, then the other. The waistband gaped, clearly too large.

"Those don't even fit you," Lisa said as Allegra shimmied out of the jeans and added them to the heap on the floor. "Why'd you buy jeans that don't fit you?"

A sudden thought struck her. She felt like slapping her forehead, so clear was the insight. Bits and pieces that hadn't made sense over the past few months now suddenly fell into place.

"You didn't buy these."

Allegra paused while pawing through a stack of shirts. "Of course I did."

"You stole them, didn't you?" Lisa watched her sister's face carefully for any sign she was right, but Allegra was good. She didn't even flinch. "Allegra?"

Allegra pulled on a t-shirt that said "Princess" on it in glittery letters. "Don't be an idiot."

Lisa touched a dangling bra from Victoria's Secret. The price tag hadn't been removed. "You didn't buy any of this, did you? You stole all of it."

Allegra whirled around, her mouth skinned back in a grimace. "Shut up, Lisa!"

Lisa took a step toward her sister. "Al, what's going on with you? Talk to me?"

"With me?" Allegra scoffed. "Let's talk about what's going on with you, Lisa. Lost anything else lately? Like maybe your mind?"

Lisa looked around the room feeling sick. "You need help."

"No, you need help," Allegra snapped. She pulled on a pair of shorts. "I'm not the one who's going looney."

The insult stung. Lisa pulled back. "Where would you find the money to buy all this stuff?"

"Why should I tell you?" Allegra said. "You obviously want to believe I stole it. You want to think your sister's a thief!"

"I don't want to think that," Lisa countered. "But tell me why I shouldn't. I know what you earn, Allegra."

Allegra smirked. "Tell me something, sis. Why are you so eager to believe I'm a thief when you won't even believe that lover-boy is really a thief? He's the one sent to jail, not me."

"We're not talking about Deacon. We're talking about you."

"It's pretty sad when you let a good lay come between you and your only sister," Allegra said haughtily.

"Where did you get all this?" She didn't want to believe her baby sister could have stolen it.

"Did it ever occur to you that I might have a boyfriend, too?" Allegra asked. "Is that too hard to believe?"

Looking at her beautiful younger sister, Lisa did not find that difficult to believe, at all. "You've never mentioned one."

"Who could with you yapping all the time about your love life?" Allegra asked.

This was completely unfair and completely untrue. "You're crazy."

Allegra flew into a rage. "Don't you call me that!"

Lisa fell back against the doorframe under the force of her sister's anger. "You're crazy *and* you're selfish!" It felt good to let it out.

"Selfish?" Allegra cried.

"I came in here to tell you how worried I was about something I found in the bathroom," Lisa yelled back. "And all you care about is yourself. That's all you ever care about, Allegra! It's always the Allegra Show. And I'm sick of it!"

"How can you say that?" Allegra put her hands on her hips. "I stayed out last night on purpose just so you and Terry could have some time alone. I'm always doing stuff for you!"

"Stop assuming you know what I want," Lisa said. She hated fighting, especially with Allegra, who always ended up turning the tables.

"You didn't want to be alone with Terry last night?" Allegra asked, her voice clearly indicating she wouldn't believe a negative answer.

"No," Lisa said anyway. "At least, not for the reason you think."

"For what, then?" Allegra asked.

"Not everything is about sex."

Allegra laughed. "Sure, it is. It's all about sex. Why even bother with men if it isn't?"

Lisa rolled her eyes. "Oh, that's a healthy attitude."

"Men are good for one thing," Allegra said, looking at her reflection again. "Buying stuff. All the rest is just sex. Give them sex and they give you what you want. Don't you know that by now?"

"Maybe I want more than that," Lisa said. "And you should, too."

Allegra's laugh was gritty. "Sure. You can want it, but you won't get it. Look at you—all pale and listless because you're waiting for the phone to ring. He said he'd call, didn't he? And he hasn't?"

"How'd you know that?"

Allegra shrugged. "They all say they'll call. But if you'd given Terry some good old- fashioned sex last night, he'd have been on the phone first thing this morning."

Terry. She hadn't even been thinking about him. Apparently, Allegra saw Lisa's expression and understood what it meant. She stopped looking at herself long enough to peer at Lisa.

"Don't tell me," she said. "You're not all teary eyed because of Ter-Bear, are you? You're waiting for that loser Campbell to call!"

Before Lisa could answer, the phone rang. Both sisters turned to the sound of the ringing from beneath a pile of Allegra's hoard of clothes. Allegra dove for it, snatching up the cordless phone triumphantly before Lisa could get to it.

"Hello?" She smirked at Lisa. "Yes, of course she's here. Can you talk to her? I don't know. Can you?"

"Give me the phone." Lisa held out her hand, but Allegra didn't listen.

"I thought you might call this morning," Allegra continued, cooing into the phone.

Lisa yanked the phone away from her sister and barked into the mouthpiece. "Hello?"

"Honey?" Her dad sounded concerned. "Are you all right?"

Allegra pointed and laughed, and Lisa left the room. "I wasn't expecting you to call."

"Apparently not," he said. "Sorry to disappoint you, honey."

"Oh, Dad." Lisa sighed. She went to her own bedroom and shut the door. "It's not that at all. What's up?"

"Your mom and I want you to come over to the house this afternoon. We want to talk to you about some things."

That didn't sound good. "What things?"

"Just some things your sister has told us. We're worried."

For once, Lisa wasn't furious with Allegra for talking out of turn. It would be nice to talk to her parents about all the things that had been going on. "I'll be there around two."

At least the ongoing Allegra drama was good for one thing. She went to the bathroom and picked up the load of soiled towels, throwing them in the hamper. After dealing with her sister, she was too tired to worry about them any more.

*   *   *

"It's too bad we couldn't stay for Joey's soccer practice," Bertha said on the ride home.

Deacon felt a flash of guilt. "I need to get home. Do some work."

"Uh-huh."

He could feel his mother looking at him, but he kept his eyes fixed firmly on the road. She could read him like a book, but he wasn't ready to go into details with her just yet. She cleared her throat. He was caught.

"Must be important work to do on a Saturday," she said.

"Yeah," he answered, glancing at the clock. It was nearly two. He still had time to call Lisa.

"It wouldn't have anything to do with the girl Maisy Eckerd saw you sparking with last night on the front porch, would it?"

Now he looked at her. "You're too good."

She laughed. "Maisy Eckerd is too nosy. So, does your hurry to get home have anything to do with her?"

He nodded, signaling to get into the passing lane. "Yeah."

Bertha sighed. "Well, finally! I thought I'd never see the day. Who is she?"

He hesitated before telling her. "It's Lisa Shadd, Mom."

Bertha gasped. "The one who sent you away?"

"Mom," he began, but Bertha was already off and running.

"Deacon Timothy Campbell! What on earth are you thinking, getting mixed up with her again? After what she did? Jesus, Mary and Joseph!"

She must really be riled to start invoking religious curses. Deacon tried to calm her. "Mom, I'm a grown man—"

"Without a bit of sense in your head!" Bertha said. "I knew you taking that job at her father's business was a bad idea! What'd she do, force you to take up with her to keep your job? I told you, Deacon, go talk to Bucky Sherman over at the plant! He'll give you your old job back!"

"I don't want my old job back," Deacon said. "Mom, listen. What happened in the past is over. I really like Lisa."

Bertha muttered, "I thought I'd raised you with some sense."

"Mom, why do you have to treat me like I'm twelve years old?"

That stopped her. "You're right," she said. "I guess I'm just a old lady—"

"Mom…"

"Who only wants the best for her children."

"Mom!"

"What?"

"Never mind."

They were home. Deacon pulled into the driveway and parked. He helped his mother out of the car, ignoring her attempts to get him talking again.

Once inside, he pulled the phone off the hook and used a trick he hadn't used since adolescence. He pulled the cord as far as it would reach, and locked himself in the bathroom to dial Lisa's number.

"Hello?"

Allegra. "Can I talk to Lisa?"

A pause. "She's not here. Who's this?"

He guessed she damn well knew who it was already. "This is Deacon."

She laughed under her breath. "Oh, well, she's not here, Deacon. I'll be sure to tell her you called."

"You do that," he said, knowing she wouldn't.

She didn't bother with goodbye. With the dial tone buzzing in his ear, Deacon left the bathroom and went back out to the kitchen. Bertha began busily wiping down the counter as though she hadn't been listening.

"She wasn't home," Deacon told her.

"Oh?" Bertha said. "Then I guess we could've stayed for Joey's soccer practice."

There was nothing quite like a mother to make a guy feel guilty, Deacon thought. But he loved her anyway. He bent to kiss her cheek, and she beamed, surprised.

"I'm going to the store," he told her.

"What for?" she asked.

"A cordless phone," he told her and ducked out the door before the flying dishtowel could hit him.

CHAPTER 10

"She's moving out?" Lisa sat back, stunned.

Marcia wrung her hands. "You know how sensitive Allegra is, Lisa. She says she feels like a third wheel. That she's coming between you and Terry."

The absurdity of the statement made Lisa laugh out loud. She saw her parents exchange uneasy glances. Doug reached out and patted her hand.

"We know how stressed you've been lately working with Deacon and everything. And that nasty email."

"Allegra says you've been misplacing things," Marcia continued with a glance for reassurance at Doug. She seemed to gather her courage before speaking again. "Lisa, honey, she says you've even accused her of taking your things."

God forbid her parents think of Allegra as anything but an angel. "It wouldn't be the first time."

"Listen, we're just concerned, that's all," Doug said sternly. "Since this Campbell fellow's been back in town, you haven't been acting like yourself at all. And it's affecting your sister."

"So she wants to move out?" Lisa said, getting up from the sofa. "Fine by me."

She wasn't upset by Allegra's unsurprising decision to flee to the safety of Mommy and Daddy's arms. What stung was that she'd thought her parents were worried for her. That their wanting to talk to her about their concerns were...well, about her for once and not

Allegra. Instead, she'd just listened to half an hour of discussion on Allegra's sensitivities.

"Lisa, don't be that way." Marcia seemed close to tears, a state Lisa wanted no part of. Her mother simply hated conflict, especially between her children, and would rather turn a blind eye to it than have to confront it.

"Allegra feels like a third wheel with me and Terry?" Lisa said. "Well, she won't have to worry about that anymore. Terry and I broke up."

"What?" Marcia cried, aghast.

"What happened?" Doug asked more practically. "Does it have anything to do with Campbell?"

"As a matter of fact, it does," Lisa told him.

Her mom's hands fluttered. "Oh, Lisa!"

"I knew it would be a mistake to hire him," Doug said. "What's he done to you?"

"Nothing," Lisa cried in frustration. Yet anyway, and nothing without her consent. But she couldn't exactly tell her parents that, could she? "Mom, Dad, listen. I have something to tell you about Allegra. Something you should know."

Again, she saw them exchange glances. "I think Allegra's been...stealing things. Clothes. Maybe other stuff, I'm not sure."

"Oh, Lisa!" Marcia cried again, covering her face with her hands.

"She said you'd accuse her of that," Doug told Lisa. "Frankly, I didn't want to believe it."

"Did she tell you why I'd be accusing her?" Lisa demanded. She put her hands on her hips, squaring off with her parents.

"She said you saw a few new things in her room and asked her where she got them." Doug's face was stony as he faced her. She'd gotten her stubborn temper from her dad, and it was times like these that it showed.

"A few?" Lisa thought of the room full of clothes. "It was a lot more than that, Dad. And there are other things, too."

"She told us you'd been giving her a hard time over there," Doug said. "Demanding she do more than her share of the chores, not sharing your things with her—"

"Are we three years old?" Lisa asked. "When she moved in with me, I told her there'd be rules. Like doing her share of the chores, yes. Like being adults, not children!"

"Nobody says you're still kids," Doug said.

"You treat her like she is," Lisa said. "You make excuses for her, you ignore the things she does—"

"Allegra has always been special!" Marcia cried. "And I won't hear another word against her from you, Lisa!"

"Fine." Lisa grabbed her purse from the end table and headed for the door. She paused, hanging her head to stop the tears from falling. She fought them back successfully before turning to her mom and dad. "I thought…I thought you wanted to talk about me today."

"We were talking about you," Doug said.

Lisa shook her head. "No, you were talking about her. You're concerned about her. You're always concerned about her!"

"We've never had to worry about you, honey," Marcia said, trying to make peace. "We know you can handle things."

So that was the way it was. Lisa nodded slowly, her hand on the door. "I'll see you guys later."

"Lisa…" Her dad was calling after her, but she ignored him.

Once outside, the hot afternoon sun did nothing to improve her mood. Lisa slid behind the wheel of her car, pressing her lips together to keep them from trembling. She pounded the wheel once before regaining control.

If nothing else good came of the past few weeks' events, at least Allegra was moving out. She couldn't pretend to be sorry about that. Lord knew, she loved her sister…but she didn't always like her.

Allegra had certainly wrapped their parents around her little finger, and was Lisa really surprised? Her sister was manipulative and sly. Of course she'd covered all the bases before pleading her woes to Mommy and Daddy. It just burned that they chose to believe Allegra and ignore Lisa.

She pulled up to her house, noting that Allegra's car wasn't in the drive. *Good. Maybe she's already gone.* Lisa went into the house and straight to the thermostat. She could keep the house as cool or warm as she liked now, instead of conforming to Allegra's insane insistence that the temperature be set only on even numbers.

She managed to hold herself together until she entered the living room. There, the sight of her carefully chosen, tapestry print couch no longer covered with Allegra's faded, tattered Penn State throw blanket suddenly made her burst into tears. Lisa flung herself onto the couch, giving herself over to the need to rage and weep and flail.

Damn, but it felt good. She punched the pillows fiercely, then lay back and kicked the cushions. That felt even better. That she was abusing her own couch, the first piece of really good furniture she'd ever owned, didn't really matter. It just felt so good to let go!

After awhile, the tears stopped and she rested, breathing heavily on the somewhat dented couch. Lisa wiped her face, pressing her fingers against her swollen eyes. A cool cloth would feel good right now.

She went to the kitchen to get one, leaning over the sink and letting the water run until it was reasonably cold. The cloth felt marvelous on her skin, and she let out a sigh of pure delight. A tantrum followed by a soothing cloth. Now she only needed some self-indulgent ice cream, and she'd be complete.

"Lisa?"

Startled at the sudden male voice in front of her, Lisa let out a shriek and stepped back. Her elbow connected squarely with the edge of the kitchen counter and she yelped in pain. Her entire arm tingled and she cradled it.

"Deacon!" She sounded exasperated when she meant to sound pleased.

He looked at her uncertainly. "Are you all right? You look like you were crying."

She touched her cheek, thinking about how she must look. "I was."

His instant look of concern made her almost glad she'd been weeping. "Did something happen?"

She thought of the night before and today's discussion with her parents. Lisa laughed, suddenly feeling much better about everything now Deacon stood so solid and real in her kitchen. "Nothing that won't go away," she said.

He looked confused. "Okay."

She felt her face again, embarrassed. "Let me get cleaned up."

She splashed water on her face, too aware of him standing so close behind her. The water felt good on her skin, which was hot now and not from temper. He was so close she could smell him...and that thought made her tense.

"What're you doing here?" she asked a little too sharply.

Last night's phone call played in her mind. I know everything you do, the voice had said. Someone was watching her. She didn't want to believe it was Deacon, but....

"You said you were going to call."

"I did call," he replied patiently. "You weren't home. I didn't know where you were...."

"So you came over anyway?" she said, her voice rising. "Even though you knew I wasn't here? Why would you come over if I wasn't here?"

She was being irrational, but knowing it didn't stop her heart from thumping or the accusation from forming on her tongue. Thankfully, Deacon stopped her before she could speak by putting his hands in the air in a gesture of peace. Lisa felt foolish...but also wary.

"Can we sit down and talk?"

Lisa nodded. "We'll go into the living room."

She led the way, entirely too conscious of how swiftly her moods and temper were changing. Lisa did not like being on an emotional roller coaster. She'd always prided herself on her ability to handle stress. The past few weeks, however, were catching up to her. *And who knew,* she thought bitterly as she and Deacon sat on opposite ends of the couch. *Maybe Allegra isn't the only diva bitch in the Shadd family.*

"What happened after I dropped you off last night?" Deacon cut right to the center of things.

His frank honesty was a quality she admired. It seemed difficult to believe she'd ever doubted his penchant for being truthful. At once, suspicion reared its ugly head again because how did she *know* he was being truthful? She'd said she believed him about the robbery, but could she believe anything anymore?

"I got a prank phone call," she told him. "It was pretty nasty."

"Dirty?" Deacon shifted on the cushions to face her, one long leg crossed over his knee.

"Why does everyone assume that?" Lisa kept her own body facing forward, aware of her stiff posture. "Not like the email, no. Just...creepy."

Swiftly she outlined what the voice on the phone had told her, ending with the part about knowing everything she did. Lisa shuddered even as she said it, though in the bright light of afternoon, she should have felt safe. She toyed with her shirt hem, plucking at the fabric with nervous fingers until she annoyed herself with the action and forced herself to stop.

"Then Terry came back because he'd said I beeped him," Lisa continued. "But I hadn't."

"Came back?" Deacon's voice played at being casual, but Lisa sensed the tension in it.

She sighed mentally, feeling machismo fill the space between them. "He was here when I got home."

"Oh."

The short declaration carried as much meaning as if he'd spoken for an hour.

"I didn't know he'd be here, Deacon. We fought. He left."

"Then he came back," Deacon said.

Now Lisa turned to look at him. "Yes, because he said I paged him."

"But you didn't." Deacon tapped his crossed leg with his fingers.

"No. I told him about the phone call and he insisted on checking all the locks before I went to bed. And he left."

Lisa didn't mention Terry's unsubtle accusation that Deacon might be at the heart of her recent disturbances, neither did she tell him what Terry had said about Deacon just leaving her without making sure she was safe. There was enough rivalry between the two men already without her egging them on.

"You should've called me," Deacon said. "I would have come over."

The thought of what that would have meant caused another sort of chill to slip down her spine. Lisa could not deny the affect Deacon had on her. Even with all that had happened, even with the doubts Terry had tried to plant in her head, the thought of Deacon spending the night still made her squirm.

"Today my parents called and said they wanted to talk to me," Lisa continued, as though he hadn't spoken. "I thought they wanted to talk about me, about the things that have been going on. Instead I had to listen to a lecture about how special Allegra is, and how horribly I've been treating her. She's moving back home to get away from me."

Deacon laughed. "Are you sorry about that?"

"No, actually, I'm not," Lisa said, and a welcome smile brushed her mouth. "Not about that. I just thought for once they'd be worried about me instead of her."

"You're too responsible," Deacon said. "They never have to worry about you."

"That's what Mom said," Lisa answered, surprised again at his insight.

"It's true," Deacon said. "It's one of the things I always admired about you."

"Being responsible isn't all it's cracked up to be," Lisa said grouchily. She finally was able to relax against the back of the couch. "Sometimes I'd like to be the needy one. The one who goes out and just does whatever she wants, who gets wild without thinking about the consequences."

She glanced at him as she said it, meaning it lightly. Seeing his face tighten at her words, Lisa's voice trailed away. She hadn't meant sex, not specifically, when she talked about getting wild. But it was there. The meaning of her words hovered between them.

Speaking would ruin it and she was glad he didn't bother. Deacon slid across the couch to her, taking her in his arms and slanting his mouth across hers in a searing kiss. She had not had time to breathe, but didn't need to, because kissing him was like drinking pure oxygen.

It was good to be touched, to be held. To lose herself in the passion that erased everything else from her mind. In Deacon's arms, she didn't have to think about Allegra, or phone calls, or missing items from the laundry.

Lisa moaned, a soft sound from deep in her throat. He pulled away, his eyes glazed. She didn't want him to let go, but he'd misunderstood the sound she'd made.

"I'm sorry," he said. "This probably isn't a good time."

Why did men have to be so difficult? Wanting it when she didn't want to give it and refusing it when she needed it? Lisa stifled a disgruntled snort and answered him by pulling him back to her.

The kissing grew more passionate, reminding her of the times they'd spent on his couch three years before. *So much for starting at the beginning,* she thought hazily, but then didn't care. His hands on her made her forget anything else.

Deacon slipped his hands up beneath her tee shirt, finding the bare skin of her stomach. His fingers traced a light pattern there, tickling. Lisa giggled, the sound muffled against his mouth, but she didn't try to squirm away. The tickling sent pleasurable shivers across her skin.

She ran her hands through the silken length of his hair, glad he was letting it grow long again. She'd liked the way it hung to his shoulders, making him seem like some sort of sexy pirate. Now her lips found the place her fingers had just caressed.

Kissing his earlobe made Deacon wriggle a little, and Lisa laughed again. She ran a line of kisses down his neck, pausing at the curve of his collar to nip the beginning of his exposed collarbone. Deacon's fingers tightened convulsively on her stomach, pinching.

"Ouch!" She sat back with a wince.

"Sorry," he said, smoothing the injured skin with his fingers. "You tickled."

"You tickled me," she pointed out, "and I didn't pinch you."

She wasn't sure, really, if she was joking or serious. The pinch hadn't hurt or even left a mark. It was that he'd reacted that way at all that made her take pause.

He kissed her cheek, then her mouth. Deacon leaned his forehead against her, looking in her eyes. "It was an accident."

In her head, she knew that.

"I'm sorry." Lisa sighed, not wanting the passion to fade and feeling it start to anyway. "There's been a lot of stuff going on lately."

He sat back. "You still don't trust me?"

"That's not it at all," Lisa said, trying to reassure herself as much as him.

"Why don't I just go," Deacon said. He pushed further back on the couch. "We can talk later."

She didn't want him to go—not now. Lisa glanced around the room quickly. She had to admit that along with the way he made her feel, she also didn't really want to be alone.

"Please stay," she said. "We could watch a movie or something. We did say we wanted to start over, right?"

She must not have been doing such a bad job of being winsome because she saw him waver. Lisa offered more incentive.

"I've got popcorn," she said. "We can even pop it in oil and add real butter."

"Damn, woman," Deacon said in a false but charming twang. "You know how to tempt a man."

"There's a Star Trek marathon on cable," she continued, making him laugh and throw up his hands.

"Sold!" Deacon shook his head at her. "Though how you can possibly convince me that watching Captain Kirk is better than kissing you, I don't know."

His teasing made warmth curl again in her belly. Lisa grinned. "Me neither."

"Are you sure you want me to stay?"

"Yes." She was sure. Not about what might happen later if their hands kept touching in the popcorn bowl because she couldn't begin to think about that now. But about wanting him to stay, to keep her company, to stop her from feeling like she had to keep looking over her shoulder... Yes, about that she was certain.

"I'll make the popcorn."

He followed her to the kitchen while she puttered with a pan and some oil. Lisa turned the electric burner on medium and began the search for the popcorn kernels. She normally kept them in the cupboard behind the peanut butter.

"I know I have some," she said aloud, running her hands along the back of the cupboard. A small twinge of alarm pricked at her. Was this going to be another disappearing act?

"Maybe it's in the pantry," Deacon suggested. "That's where my mother keeps hers."

Lisa shook her head. "I never put anything in the pantry. The shelves are loose. The last owner didn't use molly bolts to secure anything in this house. I had to redo my entire closet because the shelves pulled right out of the wall. I've been too busy to get around to fixing the ones in the pantry."

"Maybe your sister—"

"Al doesn't eat popcorn," Lisa said. "Popcorn takes too long to count."

She told him that matter-of-factly, still searching the cupboards, and was surprised to hear him laugh loudly.

"What?" Deacon said. "It takes too long to count?"

Turning, she realized how strange that sounded. "She counts everything. Food has to be in even numbers. The thermostat has to be on even numbers only. Things like that."

What had been a quirk now sounded, when spoken to a non-family member, freaky. Deacon frowned when he saw she wasn't kidding. Lisa paused to turn off the burner, not wanting the oil to catch fire.

"That's weird," Deacon said.

"I know."

"Lisa," Deacon said. "That's...that's not right. Has she ever had help for that?"

"Are you saying my sister's crazy?" Lisa snapped, though the thought had crossed her mind more than once. But to hear a stranger say it rankled. "Allegra's just...special."

Appalled to hear her mother's words fly out her own mouth, Lisa went to the pantry. "She's not crazy."

"I didn't say crazy," Deacon called from behind her.

Lisa pulled the pantry door open all the way and fumbled for the chain that would turn on the light fixture. She couldn't find it. It got stuck around the fixture sometimes if the last person to turn off the lights had let it go too quickly.

The pantry was long and narrow, and lined with shelves that made the space even tighter. Normally, Lisa never ventured beyond the first section of shelving since anything she usually used was kept there. In fact, before today, she hadn't even paid much attention to what was on the other shelves.

She stretched up as high as she could, trying to reach the cord that had tangled around the base of the light fixture. She simply wasn't tall enough. She went out to the kitchen and grabbed one of the chairs.

Only by standing on it was she able to at last reach the chain and tug it. Instantly, light blared into her eyes, blinding her. With a cry, Lisa stumbled off the chair, shielding her face.

"You okay?" Deacon asked from behind her. He moved the chair out of the way.

Lisa nodded, wiping at her eyes. She blinked away the glare. "The light got in my eyes."

Deacon let out a slow whistle. "Then I guess you haven't seen this."

Lisa looked past the first section of shelving to the back of the narrow pantry. What she saw made her stomach drop and the hairs on the back of her neck stand on end. A sudden chill swept over her.

Every shelf, from floor to ceiling, had been filled with canned goods. What made it an odd sight was the choice of goods and the way they were arranged, as well as how they'd been altered. Every can, from the simplest tomato soup to strange things like marinated fennel, had been marked with what appeared to be black permanent marker.

As Lisa stepped closer, she saw the markings were not random. Letters had been blacked out—sometimes a few in a row and others every other one. Any face on any label had been carefully colored in, too. Each can had been lined up perfectly, edge to edge, and all of them, no matter the contents, were exactly the same height.

"Oh, my God," Lisa muttered, craning her head to see up to the top shelf. "They're all like this?"

"Do you think your sister did this?"

"Who else?" Lisa shuddered. "Let's get out of here."

She pushed past him and back into the safety and brightness of the kitchen. A sour taste had collected in the back of her throat. She went to the sink and began washing her hands rapidly, uncertain as to why.

"Lisa." Deacon's voice was calm and his hands on her shoulders warm as he turned her to face him.

Water splashed between them, wetting the front of his shirt. Lisa looked at her hands and bit her lip. What was happening to her?

"Allegra is special," she whispered. Hot tears stung her eyes and she could not fight them. "Oh, God, Deacon, what's wrong with my sister?"

"I don't know," Deacon said. "I wish I could tell you, Lisa."

"I need to talk to my parents again," Lisa said. She was aware of Deacon steering her toward one of the kitchen chairs, and she let him lead her there. Sitting felt good since her legs had gone numb. "They need to see this."

Deacon chafed her hands. Lisa felt like her head was a balloon, barely tethered to the rest of her body. She'd always known her sister was different. She'd just never had to face how much.

"That must've taken hours of work," Deacon said reflectively.

"And I never had any idea," Lisa told him, forcing herself to focus. "I never paid any attention to the back of the pantry. Those cans could've been in there for years and I never would've known."

"At least she's out of here," Deacon said with quiet vehemence.

The intensity of his reply startled her. "You've never liked her, have you?"

He had the grace to look away for a moment before meeting her gaze square on. "Frankly, no. Your sister has always been a pain in the ass."

"That's no reason to assume she's..." Lisa could not bring herself to say "crazy." "No reason to enjoy it if there's something seriously wrong with her."

She heard the sharp edge of anger in her voice and wanted to soften it. She turned her palms upward so his fingers could entwine with hers. The gesture steadied and calmed her.

"She's still my sister," Lisa said. "No matter what."

"How sweet." Terry spoke from the doorway. His handsome face twisted into a grimace as he caught sight of their clasped hands.

Lisa's first instinct was to pull away from Deacon's grasp, but his tight hold refused to let her. Still, she managed to wriggle her fingers out of his. Terry saw the struggle and his eyes flickered to hers. They held no humor.

"Sorry to interrupt," he said coldly, turning.

"Terry," Lisa said, wanting to bury her head in her hands. Wanting this all to be a nightmare she could simply wake from at the sound of her alarm clock. "Wait."

He did turn, his back stiff and his face set into a cold and stony mask. He refused to look at Deacon, instead pinning his gaze on Lisa with an intensity designed to make her squirm. Deacon, too, was looking at her. Judging her. They both were judging her, waiting for her reaction. Waiting, she supposed, to see whom she'd choose.

"I came to talk to you," Terry said. "I tried calling earlier, but you weren't answering."

Another one who came over even when he thought she must not be home. Lisa frowned. "I was at my parents' house."

His face, as his look flickered briefly to the back of Deacon's head, told her he didn't believe her. Lord only knew what Terry was imagining had kept her from answering the phone, but she could guess that he was blaming Deacon. Lisa heaved a mental sigh at the posturing of men.

"I only got home awhile ago," she continued. She didn't think it a good idea to mention Deacon had been with her for most of that time.

"What about him?" Terry asked anyway, jerking his head toward Deacon.

Deacon's shoulder's stiffened and he turned his head to face Terry. "I got here awhile ago, too."

Of course he didn't mention he'd done the same thing Terry had, Lisa thought, watching the two men face off like billy goats butting heads over a nanny goat. Suddenly, she was tired of it all. She felt like a piece of meat caught between two very hungry and determined lions, and she had other things to worry about.

"Terry, this isn't the time," she said. "I've got some problems I need to take care of."

"And one of them is sitting at the table with you," Terry said. His hands fisted at his sides.

Deacon pushed away from the table slowly, stretching to his full height. Though both men were about the same height, Terry was more heavily muscled and Deacon, leaner. Deacon carefully pushed his chair back in before speaking.

"You got a problem with me?" Deacon asked.

"You know I do," Terry said.

"Why don't we let Lisa decide then?" Deacon said. Unlike Terry, whose anger was clearly stamped in every outline of his body, Deacon's stance seemed almost casual. Lisa wasn't fooled. She could see the flash of his eyes. They were going to fight like school boys if she didn't intervene.

All at once, Lisa no longer had the patience to deal with either one of them. She got up from the table, not bothering to push her chair in. Her head swam with thoughts of her sister.

"Get out, both of you," she said sternly. Both men swung to look at her, near-identical and comical expressions of surprise on their faces. "I don't have time for this."

"But Lisa—" Terry began.

"Lisa—" Deacon said at the same time.

"No," Lisa cried, shaking her head at both of them. "I've got too much to worry about without you two making asses of yourself in my kitchen. Get out! Deacon, I'll see you at work tomorrow. Terry, I'll call you when I'm ready to talk to you."

She could see both of them wanting to protest even more, but she fixed each of them with a glare so fierce it made her eyes hurt. "Leave me alone!"

They scattered like leaves before her fury and did as she asked. Only when she was alone in the kitchen did Lisa sit back down to the table and cradle her head in her hands. Try as she might, she could not forget the sight of all those cans. She would have to talk to her parents, to convince them they needed to seek help for their youngest daughter.

The problem was, Lisa thought, how was she going to do that?

CHAPTER 11

Deacon didn't mind working late when he fell behind on the job. What irritated the hell out of him was having to work late because of someone else's problems. After discovering the bizarre arrangement of cans in her pantry, Lisa had convinced her parents Allegra needed serious help.

Unfortunately for him, that meant Lisa had been out of the office for a few days dealing with the problem. He could handle most of the project himself, but now things were coming to a close and she needed to be there.

At least staying after hours meant he got to spend some time alone with Lisa, who was back on the job. She'd refused his offers to take her out, saying she needed some time to herself. *I get to see her at work, which was more than Terry can claim,* Deacon thought smugly. He watched Lisa flip through the order books at his desk and couldn't hold back a grin. They might not be painting the town red every night, but he was with her.

"What are you grinning about?" Lisa had turned and caught him in the act.

"Just thinking how pretty you look." It wasn't really a lie. He always thought that.

Lisa rolled her eyes. "I don't feel pretty. I feel grubby."

They'd spent the day on-site taking only a short break for lunch and grabbing supper to eat back at the office. The Garden Shadd's bid had guaranteed the work would be finished by the end of the summer, and

August had already begun. They would finish on time, but only if there were no more delays.

Deacon tugged at her hand until she consented to sit down next to him. "You look beautiful to me."

She sighed, not easily persuaded. "I'm sorry we're so behind. If I hadn't had to take that time off to go with my folks..."

"You had to do what's right," Deacon said. "You always do."

She looked at him, and he could tell she was remembering her testimony and how it had affected him. "Sometimes doing what's right is so hard."

"But you do it anyway," he told her, tilting her chin up with one finger.

"It wasn't even worth it." She turned her face away. "The doctors declared Allegra in perfect health. She passed all their tests. And I ended up looking like the crazy one. My parents think I'm just jealous and Allegra refuses to talk to me."

"You should've shown them the cans," Deacon said. "That would have convinced them."

She looked surprised. "Didn't I tell you? The shelves in the pantry collapsed after you and Terry left. All the cans fell down."

"They were still marked."

Lisa shook her head, looking tired. "Once they were all over the floor, they didn't look any stranger than if they'd come from the bang and dent store. Whatever was so intense about them being all lined up that way just got lost." She shrugged. "Besides, at that point, my parents weren't willing to listen to anything I had to say on the matter. I just threw them all away. It's not my problem any more."

He didn't believe she really felt that way. The bluish circles under her eyes told him she wasn't sleeping well.

Lisa shrugged again, changing the subject. "Let's get back to work, okay?"

She tried to turn back to the pile of work orders, but he stopped her. "You want to talk about it?"

She shook her head, but her shoulders heaved. "Maybe I really am the one with problems."

Her agonized whisper cut him to the core. With one smooth move, Deacon pulled Lisa into his arms and onto his lap. She didn't fight him.

"No," he said. "You're not crazy. And all this stuff that's been happening to you is not your fault. It's just someone with a sick sense of humor trying to rattle you for some reason."

She put her head on his shoulder, letting him hold her. "A lot of people seem to think it's you."

That didn't set well with him at all. "Like who?"

"Terry," she mumbled. "My parents."

"They don't like me anyway," he told her. "And Terry's jealous."

She nodded against his neck. "Don't you think he has the right?"

"To be jealous—sure," Deacon said. "But not to go around accusing me of stalking you."

"He hasn't gone around accusing you of stalking me." The soft touch of her breath on his skin was driving him nuts.

"I have an idea," Deacon told her. "Let's not talk about Terry any more, okay? Or your sister. Or your parents."

She pulled away to meet his gaze. "You'd rather talk about what kind of koi to put in the pond?"

"I'd rather," Deacon said, "not talk at all."

Her mouth was sweet and welcoming, and she returned his kiss eagerly. It had only been a little over a week since the last time he'd had her in his arms, but it felt like an eternity. Suddenly he couldn't have been happier to be working late.

She sighed when he left her mouth to press kisses along the curve of her jaw and down the sweet slope of her neck. He leaned forward, twirling the chair to allow him to press her back against the top of the desk. She didn't protest, which made him bolder.

Deacon pushed the pile of papers onto the floor, not caring if they crumpled. There wasn't much room on the desk. Lisa bumped her head on the computer monitor. She let out a muffled groan.

"What are we doing?" she asked him.

Even though her eyes a little glazed from passion, he could see she wanted a real answer. "Kissing?"

She craned her neck to look around the office, then raised her eyebrow at him. "At work? Not very professional."

He saw her eyes flicker to the shelves, and he remembered. *The surveillance camera.* He'd grown so used to just hanging his shirt over the lens, he'd forgotten about it. Lisa's wary glance told him she knew about it, though, a thought that suddenly brought back a whole lot of bad feelings he'd thought he'd forgotten, too.

"You're right," he said.

The change in his tone and manner must have confused her, but she didn't question him. Instead, Lisa just got off the desk, and straightened her hair and clothing. She bent to pick up the scattered piles of papers, putting them back into order.

She spoke to him with her back still turned, so he couldn't see her face. "I am sorry about all this, Deacon. I really would like us to start over. Everything is just crazy right now."

"Sure," he told her like he didn't care. He reached down to pick up his shirt from where it had fallen and hung it back up over the lens.

When she turned back and saw what he had done, she let her eyes linger on his for one long, silent moment. Then she turned and gathered the rest of her things. Her voice was soft when she spoke.

"I'm going home now," she said. "Will you call me tomorrow? I...I'd like to go out with you. Do something. If you still want to."

He felt as though he were being tested. "Sure."

She nodded, and he wasn't sure if he'd passed or failed. "Talk to you tomorrow then?"

"I'll just finish up here," he replied.

She leaned over to brush her lips against his cheek. "Goodnight, Deacon."

After she was gone, Deacon turned and flipped up his middle finger, right to the camera. Nobody would see the gesture, of course. The shirt would prevent that. But doing it made him feel better, and he gathered up his own things and left.

* * *

Allegra's car was in the driveway when Lisa got home. For one moment Lisa seriously considered turning the car and driving away. It was late and she was tired, and cowardice wouldn't get her anything but more grief.

It was as though her sister hadn't moved out. Dirty dishes filled the sink, crumbs scattered the counter, and a carton of milk sat on the table next to a half-filled glass. Lisa carefully hung her keys on the hooks by the door and slung her purse over the back of a chair.

"Allegra?" There was no sense in avoiding the confrontation. Lisa mentally girded her loins as she went to the living room.

Her sister wasn't there. Lisa climbed the front stairs. The door to her room was closed, just as she'd left it. The hall bath light was on and the door open, but it was empty. Lisa went through the dark and empty spare room and knocked on Allegra's door.

"You're going to come in anyway, so why knock?" came the disgruntled reply.

Lisa pushed open the door. Except for the double bed, dresser and rocking chair, the room was completely bare. Even the open closet held nothing but a few lonely hangers.

"Wow, Al," was all she could manage to say.

Allegra fixed her with an arch look. "Don't pretend you're not happy to see this, Lisa."

Lisa crossed to the rocker and sat down. "We need to talk."

"I have nothing to say to you," Allegra said. "Go talk to your boyfriend. Oops, I forgot. You dumped Terry, didn't you? So go talk to your convict lover."

"I was worried about you," Lisa began, but Allegra cut her off.

"Just shut up!" Her dark hair swung in lank strands over her shoulders. Her hands clenched at her sides and she took a step toward Lisa, her pretty face scowling. "Shut up!"

Taken aback by her sister's ferocity, Lisa got up from the chair. "Okay. I'll go."

"I'm really doing it, you know," Allegra whispered so softly Lisa wasn't sure she'd heard her right.

"What?"

"Moving out," Allegra said in a normal tone. "Moving out of here. And I know you're happy about it!"

She was happy, there was no denying it, but Lisa felt too guilty to say so. "It's probably for the best, Al."

Allegra sneered. "Sure. Then you can have this place all to your self for your little sex parties."

Every time she almost felt sorry for her sister, Allegra had to go and make sordid accusations that annoyed her. Lisa took a deep breath, not wanting to lose her temper. "Don't even go there."

"You never wanted me here." Allegra pouted.

That was true, too. "That's not true." The lie slipped from Lisa's mouth easily enough, but that didn't make it any more convincing.

Al snorted. "Right. Sure. Whatever. I had to beg you to let me move in with you so I could get away from that house, that other house..." She stopped, her voice drifting into silence. Her dark eyes blinked rapidly, as though she were remembering things. Her tongue flickered out to run along her lips.

"And you took the best room for yourself," Allegra cried suddenly. She pointed her finger at Lisa. "And you got to pick what kind of furniture we had. And you didn't share your butter!"

"What? Where the hell did that come from?" Lisa paused in the doorway, stunned.

"I wanted to use some butter to make a grilled cheese, and you said

I'd have to start buying my own!"

"Why shouldn't you buy your own?" The conversation was beginning to border on ridiculous.

"Because we're sisters, and we should share!" Incredibly, Allegra was crying. Real tears slid down her cheeks and dripped from her chin.

Lisa didn't know what to say. Her sister was frequently melodramatic, but these tears seemed genuine. "You're moving out because I wouldn't share my butter with you?"

The look of scorn Allegra shot her was enough to make Lisa wince. "Please. Like I can't buy my own goddamned butter?"

Lisa shook her head in disgust as she started out the door. "You know what, Al? I'm not going to do this with you. I'm tired, and I'm going to bed."

"I shared everything with you!" Came Allegra's cry at Lisa's back.

Lisa turned. Allegra had sunk onto the bed, her tear-streaked face half-hidden by the fall of her thick, dark hair. She held her right hand in her lap and rapidly touched the fingers with her other hand, like she was counting off a list in double time.

"I always shared everything with you," she said sullenly.

Lisa thought back to all the times she'd listened to Allegra's bragging about how many men had asked her out, how many had asked for her phone number, how many she'd kissed or slept with. How she just couldn't find clothes that fit right since her breasts were too large and her waist too tiny. How it was so, so difficult to be pretty because nobody ever took her seriously.

"You sure shared," Lisa said. "More than I ever wanted to know."

The words came out sounding petty and strained. Allegra didn't seem to notice. Now she stopped the relentless hand movement and lifted her head to stare at Lisa. Her cheeks gleamed with tears.

"I just wanted to be close to you, Lisa," she said in the little girl voice that always set Lisa's nerves on edge. "You're my big sister."

"And we're both grownups now, Allegra," Lisa told her, trying to be kind. "It's not like we're kids any more."

Allegra's eyes seemed to shift focus. "What's that got to do with it? Is that why you tried to tell Mom and Dad I'm a nutcase? Because you hate me?"

"I don't hate you, Allegra." With a sigh, Lisa went to the bed and sat next to her sister. "But if we're going to share space, we need to respect each other. And you don't respect me—"

"Respect," Al hissed contemptuously. "What do you know about it?

I adore you, Lisa!"

The vehemence of her statement belied the actual words. Lisa suddenly felt as though ants had begun crawling all over her skin. She got up from the bed slowly like the floor had tilted beneath her feet.

"I'm going to bed," she said.

"When you wake up, I'll be gone," Allegra said. "And won't you be sorry then?"

As she slipped between her cool, fresh sheets, Lisa thought about what Allegra had asked. *No,* she thought with weary finality, *I won't be sorry. Not at all.*

*   *   *

A long, hard ride always put things back into perspective for him. Deacon let the motorcycle slide into the driveway and parked it. It felt like he'd ridden every tiny back road in Elk County, and there were a lot of them. Right now, all he wanted was a hot shower, a cold beer, and maybe some boring television to fall asleep to.

"Deacon?" Bertha's voice quavered as she stepped out of her darkened bedroom.

Deacon pulled a cold green bottle of Straub's out of the fridge, then grabbed another. "Just me."

Bertha pulled her summer robe more tightly around her as she entered the kitchen. "I thought you'd got home hours ago."

Deacon twisted the caps off both bottles and took a long swallow from one. "Nope. I just got home. I went riding after work."

Bertha's brow furrowed. "Well, that's strange. I swear I heard you ruffling around up there earlier when I got home from bingo. My dogs were barking so bad I just went straight back to the bedroom to soak 'em and I guess I fell asleep watching Wheel of Fortune."

Deacon glanced up to the ceiling. "What exactly did you hear, Mom?"

She gestured vaguely. "Oh, just some thumps and stuff. I thought you must've been unpacking some of those boxes finally."

Deacon didn't want to alarm his mother, but her story made him nervous. He hadn't been home since leaving for work this morning. *So who had she heard upstairs?*

"'Night," he told Bertha and gave her the peck on the cheek she expected.

"It's cool tonight," Bertha said. "I left your windows open for you."

"You didn't have to do that, Mom," he said. "You shouldn't be climbing those stairs."

Bertha chuckled. "Gotta make sure your dirty laundry isn't growing mold up there, don't I?"

Since she knew as well as he that Deacon took care of such things on his own, he took the comment as she meant it and laughed. "I guess I can get older, but you'll never believe I've grown up."

"Not while you're still living at home." She wagged her finger.

"Point taken," Deacon replied with a grin. "I'll start looking for a place of my own."

Bertha reached out to hug him. "You always have a place here, Deacon. You know that. I just want you to get on with your life, and living here with this old lady can't be much fun."

"You're not old," he said gallantly, playing along even as the desire to get upstairs and search his room for signs of an intruder itched.

Deacon took his beers and climbed the narrow stairs. The nightlight Bertha kept burning in the upstairs hall shed a golden but dim glow that barely illuminated the built-in cupboard next to the bathroom door. To his left, the door to the small bedroom remained shut as it always did unless someone was using it. To his right, the door to his room was cracked open. He'd shut it behind him when he left this morning, he was pretty sure of it, but if Bertha had been upstairs to open the window she certainly could have been the one to leave the door open.

Still, it was with caution he pushed open the wooden door and stepped into the room he'd used since childhood. He'd hit the door with a little too much force, and it flew open hard enough to bang against the wall. In nearly the same motion, he flicked on the light switch.

The room, as far as he could see, was empty.

All at once feeling foolishly James Bond-esque, Deacon stepped further in to survey the interior. The closet door directly to his right was half open, the way he'd left it, his few "good" shirts and pants hanging nonchalantly on their hangers. In front of him and to the right was the small space carved out by the room's t-shaped divider, completely filled with boxes of his belongings. Unless the intruder was an elf, nobody could possibly be hiding in there.

Deacon moved toward the back of the room to the large space he'd set up as his. As he passed the dormer window he glanced down the short narrow space but saw only the easy chair and reading lamp he'd put there. His bed was not creased. The double window on the far wall was open as Bertha had described, and the sheer curtains fluttered in the night breeze. Directly outside the window he could see the brick of the house next door, but nothing unusual. The tv on its stand next to the built-in drawers was blank and silent, the vcr clock blinking as it always did because he was too lazy to set it.

In short, nothing out of the ordinary. If the front half of the room was a disorganized jumble of boxes, the part he actually used was clean and tidy. His coat rack, hung with baseball caps and jackets, stood sentry in the corner formed by the divider, and the battered loveseat took up the rest of that space. No place a person could hide, if indeed somebody had been up here earlier today.

Nothing seemed out of place either. He didn't have much out, not having bothered to unpack most of his things. The narrow desk with the wobbly legs under the window was the only item in the room that could possibly have garnered attention he wouldn't be immediately able to tell, since the desk was always jumbled with mail and magazines he meant to read.

Deacon tossed his heavy leather jacket onto the bed and put his helmet carefully on top of the divider. As he did, the breeze blowing through the window brought him the scent of a woman's perfume. He froze, lifting his nose in the air to try and find the smell again. It was faint and not one he recognized. Then it was gone.

Maybe he'd imagined it. His mind, prompted by Bertha's tale, wanted to find something wrong in his room. Yet, Deacon had to admit, that aside from a sense of unease, he could see nothing wrong. No sign anyone had been here. Nothing seemed missing, and nothing, so far as he could see, had been left behind.

The phone on his night stand blinked red. He had a voice mail message. Since Bertha claimed herself too old to learn how to operate the new system, it had become his responsibility to take down the messages, mostly from her bingo buddies or his siblings. He rarely got any calls himself, but this time he hoped he might hear Lisa's voice.

Quickly Deacon punched in the access number and his password, and was surprised to hear "seven messages." The messages began playing and every one of them was a hang up. His suspicions roused after the third one. That was too many to be mere coincidence, especially when their telephone barely even rang seven times a day.

He didn't have caller ID and couldn't check to see who had made the calls, but he was willing to bet they'd been made by the same person. *The one who'd been bothering Lisa?* Deacon stripped off his clothes while he thought. It was no secret there were people in town who didn't hold him in high regard. He could count several of them just off the top of his head, Officer Terry Hewitt being one of them.

128

Accusing Terry of making the calls would be childish and stupid, too. They were only hang ups, nothing threatening or obscene. Trying to link Terry to Lisa's harasser would only earn Deacon greater suspicion from the police department and maybe even Lisa herself.

So, who? He was still pondering as he showered and slid into bed with nothing between him and the sheets but the scent of soap. He thought he caught the scent of perfume again, and it vanished as swiftly as before. He thought of Lisa and the way she smelled, and stirred with arousal. Lying in the dark with the cool night breeze caressing his bare skin, he wondered if he'd ever get to sleep. It was going to be a long night.

CHAPTER 12

Lisa let the dart fly from her hands and it struck the board with a thud. She let out a whoop of pleasure and turned to Deacon. "I told you I'd kick your butt!"

He gulped his beer and set the mug on the table. "We'll see."

But his next shot bounced harmlessly off the board and hit the floor. Lisa laughed, feeling at ease for the first time in a long while. Deacon scowled and poked her in the stomach while she wriggled and giggled.

"That tickles," she protested, and he smiled.

"I let you win."

"Sheee, yeah," Lisa scoffed. "Right."

The waitress arrived at their table bearing two platters of steaming hot chicken wings, blue cheese and celery. Deacon picked up all the darts and stuck them in the board, then joined Lisa at the table to dig into the decadent feast. Each had ordered a plate, and though his eyes had shown he was dubious she could finish hers, Lisa planned to show him she could.

The first bite stung her mouth, but Lisa moaned in pleasure anyway. "Hot! But good."

Deacon dipped his wing in the blue cheese and devoured it, following the bite with a swig of beer. "When's the last time you ate?"

His question made Lisa falter a little. Truthfully, she hadn't been eating much lately. Between the phone calls, the strife in her family, and trying to finish the children's garden, she'd had no appetite. Not to mention the break up with Terry, which still made her feel guilty any time she thought about it.

"I eat every day," she said. "But I haven't had wings in ages."

They ate in silence for a few minutes. Lisa's good mood hadn't been spoiled, just tempered. There was no getting away from her problems, not even on the much-anticipated date with Deacon. He seemed to understand, though, keeping his distance and treating her like they really were just starting out.

"Have you filed a report about the helmet and jacket?" she asked after a minute.

He shrugged. "I did. But I doubt it will do anything. Someone lifted them right out of the parking lot at The Garden Shadd. They had to. I usually take them in with me, but I guess I forgot..."

He trailed off, and she didn't push the issue. He could have accused someone on the staff at the nursery of taking his things out of his office, but he didn't. It was a sensitive topic. Still, she felt bad he'd lost his leather jacket and the nice helmet, even though the ones he'd bought to replace them made him look even sexier.

"One more week," he said suddenly.

The out-of-the blue reference confused her, until she realized he meant until the Children's Garden. One more week until it was finished. Lisa nodded around a bite of blue-cheese drenched wing.

"Just in time for school to start," she said to point out the irony.

"The kids'll still have plenty of time to enjoy it before the weather gets too cold," Deacon said.

"It's been great working with you." Lisa wiped her mouth and hands on a napkin and reached across the table to touch his hand. "I mean it, Deacon."

He smiled. "I thought you were going to choke that first day when you walked into the lunch room."

Lisa thought back, deciding now was the time to be honest. "I wasn't surprised to see you, just nervous. I asked Dad to hire you."

She watched him carefully to see his reaction. To her relief, he didn't seem angry, only thoughtful. He took another drink before answering.

"Why?" he asked finally.

"Because I thought you'd be an asset to the company," Lisa told him. "And...because I felt guilty."

He quirked his eyebrow at her. "And now?"

She toyed with her smeared napkin. "I still think you're an asset to The Garden Shadd. And I'll never stop feeling guilty, I guess."

"You spend too much time feeling guilty," he told her.

Her throat felt thick with tears, but she managed to smile. "Curse of the eldest daughter, I guess."

"What's past is past. For a lot of things."

There was one more thing she'd have to tell him if she wanted to come clean. "There's something else."

His brow furrowed, and he looked at her questioningly. Lisa took a deep breath, knowing what she had to say could make or break how they continued from here. Yet she couldn't let it go unsaid.

"There's a surveillance camera in your office," she said, then waited for him to react.

Deacon grinned. "Lisa, I've known about that camera since the day I started work. I've been hanging my shirt over it every day."

"You're not mad?"

He shrugged. "I was at first. But I figured, let my work speak for itself. I knew your dad hired me for a reason, whatever it was, and that it was up to me to prove myself. I'd say I've done that."

Lisa thought about her parents' feeling Deacon might be behind her harassment, but she didn't say anything. "The Children's Garden is the best project I've ever worked on."

The rest of the bar disappeared. The noisy patrons, the loud music, even the smell of beer and smoke drifted away until all that remained was Deacon, staring at her. Lisa's breath caught in her throat and her abdomen turned to liquid fire. His gaze was intense, probing, blazing.

"Do you want to get out of here?" he asked.

She nodded. Deacon tossed some money on the table and they left the food and beer behind. He slipped her hand into his as they walked out the door in a gesture as natural as breathing.

He'd picked her up at her place on the back of his Harley, but Lisa hesitated as she took the helmet he offered. She assumed they'd go back to her house since she now lived alone. But thinking ahead to the night she imagined they were going to have made her remember the last time they'd been this close. She hadn't been prepared then, and she wasn't prepared now.

"I don't have anything at home," she said in chagrin.

He knew what she meant. She could see he thought the same thing—about the Circle K parking lot and why they'd been there, and what had happened then. *Déjà vu.*

"We can swing by my place," he said.

She thought of meeting his mother for the first time under these circumstances. She must have looked stricken because Deacon shook his head.

"It's Mom's bingo night," he said. "She won't be there."

The ride took forever and only a few minutes. When they pulled up in front of the dark house, anxiety fluttered in Lisa's stomach. Three years ago she'd been ready to do this without hesitation, but so much had changed since then. Was she ready?

Deacon's house smelled like cinnamon and vanilla, and a plate of fresh cookies beckoned from the counter. He snagged one and bit into it, sugar dusting his lips. Feeling bold, Lisa stood on her toes to lick it off.

The kiss turned fierce, taking her breath away. When Deacon let her go, Lisa had to lean against the counter because her knees were so weak. "Wow."

He rubbed the back of her neck with his fingers, easing away knots she didn't know she had. "Do you want to come upstairs with me?"

"Yes." The thought of standing in the kitchen alone, having to explain to Deacon's mother who she was and what she was doing there while he rummaged around for condoms did not appeal to her. Besides, she wanted to see where he lived. How he lived. And she didn't want to leave his side.

Lisa followed Deacon through a tidy and cozily furnished front room and up a narrow set of stairs. The size of his room surprised her, but when she saw how cleverly it had been set up, she smiled. "You have a big family."

"All three of us boys slept here," Deacon said. "My sisters shared the room across the hall. Things got pretty wild up here sometimes."

"I'll bet." She looked to her right at the huge pile of boxes.

"C'mon in. Make yourself at home." Deacon gestured and led her to the back of the room.

Lisa took in the sparse furnishings. "You don't plan on staying here much longer."

"No. Just until I'm back on my feet. And with working at The Garden Shadd, that shouldn't take much longer." He paused. "I had a lot of legal bills to pay off."

She wasn't flooded with guilt—not from the way he said it so matter-of-factly. Maybe there was hope for them after all. "I'd never move back home if I could help it. Not like my sister."

Deacon snorted. "You're much different than your sister."

He gave her that look again, the one that made her melt like butter on a hot cob of corn. Her throat dried and she had to lick her lips. She watched Deacon watching the movement of her tongue across her mouth, and knew he was going to kiss her before he did.

He tasted faintly of hot sauce and blue cheese. Tangy and delicious. Even the smell of smoke that clung to his clothes and hair from the bar couldn't put her off. Not when Deacon's hands traced circles on her back and sent stabs of tingling pleasure directly to the center of her being.

Lisa put her hands on his chest, feeling the roll of muscles as he moved. Her hands drifted lower to the hard plane of his stomach, taut even beneath the denim shirt he wore. With their mouths still locked, Lisa slipped her hands around his waist letting her fingers caress his rear.

Deacon breathed against her when she cupped the solid flesh of his behind. She tweaked him a little, wanting to make him laugh. She only got a smile before he was kissing her again.

Somehow they made it to the love seat, sinking down onto the faded cushions in a tangle of arms and legs. Lisa ended up on Deacon's lap, straddling him, her knees wedged against the love seat's back. His belt buckle pressed against her between her legs, but shifting didn't help. That only brought her in full contact with the bulge of his erection.

A whimper escaped her as he rocked his hips pressing his arousal against hers. For a moment, the sound embarrassed her, but when Deacon echoed it with a low moan of his own, Lisa forgot anything else. His tongue stroked the inside of her mouth, his lips nibbling lightly on hers.

Lisa rested her hands on his shoulders, letting her fingers play with the tender flesh under his ears. Deacon slid his hands up to cup her breasts. Instantly her nipples went hard as ice, throbbing against his palms. Deacon rubbed them with his thumbs making Lisa gasp.

"Oh," she managed to say.

"Oh?"

She nodded. "Oh." She bent to kiss him again, feeling his hands on her and wanting them everywhere.

"If we don't stop," Deacon said, breaking the kiss. "We're not going to make it to your place."

The thought sobered her, but only a little. She touched his mouth with her fingertips. "I don't think I could wait."

He looked at the bed. "Mom will be out for another two hours."

"It's almost like being a teenager again," Lisa said. And it was.

Thoughts of being discovered only heightened the passion already ignited.

"Just let me get...what we need," Deacon said. "Don't want to ruin the moment later."

She shifted enough to let him get up and reclined on the love seat. Lisa felt lazy, like a cat purring. Her nipples tingled from Deacon's touch, and she felt like she was wearing way too much clothing.

How was it possible to want someone so badly? She thought with some regret of the time spent with Terry. He'd never made her feel this way. Lisa pushed the thoughts from her mind. She didn't want to be thinking about Terry when Deacon's hands were on her.

Deacon rummaged around in his bedside drawer. "I know I have some in here."

"I'm not even going to ask why." The thought of Deacon with another woman made her pause, but she kept her word. There was no point in going there anyway. She really didn't want to know.

All that mattered was here and now. Deacon and Lisa. There could be nobody else tonight. Tomorrow would be enough time to figure out where they were going. For now, it was enough to anticipate undressing him. Allowing him to undress her.

She'd waited three years for this. Lisa wasn't going to ruin it by over-thinking now. She got up from the love seat and crossed to the bed. She ran one finger along the plain footboard, smoothing the curves of it and enjoying the feel of the smooth wood beneath her fingertips. In this heightened state, everything had become sensual. Every movement, every touch, every smell...

She smelled something familiar. Something that wasn't cinnamon or vanilla, and it wasn't the musky familiar scent of Deacon's cologne. It was lighter, like flowers. *Like a woman's perfume.*

Before she could think much more about it, Deacon found what he'd been searching for. He put the small foil packet on the night stand and turned to her. His sultry smile faltered when he saw her face.

"What's wrong?" he asked.

"Nothing," Lisa said, and forced herself to believe it. Whatever had happened before was not happening now. She was here with Deacon, and he with her.

To prove it to herself, she jumped on the bed, making it bounce. His grin returned and he slid down to lay beside her. She fit in the circle of his arms as though they'd been joined at birth. Snuggling against him, feeling his mouth press against her hair, Lisa shoved away the tickle of doubt that threatened to turn the fire of her passion into ice.

"I've waited a long time for this," he whispered, his voice husky. "It was all I thought about when I was away."

"Sure," she teased, wanting to believe him but not sure if she should. "You didn't think about anything else? Not at all?"

"Well," he amended. "Maybe I thought about beating your butt at darts. But mostly about this."

She knew he had to be gallantly lying, but the lie pleased her anyway. "Me, too."

She tilted her face to his, opening her mouth to his kisses and relishing the heat of his arousal against her stomach. There were too many clothes between them, even though she wore only a denim skort and sleeveless blouse. Too much material, when all she wanted, needed, was his flesh against hers.

"Hurry," she said against him, smiling. "Before your mother gets home."

His fingers fumbled at the buttons on her shirt, and Lisa pushed at him impatiently. She lifted the blouse over her head and tossed it to the floor. Refusing to feel self-conscious at the way his eyes gleamed, she touched the front hook of her bra. She didn't have to ask. Deacon reached out and flicked the small hook with his finger, loosening it.

The peach cotton fell away, exposing her to the air and his gaze. Though the breeze from the open window was blessedly cool, it wasn't enough to chill the fever sweeping over Lisa's body. Her nipples strained even further becoming taut pink buds that begged for Deacon's tongue.

He obliged her body's silent request, dipping his head to taste first one breast, then the other. Lisa let her head fall back, helpless against the onslaught of sensation rocking through her. It had been so long. Too long since a man's hands had touched her this way. Too long since she'd felt the slickness of arousal between her thighs and the ache of desire. And never this strong, this powerful. None of her previous lovers had ever made her feel this way.

Deacon pushed her onto her back, letting his mouth run over her breasts and down to the soft paleness of her stomach. His tongue traced tiny circles onto her skin. Lisa sighed with bliss, closing her eyes and running her hands through his dark hair. She was floating.

He paused at the waistband of her skort. "How does this thing come off anyway?"

Lisa opened her eyes, laughing. "I'll do it. And you're wearing too many clothes."

They sat up. Lisa put her hands to the buttons on his denim shirt, running her fingers along the length of them. So many to undo when she wanted to tear just them open. Instead, she kept his gaze skewered with her own as she slowly undid each one. She paused to press her mouth to the exposed flesh of his throat, feeling his pulse beating rapidly under her lips. With every button she moved down more and more, pushing the shirt from his chest.

She stopped to pay attention to his twin brown nipples surrounded by dark, curling hair. Deacon moaned as she flicked them each with her tongue, and Lisa hid a grin. Two could play the same game. She nuzzled her nose in his chest hair letting it tickle her eyes and cheeks before following the line of it down past his navel to where it disappeared into his waistband.

She didn't have to ask how to undo his jeans. She unbuckled his belt and undid the snap, but hesitated before unzipping. She looked at him, saw the same desire clouding his eyes she felt covering her own. She put her hand on the bulge trying to escape the confines of his jeans, and felt him throb at her touch.

Lisa quickly undid the side buttons of her skort and slipped it off. Now she wore only the sheerest of panties that hid nothing. She helped Deacon slip down his jeans, prepared to see boxers or briefs. Instead, she saw more dark hair, pale flesh, and the length of him rising from between his thighs.

"You don't wear underwear?" she cried, shocked into laughter.

Deacon kicked off his pants onto the floor and stretched out fully on the bed. "Nope. Saves on laundry."

Lisa shook her head. "Don't you...chafe?"

Deacon rolled his eyes. "Let me show you."

She was in his arms again kissing his mouth, his neck, the curve of his jaw. Deacon ran his mouth along the line of her shoulder, and all she could do then was lie back and enjoy the sensations rushing through her. He moved back to her breasts, circling her nipples with his tongue and leaving wet patches to cool in the night breeze.

He pressed kisses past the cup of her navel and to the line of her panties. Lisa sucked in a breath of anticipation waiting for him to slip them off. Deacon surprised her, stroking her through the sheer cloth, trailing his finger lightly. The sensation, muffled as it was through her panties, was nonetheless enough to make her bite her lip and rock her hips. He pressed his fingers against her again, trailing along the ridge of her opening, then stopping to press gently on her aroused bud. He was driving her crazy.

She wanted to be open before him, without the barrier of the cloth, but Lisa could not speak. Could not ask. Could do little more than spread her legs at his touch and throw back her head willing him to continue.

He took his hand away and a low sound of protest tore itself from her throat. Seconds later, she felt the heat of his mouth against her, kissing her through the panties. His tongue flicked out and repeated the slow, teasing movement his fingers had made pausing at each stroke to provide the same tormenting pressure. The cloth, sheer as it was, muted the feelings of his movements just enough to make them that much more infuriatingly sensual.

Lisa breathed deeply letting the feelings wash over her. She was on the ocean, rolling with the waves. She was soaring in the sky on eagle's wings.

His hands rested on her hips tugging lightly at the string sides of her bikini panties. Without being asked, Lisa lifted her hips to let him finally pull down the last piece of cloth between them. Then she waited, eyes closed, breathless.

The touch, when it came, was torturous. She longed for him to plunge into her, against her, to stroke her and fill her. Lisa's moan came from low in her throat, but there was no longer any thought of being embarrassed. This was what happened when lovers joined. Noise and smell and tangled movements. It was ecstasy.

She felt his hands drifting along her thighs, stroking. His kisses were fire against her, licking and tasting. Lisa rocked with Deacon's movements.

Her fingers clutched at the bedspread, crumpling it. She was so close, so close. Every touch of his tongue and hands moved her a fraction closer to the edge. Deacon slipped one finger inside her, and Lisa cried out again overcome with sensation.

"I want you," she told him.

He pressed one last kiss to her and slid up her body to meet her mouth with his. She felt him again on her stomach, and this time there was nothing between them. Nothing to keep the sensation of his hot, silky erection from the softness of her belly.

She slipped her knee between his, pressing their bodies even closer. Without the direct pressure of his mouth on her, the proximity of her orgasm had ebbed enough that she didn't feel so dangerously close. It was her turn to do a little torturing. Swiftly, Lisa pushed Deacon onto his back.

"Hey, I like this," he said.

"Shh," she said. "It gets better."

She didn't waste time teasing him too much. She was too eager to hear him moan and feel him squirm beneath her. She did take the time to cup his weight in her palm before sliding her mouth along his length.

Deacon rewarded her instantly with a groan. The sound of it sent a bolt of fire directly between her thighs. Lisa closed her lips around him again drawing forth a muffled curse this time. She laughed silently, shoulders shaking.

It felt good to laugh even while her body sang with desire. It was good to be so comfortable with him. She'd never felt this way with anyone. Nakedness had always brought shyness. Lovemaking had brought uncertainty. What seemed all right in the dark made meeting her lover's eyes in the light of day awkward.

Tomorrow she would not have trouble looking at Deacon. In fact, the only regret she had was that they'd been unable to wait to get to her house, so she would not wake up in his arms.

"We'll just have to go over there and do this again," she said, finishing her thought out loud.

"What?" Deacon's voice was slurred, but he tilted his head to look at her. "What did you say?"

"I want to wake up in your arms tomorrow," Lisa said, crawling up next to him and nestling into his arms. "I want to finish making love to you and fall asleep with you."

He didn't say anything. Lisa didn't look at him, suddenly nervous that she'd gone too far...said too much. She fought the awkwardness threatening to creep in.

Don't think! Don't think too much!

But her fears were groundless. Deacon pulled her tighter against him and kissed her hair. "Me, too. But we can't do that here. Sorry. Mom would probably keel over."

"So, we'll have to go back to my place and do this all over again," Lisa said.

"Lisa," Deacon said sternly. "What do you think I'm made of? Let's just get through this once okay?"

"I'm sure—" Lisa said as she grasped his erection and squeezed gently. "—that you'll be able to rise to the occasion."

His groan was not of pleasure this time. Lisa poked him. He poked her back, but gently, then pulled her on top of him and wrapped his arms around her.

Slowly, softly, they kissed, their passion ebbing and flowing in a rhythm all its own. They turned to their sides, shifting on the bed and sliding arms and legs around each other. It seemed impossible to get close enough.

"Deacon," Lisa sighed, holding him tightly. "I've never felt like this before."

"I have," he said.

His unexpected answer threw her and she pulled out of his embrace. "What?"

He grinned. "With you. Before. I felt like this all the time."

He took her hand and drew it back to his length. "Just like this. It made riding the bike difficult."

She poked him again, then kissed him. "I'm sure it did."

They kissed some more, rolling on the bed without caring which way they went or why. Pillows went flying and the bedspread crumpled. Deacon konked his head on the headboard, and when Lisa laughed, he began to tickle her mercilessly.

She'd never been tickled naked before and she thought she'd hate it. In her aroused state, though, even this normally annoying touch set her nerves tingling as he stroked her back and forth along the belly. When he bent to blow raspberries against her stomach, though, Lisa had to cry out for him to stop.

"Enough," she cried, wiping away tears of laughter. "Isn't your mom going to be home soon?"

Deacon looked at the clock. "I don't want this to be over."

She became serious. "Neither do I."

The mood, which had gone from sultry to silly and back again, deepened once more into sensuality. Gently, softly, Deacon pressed Lisa to the bed and covered her body with his. Their mouths joined, opening and closing in perfect time. His hands drifted through her hair, and she let hers run along his back.

"Let's not wait any more," she said. "I want you, Deacon."

He reached for the foil packet on the nightstand, but pushed it too far with his fingers. It fell off the stand and behind the bed. With a defeated groan, Deacon buried his head against her shoulder.

"I'll get it," she said, kissing his ear. "Butter fingers."

He moved aside to let her roll over. Lisa hung her head over the edge of the bed, searching for the glint of silver in the dim light.

Deacon's touch, drifting lightly along her buttocks, was a pleasant distraction.

Lisa wiggled further to the edge, hanging her head down more to see beneath the bed. There it was, the oblong packet glimmering seductively among the dust bunnies. She hooked it with her finger, pulling it into her palm just as something else caught her eye.

"Oh, my God," she said, stunned.

"Something wrong?"

Lisa pushed forcefully away from him, sliding down onto the floor. With one hand she reached beneath the bed again, dragging out what had so shocked her. It was her purse.

"No," Deacon said. "Lisa—"

"Don't you talk to me." She took the bag and flung it onto the bed. Tears sparked her eyes. She simply could not believe it.

"Lisa, it's not—" He reached for her hand, tugging it.

"Shut up!" She didn't care if the entire world heard her. She yanked her hand away and slapped his cheek to get free. Through tear-blurred vision, she scrambled for her clothes, pulling on her shirt and panties without bothering to find her bra. "Just shut up!"

She fumbled into her skort and managed to find her sandals. The bag she snatched up from the bed. Lisa felt as though she might just fall.

Deacon did not move except to sit on the edge of the bed. His face had grayed with shock, but Lisa did not want to hear him speak. That she'd been about to let him make love to her suddenly made her nauseous.

"Don't tell me it wasn't you," she said. "Because this time I know you're lying!"

He said nothing, as if he could tell there'd be no convincing her. Lisa fairly ran to the door, pausing only long enough at the top of the stairs to be sure she wasn't going to tumble down them headfirst and break her neck. At the bottom, she flung open the front door and ran out into the night, clutching the stolen purse to her chest like it was a wounded bird.

CHAPTER 13

Lisa ran and ran, the stitch in her side like a knife stabbing her. Through the dark streets, past the statue of the Holy Virgin in somebody's yard, her hands raised in eternal supplication. Ahead of her was the police station, a single light burning above the door.

She paused long enough to smooth her hair and straighten her clothes. There'd be no help for her tear-stained cheeks and swollen eyes. Lisa scrubbed at them briefly, knowing she still looked a mess.

She climbed the stairs, her sandals clanging on the metal. The building still smelled new, like paint. The scent tickled her nostrils and she wanted to choke.

She pushed open the door on the second floor and faced the empty desk. Behind the glass panel she could see a chair and some filing cabinets. It looked a lot like the ticket window at a movie theater except there was no tantalizing smell of popcorn to tempt her. The sign pasted on the glass informed her that if the desk was empty, she should ring the buzzer.

She did, shifting from one foot to the next. Without the running to occupy her, she'd begun to feel stupid. What was she doing here anyway? Terry didn't want to see her. He'd made that perfectly clear. She couldn't automatically turn to him just because she was afraid.

But I could, Lisa reminded herself, hearing the sound of footsteps approaching from down the corridor. He was a police officer. No matter what his feelings toward her were, and no matter what had passed between them, he would do his job.

The uniformed officer who swung open the heavy door was not Terry, but she recognized the woman. "Hi, Karen."

Karen fixed Lisa with a look that was at once both professional and cool. "Can I help you?"

Word got around fast. "I need to talk to Terry."

"Officer Hewitt isn't on duty right now," Karen said. "If it's something personal, you'll have to try him at home."

"It's not personal," Lisa said, though in a way, it was.

"One of the other officers can take your statement or help you with your problem, if you need assistance," Karen said formally, as though she and her boyfriend Jake hadn't double-dated with Lisa and Terry dozens of times.

Lisa didn't want to talk to one of the other officers. "No, that's okay."

Now Karen's reserved façade softened. "You don't look good, Lisa. What happened?"

Lisa pulled her purse closer to her body noticing the way Karen's trained gazed flicked over her. Assessing. Noting, Lisa was certain, her mussed hair and lack of bra.

"I just needed to talk to Terry," Lisa mumbled. "I'll try him later."

"He's on duty at eleven," Karen offered, though her face made it clear she didn't want to give the information.

"I'll try later," Lisa repeated, turning to go.

"Lisa, what happened?" Karen asked again. "And I don't mean tonight, though if something did happen, I think you need to tell me. But what happened with you and Terry? I thought you two were so happy together."

Lisa tilted her head to keep tears from bursting from her eyes. "Just…leave a note for Terry, okay? That I was here?"

"Sure," Karen said, the small slip into camaraderie replaced with professionalism again. "Sure, I will."

"Thanks," Lisa whispered as she let herself out the door to the stairwell again. For a moment she paused on the other side of the door, holding the purse to her and fighting back sobs.

She realized she hadn't even checked to see if anything was missing. With trembling fingers she opened the clasp and fumbled with the contents. *Lipstick. Gum. Eye drops.* She pulled out her wallet and snapped it open.

Nothing was missing. The money—a twenty and two tens—still nestled in the bed of receipts and coupons. Her credit cards were untouched. She touched the plastic accordion folder that held her pictures, looking at the one of her and Terry. Taken last summer, it showed them holding hands and smiling.

"What did happen?" she asked aloud, her voice echoing grotesquely in the empty stairwell.

Then she was running again, pell mell down the stairs and out into the night. Running home. Her feet slapped on the pavement and her breath began to come in labored gasps. Still, Lisa pushed herself, running through the dark to get to her house.

By the time she reached the side door, she was out of breath and her feet were numb from misuse. She leaned against the handrail and tugged off her ruined sandals, then tossed them immediately into the nearby trash pail. The pretty shoes had been made for dancing, not running.

She waited there a moment, her head hanging. Spots flashed in front of her vision, and her tongue clove to the roof of her mouth. Lisa wondered if she might actually faint.

A few more minutes of sucking in the cool night air and she felt much better. Now her feet, no longer numb, began to throb. Her entire body ached. She needed a hot bath.

Instead of going inside, Lisa sat on the porch steps. The houses on either side of her were dark, as they often were. Her neighbors were all elderly and went to bed early. It was peaceful to sit in the dark letting her body recover from the abuse she'd just put it through.

It was calming to breathe the sweet night air and rest her face in her palms. Thinking. Why had Deacon taken her purse, but left the contents intact? If not for the money inside, why take it at all?

The small groan she heard was her own. Lisa bit her lip. She'd been about to make love to him. Why hadn't she learned?

Terry was right. Once a thief, always a thief.

Worse than a thief. A liar.

She shook her head, disgust rising in her throat. The man had lied to her and used her, and she'd let him touch her. Kiss her. She'd let him start making love to her…

She stood so fast the stars tilted and she had to grasp the railing again to keep from falling. She would file a report against Deacon first thing tomorrow. She would settle this once and for all, and this time, she would feel no guilt about the matter.

Her key stuck in the door and she jiggled it. The house and all its doors were old and warped. The locks were tight, stairs creaky, drawers sticky and unyielding. Normally none of those things bothered her, but tonight the stubborn lock worked on her nerves worse than a pair of yapping dogs.

She finally burst into the kitchen with a muttered curse and tossed her keys onto the counter. The light flickered when she flicked the switch, but at last came on. The bulb was probably loose.

The rest on the porch had calmed her. Slowed her breathing. Lisa ran the cold water in the sink and splashed her face with it, washing away some of the sweat that coated her skin.

Instead of a hot bath, maybe she'd take a refreshing cool shower. Lisa bent to splash more water against her skin. Then suddenly, she was weeping.

She bent her head to the sink gripping the counter with both hands. Everything was turning and twisting beneath her, and without something to hold on to, she thought she just might fly away. Her sobs came easily like they had when she was a child and not afraid to cry. Her nose ran and her eyes burned. Her forehead ached from pressing against the sink's cold metal rim, but she didn't move. The water running from the faucet grew colder as the minutes passed, wetting her hair and drowning out even the sound of her crying.

He couldn't have done it. Not Deacon. But if he hadn't stolen it, how had her purse gotten under his bed?

Her thoughts whirled, back and forth. She trusted him. She didn't. She believed in him, and then she didn't. What was going on?

She thought she might have stayed that way for an hour, but when she finally forced her back to straighten, Lisa saw by the wall clock it had only been a few minutes. She peeled her hand from the counter with a grimace. She'd been holding on so tightly her fingers were tingling. She closed the faucet, and the silence that filled the kitchen when the water ceased its sputtering was enormous.

Lisa ran her hand across her face, feeling the puffiness around her eyes. Her skin was hot, and she was sure she looked like a wreck. But she felt better. Not a whole lot better by any means. Only time would do that for her. But better than she had a while ago.

She didn't remember tossing the purse onto the table, but when she turned to face the kitchen that was where it was. A simple leather bag, not expensive. Nothing she could not have lived without. The money inside was minimal and the credit cards easily replaced. She could have lived without finding it again.

But she had found it, and everything had changed.

"Damn it," she said aloud to the kitchen. "Damn him!"

She'd trusted Deacon, the lying bastard. She'd broken off her relationship with Terry for him. She'd gone against her family's advice to trust him!

A chill tickled her spine. *Had they all been right about him being a thief?*

Had they been right about the other things as well?

Could Deacon have been behind the strange things happening to her lately? The email, the phone calls, the missing laundry.

Her glance flew to the kitchen door, still standing open as no protection against the night. Lisa crossed the kitchen in a few lengthy strides to slam it shut. Then she locked it.

There had been all those other things, too. The mess in her bathroom. The unscrewed light bulbs. She'd blamed poor Allegra, but perhaps they hadn't been her sister's doing at all.

Had they been Deacon all along?

Lisa rubbed her bare arms, uncomfortably aware that the cold water and her own nervousness had urged her nipples into iron-hard bumps. She'd forgotten she wasn't wearing a bra. She looked down and saw her feet were dirty and scratched from her careless flight through the streets of St. Mary's.

She looked once more around the kitchen, taking comfort in the familiar. This was her home. She would not be afraid in it any longer.

Lisa went to the living room to check the front door, too. *Locked.* The room was dark and silent, and it was difficult to see after the harsh brightness of the kitchen. Menacing shadows lurked in every corner. Lisa rattled the front door again, and without looking back, started to climb the front stairs.

The light coming in from outside had been turned a dull, bloody red from the stained glass in the stairway's circular window. Not very reassuring. She fiddled with the hall switch, grateful but unwilling to admit it when the light came on upstairs. She wasn't in a horror movie, for crying out loud.

The hall bath door was closed. Had she done that? She couldn't remember and pride forced her to stop trying. Lisa ducked into her bedroom, closing the door behind her and laughing when she saw that her hands trembled.

"Fraidy cat," she whispered to herself in the dark room. Unlike the living room or the stairs, the dark in here was comforting. Welcome. Normal. She often kept the shades pulled tight to prevent early morning sun from waking her on the weekends. The dark in here wrapped around her like a warm blanket.

Even so, because she was afraid, she turned on the light. The only one hooked to the switch in here was the lamp on her dresser. It lit the room with a soft amber glow not strong enough to dispel all the shadows, but it would be enough.

"Shower," she said. "Pajamas. Bed. In that order."

She expected to find something when she stepped into her tiny bathroom. She didn't know what, but something bad. The crumpled pile of her bathrobe became a dead body for ten horrifying seconds until her mind allowed her eyes to see it for what it truly was.

Lisa let out a shaky laugh, blowing sticky strands of hair from her cheeks. She crossed firmly to the clawfoot tub and twisted the faucet handles. Water spurted out, hissing and spitting like a bag full of cats before smoothing into a heavy stream. It bonged against the tub's cast iron sides.

Lisa suddenly thought of that horror movie with George C. Scott— *The Changeling*—with the little boy drowning in the old iron bathtub. He'd flailed his hands against the sides, banging away, sending the same bonging sound throughout the old house while George wept in his bed for the wife and daughter who'd died.

In *The Changeling*, there was also a scene where they taped a séance, playing back the tape later to hear the little boy's ghost whispering his name. Joseph. The thought of it now sent the hair springing up on the back of Lisa's neck, and she shuddered.

"Lisa."

She yelped and spun away from the tub, slipped on the old linoleum floor and landed hard. Her shoulder hit the pedestal of the sink, her head the bottom of the sink's bowl. Pain bloomed in both spots at once, and she rubbed them to take away the sting.

There was nobody in the room with her. Nobody in her bedroom, either, because she could see clearly out the bathroom door to every corner of her bedroom. Unless somebody stood in the narrow space between the open bathroom door and the wall.

Her gaze instantly flew to the crack in the door, expecting to see a face staring back at her. Jack Nicholson in *The Shining*, ax at the ready and a big, sneering grin just for her. "Heeeeere's Johnny!"

There was nobody there. Lisa let out a strangled, shuddering breath and sagged against the tub's rim. The water still boomed. Nobody had whispered her name into her ear because nobody was there. She was imagining things. That was all.

Just as she reached over to twist the knob that would divert the water from the spout to the shower, a thump vibrated the wall behind her. Her fingers pulled back from the knob and she turned. She had not imagined that.

This wall backed against the hallway. She waited, tense, the breath growing stale in her lungs, for the thump to come again. It didn't, and when she finally breathed bright spots flashed in front of her eyes again. She forced herself to breath again, slowly, so she wouldn't faint.

Lisa pressed her fingers against the wall, waiting. *Nothing.* Behind her, the water splashed. It blocked any sounds she might have heard, but she reasoned it also blocked any noise she made herself. She didn't turn it off, but she did pull out the plug to prevent the tub from overflowing.

She got up from her crouch, rubbing her thighs to make sure the blood flow hadn't stopped. Her knees felt weak, but that was from nerves. She stretched, her back cracking, then stepped softly through the bathroom door.

The bang and crash of the water continued behind her, though it was softer in here. Lisa pressed her ear to the bedroom door, listening. She'd finally convinced herself the noise had been nothing, after all, when she heard it again. Not a thump in the hallway, this time, but a more subtle noise and one she couldn't quite identify.

She strained, trying to hear. Some thudding, muffled through the door and sounding far away. *Allegra's room?*

Relief flooded her. *Of course!* It was only Allegra. Though her sister had moved out, she'd been back before. It must have been her making the noise.

Lisa's laugh sounded more like choking, and she still felt as though she might be sick. She rubbed her sweaty palms against the denim of her skort, then brushed away the hair from her face. It was just her sister out there, not the ghost of a little boy or an ax-wielding maniac.

The door stuck when she tried to open it, but a sharp tug finally got it open. Lisa peered out into the hallway, which was now dark. She reached out to her left, just above where she'd felt the thump against the wall, and hit the switch. The hall stayed dark.

Just down a few feet to her right and across the hall was the closed door to the empty spare room. Now the noises weren't so subtle and their location was identifiable. Someone was in the spare room or maybe Allegra's room.

"Allegra," Lisa tried to say, but her throat had closed. Despite her self-reassurance that it was her sister in there and not the bogeyman, she could not find her voice to speak.

She straightened her back, forcing a bravery she didn't really feel. "Who's there?"

The booming sound of her own voice startled her. She didn't sound afraid. That, in turn, made her confident enough to step out of the bedroom and into the dark hallway.

Enough light shone from her room to illuminate the door to the spare room. The brass doorknob gleamed dully. Lisa reached a hand to it, then pulled back. This was insane. This was exactly the kind of thing stupid movie heroines did; the same thing that always made her scream at the screen, "Don't go in the basement/deserted alley...spare bedroom!"

Another muffled thump, then the soft beat of music. It was Allegra. It had to be, if for no other reason than her mind strictly refused to comprehend it could really be anyone else. No ghost, no lunatic. Only her sister.

Lisa put her hand back on the knob, and turned, stepping through the doorway into the black room beyond.

"Hello?"

It took her eyes a moment to adjust to the greater darkness inside the spare room. Squinting, she stepped further into the room, meaning to knock on her sister's door. Before she had the chance, the door to Allegra's room opened. Lisa squinted, turning her head against the blast of bright light pouring out. Blinking, she expected to see her sister's tall frame.

She saw instead a blank-faced alien. In the next instant she recognized it was no alien, but instead a tall figure wearing a motorcycle helmet. The light shining from behind the figure made it seem to glow. As it stepped toward her, Lisa saw the person not only wore the helmet but the jacket, too.

Deacon's helmet. Deacon's jacket.

She knew them both on sight. The ones he'd claimed had been stolen at work. Another lie, because he was wearing them!

This was her worst nightmare come true. He'd come after her. Before Lisa could run or scream, Deacon reached out and grabbed her by the upper arm. His fingers, even through the thick motorcycle gloves, pinched mercilessly. Pinning her.

"Let me go, you son-of-a-bitch!" Lisa twisted without effect.

She kicked out and up, but her position was not good and she couldn't connect. Deacon said nothing, just pinched down on her bare arm. His silence, coupled with the bizarre outfit, frightened her as much as anything else.

"Let me go!"

She flailed with her other arm, knocking against the helmet with a loud thunk. Deacon dropped her arm, holding his head and stumbling back. Lisa turned, meaning to run. He recovered faster than she'd thought possible and grabbed the length of her hair.

Her head snapped back and Lisa went down. Deacon lost his grip as she fell making him stumble forward to land on one knee. Lisa rolled to her knees, seeking to regain her footing, but again Deacon was too swift. As she got one foot beneath herself, he grabbed her shoulder and spun her around.

Being on the floor gave Lisa an unexpected advantage. On her back, she could brace herself for another kick. Lisa's foot shot up and out, connecting with Deacon's stomach. With a loud oof, he flew back surprisingly easy for such a large man. She'd never have thought she could move him so far.

Deacon groaned, bending over at the waist. Lisa lost no time in scrambling to her feet. Once upright, she immediately went back to one knee with a shout of pain herself. Somehow she'd twisted her ankle, and badly.

Lisa threw a glance over her shoulder. Deacon was no longer groaning and holding his stomach. Now he was reaching for her again. His hands reached for her, still sheathed in the menacing black gloves. He shook his head, rattling the helmet almost as though it were too large.

Something was wrong. Something didn't mesh, but Lisa didn't have the luxury of time to figure out what it was. Limping, she managed to get to the doorframe where she paused out of sheer necessity. If she took one more step, the pain was going to make her pass out.

She felt him grab her shoulder and she didn't try to get away. Instead, Lisa turned to meet his grasp, ducking and bobbing as she did. Her shoulder slipped out of Deacon's hand and she ducked beneath his outstretched arm. Now she faced the inside of the room.

Deacon was moving slowly. She must have injured him. Lisa took advantage of his lack of reaction and broke toward Allegra's door. Her eyes had adjusted to the dark, and when she entered the bright light, it momentarily blinded her.

She didn't have time to waste. Behind her she could hear the thump of Deacon's heavy motorcycle boots on the wooden floor. The rooms were small and his stride long. He'd be on her in seconds.

Blindly, Lisa kept hobbling toward where she thought the second door, the one leading to the back hall stairs, must be. She misjudged by just an inch or so, slamming her shoulder into the other doorframe. She kept going, gritting her teeth against the pain and hoping his helmet impeded his vision as much as the light had hers.

Apparently, it did because Lisa heard the thud and crash of Deacon falling as she flew out into the back hallway. Here it was dark as well, once more an adjustment for her eyes. She skidded to a stop before she could tumble headfirst down the stairs.

In Allegra's room, she heard muffled cursing, a string of phrases so foul it made her catch her breath. The voice was low pitched and growling. A sick voice. A mad-dog voice. It made her stomach churn to hear it.

Lisa grabbed the banister and began hopping down the stairs as fast as she could. She dared not look behind her, afraid to see the looming, helmeted figure at the top of the stairs. She reached the narrow landing and kept going, favoring her injured ankle as best she could.

The kitchen light was still on, just as she'd left it. Her feet slapped the faded linoleum as she jumped down the last two steps. Her ankle screamed and her voice with it, but Lisa barely noticed. She had to get out of the house.

She took two steps and ran straight into a brick wall. Arms grabbed her, holding her, and Lisa went crazy in reaction. She shrieked, her voice like a fire siren, rising and rising until she thought it just might break. She kicked out, feeling her toes connect with something solid, even as she punched and slapped. He would not get her! He would not hurt her!

"Lisa! It's Terry!"

He managed to pin her arms, and as the sense of his words sunk in, Lisa stopped struggling. She sank into Terry's arms dazed.

"Terry? What're you doing here?"

"My God, Lisa, what happened to you?"

"What are you doing here?" she asked again, knowing the question was stupid, but having to ask it anyway.

"Karen told me you'd been by, and when I got your page, I came right away. What happened?"

She couldn't seem to make her lips form the words. Terry tried to lead her to a chair, tried to make her sit, but Lisa's gaze fixed on the back stairs and what she expected to see appear there any moment.

"He's coming," she managed to cry out. "Look out!"

But there was nobody there. She let Terry push her into the chair and watched while he looked up the staircase. He came back to her, kneeling in front of her. Concern filled his handsome face.

"Who's coming, Lisa?"

She'd calmed somewhat under Terry's comforting gaze. "Deacon," she said, voice trembling. "He came after me. Out of Allegra's room. He had on the helmet. And the jacket. He said they were stolen, but he lied!"

Lisa began to shudder, her body shaking as though she was being touched with a cattle prod. Terry put his hands on her shoulders briefly, soothing her.

"Campbell was here?"

"Upstairs," Lisa said through chattering teeth. She thought she might never be warm again.

Terry stood, pulling his gun. "I'll go check."

"Don't leave me!"

He looked from her to the stairway. "I have to see if he's still up there, Lisa."

He was right. Lisa nodded. "Okay."

Terry put a kiss to her forehead. "I'll be right back."

He disappeared up the stairs. Lisa closed her eyes waiting for the sounds of struggle. She heard Terry's footsteps cross through Allegra's room, into the spare room, into the hall. She heard him enter her room.

"Lisa?"

Her eyes flew open, her neck whipping around to face the back door. Deacon stood in the doorway.

It was like being a child again, struggling to call for her mother after a bad dream. She opened her mouth to scream, but only a hiss of air came out. Her body convulsed, scooting the chair back from the table.

"Lisa, are you all right? I came as soon as you called."

He crossed the kitchen toward her. He wasn't wearing the helmet or the jacket. Not even the gloves. A darkening welt marred his tan cheek.

"Stop! Don't move!"

Terry appeared from the back stairs, aiming his gun at Deacon. Deacon put his hands immediately into the air, taking a step back from Lisa. Terry moved closer, stepping in front of her.

"What's going on here?" Deacon asked.

"I should ask you that," Terry said. "Turn around and put your hands on the wall. Slowly."

Deacon did as ordered, talking over his shoulder. "Lisa called me—"

"I didn't," she retorted, finding her voice again. "I didn't call you! You were here!"

"What?" His outrage sounded real.

Terry pulled a pair of handcuffs from his belt and hooked them around Deacon's wrists. As though satisfied Deacon would no longer be a threat, Terry holstered his weapon.

"She says you attacked her upstairs." Terry's voice was grim.

Deacon shook his head. "I swear to God—"

"Tell it down at the station," Terry interrupted.

Lisa could only watch numbly as Terry yanked Deacon around. For one instant, Deacon's eyes met hers. She found she could not look away.

"You have to believe me," he told her. "I was at home until ten minutes ago. When you called me."

"I didn't call you," Lisa said.

"Don't talk to him, Lisa," Terry ordered. "I'm going to call for someone to come sit with you while I take this jerk down to the station."

"I swear to you, someone called me," Deacon said. "I thought it was you. She said she was sorry about what happened and could I come over right away? And I did, but the minute I walked in that door was the first time I've been here all night. I swear to you, Lisa."

"You're a liar," Lisa said, ignoring Terry's order.

"She says somebody attacked her upstairs," Terry spat. "Somebody wearing your helmet and jacket. Take a look at her face, Campbell. She's obviously been assaulted. And you want to tell me you didn't do it?"

"If I did it, how come I just showed up in the kitchen now?" Deacon spat back. "It wasn't me."

"The front door is wide open," Terry said. "You had enough time to run down the stairs, get rid of the clothes and come to the back door."

"But I didn't," Deacon growled.

"How'd you get that bruise, Campbell?" Terry asked.

Deacon looked at Lisa. "I didn't get it upstairs."

Terry turned away from Deacon, as though the other man's words weren't even worth listening to. "Someone will be here in a few minutes."

"Believe me, Lisa," Deacon said, ignoring Terry as the man ignored him. "Look inside yourself and decide if you can really believe I'd ever try to hurt you."

Lisa shook her head, wanting his words to go away. "You can't trick me this time, Deacon."

"I don't want to trick you," Deacon said.

Terry jerked him upright. "Shut up, Campbell. You'll sit out in the patrol car until someone gets here."

As he was being dragged away, Deacon struggled only to call over his shoulder. "Someone stole my helmet and jacket, Lisa! I didn't lie about that! They took them from my office. Check the video!"

Then Terry had yanked him through the doorway. Lisa sat back in her chair, unable to move. Her ankle throbbed, as did a dozen places on her body she hadn't noticed were in pain until just now. From upstairs, she could still hear the faint sound of running water.

She heard the crackle of static from Terry's radio, then the burst of voices. Someone would be here soon to sit with her while Terry took Deacon to the station and threw him in a cell. Someone would protect her even as the man who'd assaulted her was locked away.

Chill doubt still assailed her with its skeletal fingers. Something was not right. It was not right. She ticked the fingers of one hand against the palm of the other, before looking down and stopping the motion with a shudder. That was Allegra's nervous habit, not hers.

Lisa shook in the kitchen chair, wishing for a sweater and unable to force herself to find one. Something was not right. What was it? What still nudged at her brain?

Deacon had said she called him. She didn't. Terry said she'd paged him…and she hadn't done that either. Lisa got up from the table so fast she knocked over her chair. She didn't call and she didn't page. But someone did.

Someone wearing a helmet and jacket attacked her. Deacon said those items had been stolen. Check the video, he'd said. Barely aware she was moving, Lisa grabbed her keys and headed for the back door.

Check the video. The video would tell her the truth. About everything.

CHAPTER 14

Terry hadn't put the lights on his patrol car on, but there had been enough commotion to get the neighbors peeking through their blinds. Lisa paid them no attention, focused on her mission. The car keys bit into her palm as she slid behind the driver's seat.

"Lisa!"

She heard Terry calling, but ignored him. She could see the dark outline of Deacon's head in the back seat of the patrol car, and Terry began heading her way. Lisa yanked the gear stick into reverse and backed out of the driveway. She didn't bother to see if Terry ran after her.

Her mind raced along with her car as she sped down the dark and narrow streets. She should not believe Deacon, not after finding her purse under his bed. Not after she'd seen the figure in his helmet and jacket looming up, outlined by the light from Allegra's room.

Her foot twitched on the gas, making the car buck, as she remembered the kick. Even though she'd connected with force, her assailant had been too easy to shove away. Too light, not heavy as she knew Deacon's weight to be.

Her cheeks flushed hot as she thought of exactly how well she knew the weight of Deacon against her. Lisa's fingers tapped nervously on the wheel as she waited for the light to turn green. Checking the videotape would only take a few minutes. One way or another, it would set her mind at ease.

Her mind whirled as she thought back over the past few months.

While she had been falling back in love with Deacon, could it be possible that he'd been the one behind all the strange things? He had a motive as her family and Terry kept reminding her. But could he really have done those things?

"I don't want to believe that," she said aloud.

The group of kids out joyriding in the car beside her looked over and started laughing. They'd been singing along with the radio, but apparently talking to oneself wasn't the same thing. Lisa shot a glare their way, not in the mood for teenage games. One of them flipped her the finger as the light changed and they revved their engine to beat her.

She rolled her window up and punched the air conditioner button. Her earlier chill had been replaced with an almost feverish heat. She forced herself to maintain the proper speed limit, though she was dying to race through town. She didn't want to get into an accident or get a speeding ticket on her way to The Garden Shadd.

"I don't want to believe it," she said again, not caring who saw her lips moving.

She had not made the decision to go to bed with Deacon lightly. Despite their past, the last few months had proven him to be a man of talent, integrity and kindness. Had she been wrong about all that? Was Deacon the liar she'd accused him of being, and such a good one he had fooled her into falling in love with him?

The brakes squealed as Lisa jammed her foot down. Thank God there was nobody behind her. She eased up on the brake and took deep breaths to steady herself as she pulled off to the side of the road. She was suddenly shaking too much to drive.

Love. She loved him. All at once it seemed so clear. The way his touch made her tremble was more than just chemistry, more than hormones rushing through her body and urging her toward sex.

Lisa thought back over the past several weeks and one thing stood out startlingly clear. Deacon's face was the first thing she thought of in the morning when she woke, and the last thing she thought of before she slept at night. She loved him.

She let out a small groan, letting her head rest against the steering wheel. Her entire body ached, and now, so did her heart. She'd fallen in love with a man, who at the minimum, was a thief. At worst, he was the man who'd just attacked her.

She had gone her entire life without encountering danger until Deacon moved back to town. Everything had started with the kids in the parking lot who tried to steal her underwear. If so much had not happened since then, she might now be able to look back on that and laugh. As it was, that night had been only the beginning.

He had come to her rescue—a dark knight on his rumbling metal steed. Why would he have saved her only to continue harassing her? Only someone mentally unsound would do something like that... Lisa gasped.

Allegra.

Lisa had come to believe Deacon when he declared he had not robbed The Circle K. If she believed that, she could not believe he'd been behind the phone calls, the thievery, the subtle but frightening harassments she been subjected to. If she did not believe it to be Deacon, she had to believe it was her sister.

"Allegra is special," she whispered, feeling tears stinging at her eyes. "Oh, no. No."

What would be worse? The man she loved or her only sister? She didn't always like Allegra, but blood would always be thicker than water.

Lisa checked traffic and eased back out onto the street. The office was only a few minutes away. She kept her attention fixed firmly on the road, but she couldn't force her mind to stop its whirling.

The pantry, with its eerie arrangement of cans, was a sign she should not have ignored. It had been too easy to go along with the doctors who'd said Allegra was fine. Admitting her sister was not just special, that perhaps she was sick, was something Lisa had not been prepared to do. Until now.

Now, when her love for Deacon was the one bright and shining thing in her life. He might be a thief and might not love her as she loved him. He might even have only been wooing her to seek revenge for the past three years he's spent incarcerated because of her.

Lisa discovered it didn't matter. Because she loved him, she had to find the answers. She'd risk a broken heart to face the truth.

Just ahead The Garden Shadd sign beckoned. Though the sign was lit, the building was dark but for the pair of lights on each side of the front door. Lisa pulled her car into the parking lot, then around back to the employee's spaces. It was even darker back here.

She parked the car and sat in the dark, her breath coming fast in her chest. She was scared. The air-conditioned air which had been a welcome breeze against her face now sent chills capering over her spine. She shivered and switched it off.

Silence filled her car making her thoughts seem too loud. Lisa yanked the keys from the ignition, tucking one between each knuckle until her hand bristled with metal. With her other hand, she opened the car door, then got out.

She squared her shoulders, breathing in the scent of mulch and flowers that permeated the air. She had been here a thousand times, even after hours, even in the dark. Tonight should be no different, but it was. She felt it on her skin and the way her eyes leaped to search out the faintest of noises. Something was different here tonight, and maybe it was only her imagination. Or maybe it was not.

She crossed the short, sloped ramp and unlocked the gate leading into the outdoor nursery. Inside, even the faint glow from the street light was masked by the multitude of lush, growing things. The plants seemed to whisper as Lisa stood among them, and in their familiar presence, she had a moment of comfort. Surely no harm could come to her here.

The feeling of unease returned, however, as she stepped out of the friendly rows and unlocked the door into the back offices. The key jittered coldly in the lock, betraying the trembling of her fingers, and Lisa paused a moment to get control. Then she tucked the keys back between her fingers and stepped into the dark hallway.

A glowing exit sign lit her way to Deacon's office. Even from this distance, she could see the door stood open. What she needed to find, though, was not in Deacon's office, but her father's. That was where Doug kept the surveillance equipment that was part of The Garden Shadd's minor security system.

Instead of turning left, though, Lisa went to her right toward Deacon's work space. She had no idea exactly what she was looking for. It wasn't until she actually reached the doorway that she realized she had not yet turned on any lights.

Her hand instinctively went to the switch on the wall before she stopped herself. Her decision to stay in the dark had been unconscious, but it made sense. The dark was her ally as well as her enemy.

Lisa closed her eyes, envisioning the layout in Deacon's small and cluttered office. To her right, just inside the doorway, would be a battered chair. To her left along the wall was a workspace with computer equipment. Behind that and along the back wall, the rows of shelves were filled with supplies and the video camera.

When she opened her eyes, the room wasn't any brighter. With no window to let in the outside light, it wasn't going to be any brighter unless she turned on the lights. Lisa nudged her foot carefully in front of her until it connected with the chair's edge. She had her bearings.

With her hands out in front of her, she took one hesitant step forward. Immediately, she felt something beneath her fingers that had not been in there in her imagined perusal of the room.

It was a face.

*   *   *

"I don't give a rat's ass about your excuses," Hewitt spat into Deacon's face. "Save it for the judge."

Deacon's wrists ached from the biting metal of the handcuffs, but he couldn't stop himself from lunging uselessly forward. "You have to listen to me!"

Hewitt's laugh was cold. "Shut up, Campbell."

"Aren't you even going to go after her?" Deacon asked, slumping back against the seat, ignoring the pain that bit at his wrists as he did. "She's in danger!"

"From what?" Terry asked. "I've got you right here."

Deacon gritted his teeth and fixed the officer with a look that would have made a lesser man flinch. To give him credit, Terry's gaze didn't even flicker. Under other circumstances, Deacon might even have felt a certain grudging admiration for his rival.

"I am not the one who attacked her."

"How'd you get that bruise?" Terry asked again. "It looks like a hand print."

Deacon didn't want to tell Terry the truth about the wound, not now when the other man would just think he was bragging. He didn't have a choice, though. "She slapped me. But not here. At my house earlier tonight."

Now the other man's gaze flickered, just a little. Terry smiled thinly. "So Lisa did hit you. In self-defense."

"I wasn't attacking her," Deacon gritted out. "She was running away and I tried to catch her, to get her to listen to me—"

"Why was she running, Campbell?" Terry interrupted. "Though I think in light of the Miranda warning I read you a while ago, you'd want to keep your mouth shut at this point."

"She's in danger, damn it!" Deacon's yell echoed through the dark street. He saw the curtains shake from the window across the street, and he bit down on his tongue to keep from yelling again. "Just check it out, man. This is Lisa! Don't you even care?"

"Of course I care," Terry hissed. "And if I thought you weren't full of shit, I'd be after her in a heartbeat! But I have a job to do here, and based on what she and you both told me, it's my job to take you in and see you remanded into proper custody."

"I love her," Deacon said, his voice low and his head hung lower.

"What?" Terry asked, bending low to hear him. "What did you say, you scumbag?"

Deacon lifted his head, no longer caring about competing, or about being more of a man. Lisa was in danger. He felt it in every cell of his body. "I love her. I would never have hurt her."

Terry sneered, though it seemed forced. "Shut up. Keep your filth to yourself. You can't love her. You don't have it in you. She deserves better than you!"

The other man's voice broke even as it rose and Deacon heard the truth in it. "If you love her, too, you'll get behind the wheel and take us both to The Garden Shadd. Before it's too late."

Terry closed his eyes briefly, sagging against the car door. All at once the shine seemed to vanish from his badge. When he opened his eyes, his expression was grim.

"You'd better be right or I'll kick your ass," he said. "With or without permission of the court."

Then he slammed Deacon's door and slid behind the wheel, gunning the engine and turning on the sirens.

*   *   *

Lisa couldn't even scream. She felt her wrists grabbed, the fingers gripping like pincers against her flesh. She fell back, but was supported by the grip of her phantom attacker. Desperately she kicked out, but whoever held her had long arms. In the dark, with no frame of reference, Lisa couldn't even see to defend herself.

"Lisa."

It took a second for the voice to register, but when it did, Lisa let out a sharp sob of relief. She yanked her wrists free, sucking in the air she'd forgotten for a moment to breath. "Al! My God, you scared the hell out of me!"

She felt her sister's form lean forward, brushing against her, to flick on the lights. Lisa threw her hand in front of her face against the sudden brightness. It took her a few moments of blinking to be able to focus on her sister's face.

Allegra looked like a refugee from a horror movie. Her dark lustrous hair, usually so smooth and shining, was now tangled and dull. Purplish half-moons shadowed her brown eyes, though the rest of her face was sallow-pale. She'd been chewing at the skin of her lips, leaving them raw and bloody.

She wore a pair of jeans so loose around her hips that the hip bones jutted like butterfly wings on either side of her sunken belly. Dark tufts of pubic hair peeked out with every shift of her hips, but what might have been meant as an erotic turn-on looked only scary. Her shirt, a red button-down, had lost most of its buttons. It gaped open to Allegra's navel, barely concealing the fullness of her clearly naked breasts beneath.

She was covered in writing from the edge of her collar bone down. Words, scrawled in blue and black ink, began a long litany of items, which read together, almost became poetic.

Eyeliner
Underwear
Red shirt
Sunscreen
Black skirt
Pantyhose
Umbrella
Dungarees

Those were just the words Lisa could read. The writing curved around Allegra's skin, disappearing beneath her clothing. The sight of it made Lisa want to gag.

"Allegra," she said carefully to her sister's dull eyes. "What have you done to yourself?"

Allegra touched her skin lightly. "Nothing. Everything. I thought if I made a list it would make me feel better."

"A list of what?" She had to look away.

"You've never stolen anything," Allegra said. "You don't know what a rush it is. Almost better than sex."

Her throaty laughter contrasted sharply with her haggard face and dark-circled eyes. Allegra ran her fingers from the base of her throat to the first row of words. Then she brought her fingers back to her lips and kissed them.

"You'd think people would pay more attention," she said. "But they don't. You can walk right out—right under their noses. And they never know."

"You did steal all that stuff."

"Get with the program, Lisa," Allegra snapped, breaking out of her dreaminess. "The train is leaving the station. Try to stay on it, okay?"

"Okay." Lisa wanted to soothe her sister. Wanted to make this all stop.

"I didn't steal it. I liberated it." Allegra paused. "It was like being invisible."

Her fingers clawed the skin at her throat suddenly leaving red welts behind. "I hate being invisible! I hate it! I don't like being ignored!"

"Nobody's ignoring you," Lisa replied. The thought Allegra had ever felt invisible was unbelievable. She's always been impossible to ignore.

"You never listen to me," Allegra muttered. One hand flew up to softly touch her ravaged lips. The fingertips came away sprinkled with blood.

"I'm listening now," Lisa said, as soothingly as she could with her voice shaking.

Allegra's eyes flicked to look at her. "You weren't supposed to come here. You were supposed to be breaking up the fight."

"What fight?" Lisa asked gently.

"Of the knights for the lady fair," Allegra said without a trace of her usual wry humor. "Officer Friendly and Jailbird. Both were supposed to show up at the house and battle for your hand."

"You called them?" It was apparent to her now that her sister was indeed behind everything.

Allegra nodded with a movement that made it seem as though her head was too heavy a weight for the delicate stem of her neck. "And they came, didn't they? Came for you?"

"Yes, they did." Lisa wanted to reach out to pull Allegra's fingers away from the ruins of her mouth, but she was afraid to touch her.

"Nobody would do that for me," Allegra whispered, her words muffled behind her fingers. Her shoulders shook. "Nobody."

"That's not true," Lisa said. "Mom and Dad…"

Allegra made a sound of disgust so low in her throat it sounded as though she were growling. "I'm not talking about Mom or Dad, Lisa! Holy wounds of Jesus, I'm talking about someone who loves me."

"We all love you—"

But Allegra would have none of it. "Shut up!" she screamed, digging ugly furrows into her cheeks with the tips of her fingers. "Just shut up, Princess Lisa!"

Lisa wisely kept her mouth shut. She felt like she'd drunk an entire pot of coffee in one gulp, every nerve jangling. Her eyes felt like they were open too wide. Her mouth had dried.

Allegra appeared to calm herself, shifting her hands from her cheeks to smooth through her matted hair. Her smile was bright and shining when she spoke.

"I'm not like you," she said, her tone biting despite the sunniness of her smile. "I'm special."

The bitter way she said the word brought tears to Lisa's eyes. "Oh, Al. Of course you are."

"I don't want to be special," Allegra whispered, sagging against the desk. "I want to be normal."

Lisa had no response to that because anything she said would be merely placation. Platitude. Something to say just to make her sister feel better, and it was obvious Allegra was beyond the help of mere words.

Her sister looked up at her with naked, wet eyes. "Is that such a big thing to ask?"

"No."

Allegra sneered. "Easy for you to say. Easy for you to say. Easy...For...You...To...Say!"

"What can I do to help you?" Lisa held out her hands. "Allegra, just tell me what to do."

"You can die," Allegra said conversationally. "That might make me feel better, at least for a little while."

*   *   *

"I don't believe this," Deacon moaned as the cop car came to an abrupt stop. "Terry, forget them! Let's go!"

Terry glanced over his shoulder while unbuckling his seat belt. "What do you want me to do, Campbell? They're blocking the road."

A car full of teenagers had rear-ended a luxury car carrying an elderly couple. Though the accident was clearly minor, the light traffic had snarled to a stop. One patrol car, lights lazily spinning but no sirens, had already arrived on the scene.

"Hey, Terry," called the other officer. She jerked her head toward the mess. "Can you lend a hand?"

Terry hesitated, glancing into the back seat where Deacon scowled. "Sorry, Karen. I've got a call already."

Karen sighed heavily, glaring at the sheepish teenage driver whose license she'd confiscated. "I ought to have you take the whole pack of these yahoos in."

The sheepish looks turned to terror and a babble of protest sprang

CONVICTED

up simultaneously from all the teens. Karen just shook her head, still writing her ticket. "Kids."

"I'll talk to you later," Terry said, slipping back behind the wheel.

He eased the car around the accident and whooped the siren enough to get the rubberneckers moving out of the way. When finally the car had moved out onto the road again, Deacon breathed a sigh of relief. It felt like ants were crawling over his skin, so anxious was he to get to Lisa.

"You think she went to the office?" Terry asked for the third time.

"Yeah." Deacon managed to keep his temper, recognizing he was at the other man's mercy. At least for now. "To check the video."

"So Doug had you under surveillance, huh?" The amusement in Terry's voice made Deacon frown.

"Yeah."

Terry snorted. "Can't say I blame him."

"Just drive," Deacon said. "If we get there and something's happened to her..."

He let the comment ride the air between them. Terry cleared his throat, pressing on the accelerator. The car sped through the night, just minutes from their goal. Deacon could only hope they weren't minutes too late.

*   *   *

"Don't worry," Allegra continued calmly even as Lisa wheezed in terror. "I won't kill you or anything." Her grin was feral and terrifying. "I'm not that crazy."

"Al, this isn't funny." Lisa found her voice, the big sister disapproving tone of it making Allegra flinch.

"I'm not trying to be funny." Al's eyes wavered, glancing around the office like she was watching for something that wasn't there. "You want to see something funny? I mean funny ha-ha, not funny weird."

"No," Lisa said. "I want to go home."

Allegra cocked her head. "I sorta kinda figured you were here to see the video."

"I don't need to see it," Lisa said. "Come on, Al. Let's go home. We can talk to Mom and Dad—"

"We can talk to Mom and Dad!" Allegra's voice mocked her. "No, thanks. I have something you need to see."

She held out a stack of videos. Lisa reached for them, but drew back her hands when Allegra yanked them away. The pile shifted in her sister's hands and fell to the floor with a clatter.

164

"Stupid bitch," Allegra yelled, but Lisa couldn't be sure which one of them her sister meant. Allegra bent to scoop up the tapes. "Now they're out of order."

She began counting under her breath, rocking while sorting the tapes, all of which were blank and unnumbered. She fit them into an order only she could comprehend, piling them on the floor, then rose to her full height. With the light shining from behind her, she looked entirely too familiar.

"It was you," Lisa cried, cringing back against the doorway. "Oh, my God, Allegra! At the house, it was you."

As Allegra stepped to one side to expose the desk, and Lisa saw Deacon's helmet and leather jacket.

"Of course it was," Allegra said. "Dummy. You didn't recognize me then—or three years ago either."

"What do you mean?" Lisa asked, her mind still trying to wrap around the concept her sister had actually attacked her.

"At The Circle K," Allegra told her. "That was me, too."

* * *

Just as they reached the stretch of road that led to The Garden Shadd, Deacon saw something in the ditch along the road. "Stop!"

Terry glanced in the rearview mirror, his eyes annoyed. "I thought you were in a hurry, Campbell."

Deacon couldn't point, not with his hands cuffed. He jerked his chin toward the ditch. "Look!"

Terry slowed the car and pulled over. "Looks like a car."

The car had settled in such a way that only the back fender was clearly visible. It was the license plate that had caught Deacon's eye. BADGRRL.

"Allegra's car," he said.

"Shit." Terry climbed out, leaving Deacon to strain his neck trying to see. "She's not in here!"

"No," Deacon said to himself, watching Terry shine his flashlight all around the vehicle. He looked up the small hill to the dark Garden Shadd. "She's up there."

* * *

Lisa clutched the doorframe feeling woozy. "I don't get it."

"You don't?" Allegra asked. "And I thought you were supposed to be the smart one. I'm the pretty one and you're the smart one. Lisa's the smart one. The smart one. Not so smart now, are you?"

Her sister's words had begun to take on a rambling, repetitive quality Lisa didn't like. Allegra seemed about to break from reality. Lisa didn't know much about psychology, but she knew that couldn't be good.

Allegra stretched herself up, then slipped on the helmet. Only the ends of her dark hair showed. She pulled on the bulky jacket. Her stance became more masculine, even menacing. In the dark, she'd easily pass for a man.

She flipped open the visor top. "I'm tall. Surveillance videos aren't very clear. You were ready to believe it was him. What can I say?"

"No," Lisa said softly. "I didn't want to believe it. But I had to answer them honestly when they asked me if it was him in the video, and I had to say yes. I thought it was. But I never wanted to believe it."

Allegra shrugged, the shoulders of the leather jacket creaking. "What's the difference?"

Lisa thought of three years lost and knew it made a lot of difference. "Why, Al? Why would you do that?"

In reply, Allegra tore off the helmet and tossed it to the floor. She struggled out of the jacket and let it fall, too, her lip curled in disgust. She kicked the clothes vehemently. She paced the tiny office rubbing her arms. Every movement pulled up her shirtsleeves to reveal more of the freakish writing.

"You were spending all your time with him," Allegra said. "All. No time left for me. Your sister! And you were going to marry him and go away. Then who would I live with? What would I do then, Lisa? What would I do then?"

Her sister's assessment of the situation startled Lisa. "We never talked about getting married."

Allegra shot her an empty look, continuing her pacing. "I could see it in your eyes. Smell it on you like bad fish. You loved him. Love him. You love him!"

Lisa reached out to stop Allegra and force her to look at her. "I do love him. And I probably did then, too, but—"

"See?" Allegra's pretty mouth turned down in a frown so deep it carved lines in her normally smooth cheeks. "You'd leave me!"

Lisa felt like a tightrope walker. One wrong word and she'd plummet into the precipice. She let go of Al's arm.

"It has to happen someday," she said.

"Not with him." Allegra frowned. "He's not good enough for you."

"You don't have to protect me," Lisa began, but Al's hot glare stopped her.

166

"And Terry Goody-Two-Shoes," Allegra continued. "Boring Mr. Perfect. You didn't really want to spend the rest of your life with him, did you?"

"My life is for me to decide," Lisa cried. "How dare you try to interfere, Allegra!"

Lisa's anger did nothing to affect Allegra, who merely kept her pacing. Now she began the peculiar habit of ticking off the fingers of one hand with the other like she was constantly making a mental list.

"You just wouldn't see them for what they were, would you?" Allegra questioned. "No matter how hard I tried to show you."

All the pieces fit together like a puzzle after hours of bleary-eyed concentration. "You took my purse that day. You put it in his office and wanted me to find it, didn't you?"

"But you wouldn't look."

"So you put it in his house where you knew I'd find it someday."

"It worked, didn't it?" Allegra asked, for the first time focusing on Lisa. "You ran out of there like a scalded dog, didn't you? Right to where I was waiting for you."

"You tried to hurt me," Lisa accused. She swallowed heavily, fighting the urge to choke on the sick feeling of betrayal.

"Only a little bit. I only ever wanted to scare you," Al said with her old guileless smile. Her voice changed, but remained eerily familiar. "I see everything you do. Remember?"

Where would it end? "You made the phone calls? You stole my laundry?"

"Oh, you were so easy," Allegra said. "So wrapped up in your daydreams. It was easy to misplace your stuff for you. Do you want to know what my favorite trick was? The light bulbs. I could tell that was just driving you crazy!"

Lisa wanted to slap the laugh right out of her sister. "And you hired those boys to mug me in the parking lot?"

"I thought that would be a nice touch."

"It's been you all along," Lisa muttered, not wanting to believe.

Allegra waved the accusation away as though it were smoke. "It's all going to work out. He'll go back to jail. I paged Terry to come. So it's going to work. He'll go away, and Terry will never forgive you, and things will go back to the way they were before. I'll move back in. It'll be great!"

Lisa shook her head. "You need help."

Allegra let out a low, guttural sound. "I do. I do. Maybe I do, yes.

But so what? I just want things to be the way they were—"

Lisa shouted, "Things will never be the same again!"

Allegra winced. "You just won't believe me, will you? He's not right for you. Lisa, when you find the right man, I mean the right man for you, I'll be so happy and proud to be your maid of honor. But he's not right for you and I can prove it!"

"I don't want any more proof." As Lisa turned to go, Al's hand flew out to grab her hair. With a cry of pain, Lisa fell back.

"Don't walk away from me." Allegra emphasized each word with a tug that made Lisa squirm in pain. "Come on. I have to show you."

Lisa resisted, but despite being thin, Allegra was strong. She let go of Lisa's hair, but grabbed her wrist in a pincer grip instead. She pulled Lisa nearly off balance while bending to pick up the pile of videos. Then Allegra began pulling her out the door and down the hallway.

"Al, let me go."

Allegra shook her head. "I want you to see. I want you to 'get it.'"

"You don't have to do this," Lisa said.

Her sister only tugged harder. "Yes, I do."

"This can end now." Lisa dug in her heels and managed to get her sister to stop, if only briefly.

"No," Allegra said with a shake of her head. "It can't. It's not over until it's over."

"And when will that be?"

Allegra shrugged, tugging Lisa's arm upward with the motion. "We'll see, I guess."

*   *   *

Terry parked in the back next to Lisa's car. He got out, then opened Deacon's door. He didn't remove the handcuffs, and he didn't help Deacon out of the back seat.

"She's in there," Deacon said.

Terry glanced around. "This doesn't feel good."

"Of course it doesn't feel good," Deacon snapped. "She's in there with that lunatic!"

Terry reached for his radio. "I need to call for back up."

Deacon forced himself out of the back seat through sheer will power alone. Standing, he felt less immobilized, though he still could do nothing without the use of his hands.

"Take these off," he demanded.

Terry looked at him. "No."

Deacon kicked the car. "You're wasting time! Let's just go in there and get that crazy bitch!"

Terry shook his head with another glance at the dark building. "I can't risk that. We need back up."

"Coward," Deacon muttered.

The next instant he found himself slammed onto the hood of the car. Terry's scowl was inches from his own. Even as his muscles screamed in protest, Deacon didn't show the pain. He braced himself for a punch that didn't come.

"I love her, too, asshole," Terry breathed before letting Deacon go. He wiped his hands on his dark blue pants as though touching Deacon had made him feel dirty. "Which is why this needs to be done right."

"Uncuff me, then," Deacon said. He added, "Please."

Terry shook his head again. "You think I'm an idiot?"

Deacon didn't answer. The challenge in his eyes was enough reply. Terry sighed, then reached for the cuffs. Deacon rubbed his freed wrists, then clapped Terry on the shoulder. "Thanks."

"Don't play the hero," Terry warned. "You'll get both of you killed."

"What you don't see, you can't stop," Deacon said. "You call for back up."

He waited until Terry had bent again into the cruiser, and he ran toward the building.

CHAPTER 15

Allegra knew just where to find the surveillance equipment. Relying only on the light shining in from the window, she pulled Lisa through Doug's doorway and into the center of the room, then tugged her toward the small closet to the right of the desk.

"I thought you were afraid of the dark," Lisa snapped, trying to free her wrist from Allegra's grip.

"I am," Allegra said with a shudder. "But I've had to learn to face my fears, Lisa."

It was the first sane thing her sister had said, but Lisa could take no comfort in it. There was still too much craziness to wade through.

Allegra continued airily, as though she wasn't struggling one-handed with the closet door while she bruised Lisa's arm with the other. "I left it all in the note."

"What note?" Lisa stopped tugging, recognizing the gesture as futile.

Allegra paused to look over her shoulder. Her eyes flashed in the light from the window. "The note I left you. It explained everything."

"I don't know what you're talking about."

"You saw it! I know you did!" Allegra smacked the stubborn closet door. "It's what made you go to Mom and Dad and try to convince them I'm a nutcase!"

You are a nutcase. It almost flew out of Lisa's mouth, but a sudden, unbidden memory of her sister as a baby stopped the evil words. Allegra had been a sunny baby, and Lisa had loved to tickle her belly until she laughed. "She loves you," her mother had said, watching the girls play together. "She loves her big sister."

Love for her sister washed over Lisa in a wave so fierce it nearly forced a sob from her throat. What had gone so wrong? "I didn't get a note."

"In the pantry," Allegra said. "I left it for you."

"The cans?" Another puzzle piece slipped into place.

"I was very careful," Allegra said, finally tugging open the door. "I marked out the letters I didn't need."

Lisa thought of the rows of cans, so precisely lined up. There had been a message there, but she had not received it. She guessed it didn't really matter what the message said.

"Let's get out of here," she told her sister gently. "We can go home, Al. Just you and me. And we'll talk."

"Just a minute," Allegra muttered, never letting go of Lisa's wrist.

Lisa dug her feet into the carpet. "Stop this! You're hurting my wrist!"

Even in the dim light Lisa could see Allegra roll her eyes. "Just a minute."

She didn't let go. The bones in Lisa's wrist ground together painfully. "Let me go. I'll watch what you want me to watch."

Allegra turned from her fumbling with the closet door. "You'll run away."

"No. I won't."

"You're lying."

Lisa let out a growl of desperate exasperation. Her initial fear had fled. She was used to Allegra being a pain in the ass. She could deal with this.

"I'm not the liar," Lisa said.

Allegra nodded as though thinking. "Not telling the truth isn't the same as lying."

"Whatever," Lisa said calmly. "I wasn't accusing you. Just let go of my wrist."

Her sister did. Lisa rubbed the bruised flesh, but stood her ground. Allegra watched her warily for a moment before turning back to the closet.

"Watch," she said, finally pulling open the door to reveal a set of floor-to-ceiling shelves. Several vcrs were lined up along one shelf while the rest had been used for office supplies. A small and ancient television set rested next to the vcrs.

Lisa's eyes had adjusted to the dim light, and she had no problem seeing her sister slip one of the video tapes into the first machine. Allegra twisted the tv knob.

Lisa blinked against the bright gray light flaring from the machine. After a few seconds of static, a picture appeared.

"Oh, crap." The tape showed her and Deacon the day they'd let themselves get carried away. Her cheeks flushed hot as she watched her video self let him kiss her. "Al, turn that off."

"Why?" Allegra tapped the screen with her finger. "Don't you like to watch?"

"No, Al. I don't." Lisa reached forward to snap off the set, but Allegra stopped her.

The pictures of her and Deacon kissing were replaced by a blank screen as he reached over on the tape and hung up a shirt to cover the camera lens. A second later, the tape showed Deacon at his desk. The helmet and jacket sat on the architect's table, almost out of camera range. He bent over his work, scribbling on his pad of paper with a look of concentration apparent even in his profile.

A woman entered the office, and Allegra breathed "See?"

Lisa wasn't sure what her sister wanted her to see. The woman was tall, dark haired, with a lively smile. She wore a casual outfit and carried a straw shoulder bag. Nothing about her seemed out of place.

Deacon looked up, then got to his feet. He and the woman embraced, and the woman kissed his cheek. Deacon smiled at her as though he clearly knew her. He put one hand on her back and they left the office together.

"He doesn't love you," Allegra said triumphantly.

"That's his sister," she told Allegra. "She came to take him home when his motorcycle needed some repairs."

"No." Allegra's tone said she would take no disagreement. "No. It's his lover. And he loves her, not you. Don't you see, Lisa? Don't you?"

Allegra's voice had taken on a slightly desperate quality that matched the increased frequency of the ticking-off motion of her hands. The tv screen went briefly blank, then on again to show a tall figure with dark hair entering Deacon's office. Because the interior lights had not been turned on, it was difficult to tell who the figure was, but Lisa knew it was her sister.

On the tape, Allegra reached for the dark shape draped over Deacon's chair. The leather jacket. She picked up a round dark shape and slipped it over her head. The helmet. The figure turned to face the camera, but Lisa could tell Allegra didn't know about the surveillance device. On the tape, her sister left Deacon's office. Then the screen went staticky again.

"When did you find out about the cameras?" Lisa asked.

Allegra shrugged, her eyes shining glassy in the white light. "I was going back into the office to put his stuff back."

"Why?" There was more to her question than just about the helmet and jacket.

Allegra gave her a familiar look—the one that meant she thought Lisa was being incredibly dense. "So they'd find it here. Duh. So even if he said he didn't have the helmet and stuff, they'd find it here and not believe it had been stolen. So they'd believe he was the one who attacked you, Lisa!"

"Why?" Lisa repeated. "Why did you do all this, Allegra? What did I do to make you hate me so much?"

Allegra looked stricken. "But I don't hate you, Lisa! I love you! I did all this because I love you!"

*   *   *

Deacon navigated the familiar rows of greenery easily. He headed for his office and the light which shone forth. A shout hovered on his lips, but even as he flung open the glass door into the building he could see inside. His office, though well-lit, was empty.

He spotted the helmet and jacket he'd thought stolen on the floor. "That bitch," he muttered, not bothering to touch them. She'd been trying to set him up.

If they weren't in his office, where were they? He strained his ears, listening for any sign. He thought he heard a raised shout, but couldn't be certain if it was inside the main building or out in the parking lot.

He had no idea how long it would take for Terry's backup to get there, but one thing he did remember about the City of St. Mary's Police Department. It was prompt and efficient when it came to covering crime scenes. Even so, there wasn't time to spare, not when Allegra might be hurting Lisa. Or worse.

He hurried through the nursery area and went back inside the main building. Everything in here was dark, lit only by the EXIT signs posted periodically along the corridor. Even the outside light had been brighter than in here. With one hand on the wall to help him guide his way, Deacon started running toward the main office.

He heard shuffling and a thumping. Heart pounding, he stepped into the main office. Along the back wall, Doug's office door stood open. A flickering light came from inside and he heard voices.

Without stopping to think, Deacon launched himself around the front desk and toward Doug's office door. In seconds he burst through it, fists up and ready to fight. He saw two figures outlined in the flickering light coming from a small closet, but from this angle he could see little more.

Two figures—locked in a clinch that could be embrace or battle. He had no time to think, no time to decide. He reached for the closest one, grabbed it by the shoulder, twirled it around.

Beneath the swirling hair he saw a familiar face. "Lisa!"

"Get your hands off her," Allegra shouted.

Deacon pushed Lisa out of the way just as Allegra kicked out at him. Her foot connected squarely with his thigh and he stumbled back. Allegra came after him, fists swinging.

He'd never hit a woman in his life, but Deacon didn't hesitate. His fist struck Allegra's jaw, sending her into the desk. He didn't let her cry of pain deter him from grabbing her by the shoulder. Her fist came with the turn. He didn't have time to duck, and she caught him just above the eye.

"Stop it," Lisa cried, but he didn't know who she meant.

Deacon didn't let go of Allegra even as she swung at him again. Lisa came from behind him, trying to pull them apart, and Allegra's next swing hit Lisa right in the nose. The crunch was loud and sickening in such close proximity. Lisa stumbled back, and Deacon reached to help her.

He should have known better than to turn his back on a crazy woman. Allegra snatched up a stapler from the desk and hit him on the head with it. He felt a gush of blood and he cursed.

"Damn it, Allegra!"

Her laughter sent him over the edge, but it was watching her grab for Lisa that made him reach out to seize her once more. He didn't want to hit her again. Even just doing it once had made his mouth taste bad. He struggled for a good grip on her, but her shirt was loose and kept slipping from his fingers.

"My sister not enough for you?" Allegra taunted. In the weird light, her eyes looked like silver fire. "See, Lisa? He'll take a chance on anything with tits!"

Lisa only groaned, sagging against the desk. The blood on her face looked black. Deacon finally got a good grasp on Allegra's shirt and yanked her toward him.

"Just shut up," he warned her.

Allegra drew up her knee and hit him in the groin with it. He didn't even have time to groan before he hit the floor. A red, hot haze of pain filled him. He was still trying to rise above it when the room suddenly flared with light and noise.

"Don't move!" Police officers, guns raised, filled the room.

Deacon couldn't have moved, even if he'd wanted to. He couldn't speak. Could barely breathe. He could only watch through the haze of pain as one of the officers yanked him to his feet and slapped a pair of handcuffs on him again.

Two more officers went to Lisa who still stood with her hands to her bloody face. Allegra sobbed against the shoulder of one of the officer's, her crocodile tears completely convincing.

Deacon didn't know the cop who hauled him to his feet, but he knew the one who stopped them at the office door.

"You son-of-a-bitch," Terry said, his face livid with anger. "If you've hurt her, there's no jail in the world that'll keep you safe from me."

As much as Deacon wanted to protest his innocence, speech had escaped him. He looked to Lisa and tried to make her see what was happening to him. Tried to make her save him.

She looked right at him and didn't say a word even when the cop shoved him out the door.

*   *   *

Terry's face loomed up in front of her and Lisa blinked. Her face was on fire. Blood stained her hands. Someone had hit her.

Allegra. Al had hit her in the face. Not Deacon who they were taking away in handcuffs. She caught sight of his face, his beseeching eyes, and knew she should speak.

Terry was talking to her. Allegra was crying. Lisa took her hands from her face and stared at them as though they belonged to somebody else. Then she remembered everything that had happened.

"Wait," she cried. "Wait, don't take him away!"

"Don't listen to her," Allegra said, her voice calm despite her tears. "She's just upset."

Lisa turned and looked deep into her sister's eyes. "I love you, Al. I really do. But you need help, and I want to make sure you get it."

She turned to Terry. "Deacon didn't do this to me. He didn't do anything."

"No!" Allegra shouted, struggling away from the officer who'd

175

been tending her. "No, Lisa!"

"It's been Allegra all along." Her voice broke. Suddenly, it became very difficult to remain standing, but she did. She didn't look away from Allegra at all. "It was my sister."

She'd seen Allegra cry before, plenty of times. This time, watching the silver drops fall from her sister's eyes, Lisa knew they were real.

*   *   *

Again the night sky had been painted with the swirling red and blue of police car lights. Lisa watched Terry revel in his element, directing the action. He steadfastly refused to look in her direction.

She pressed her fingers to the window behind which her sister sat, but Allegra wasn't looking at her either. Lisa stepped back to let the car pull away, watching them take her sister. She felt a presence behind her, and she didn't have to turn around to know who it was.

Deacon didn't touch her, and she almost didn't turn. So much had happened. So many things needed to be said. He waited patiently for her to decide, and it was his patience that made her turn.

"We'll both still need to go down to the station and make statements." His voice was husky.

She nodded. "I called my parents. They'll be waiting there."

She raised her eyes to his, searching for the answers she needed. Deacon returned her gaze seriously. His face was already purpling with the bruises he'd endured for her. He had come to save her. It was no declaration of love, but it must mean something. *Mustn't it?*

"What do you think will happen to her?" he asked.

"She needs help," Lisa said. "And we'll make sure she gets what she needs."

"And what about what you need?"

They stared at each other in silence until the lights flashing around them and the noise of radios faded away. There was only Deacon in front of her. Deacon, who had filled her thoughts for so long she could not imagine a time when he had not been in her mind.

Lisa reached out and took his hand, feeling the warmth of it press against her palm. "I think what I need is right here."

Deacon's kiss brushed her lips with feather softness. In Deacon's arms, Lisa found what she'd never known she needed until that moment. No matter what happened from then on, there was nothing else to fear.

MEGAN HART

Megan Hart began her writing career in grammar school when she plagiarized a short story by Ray Bradbury. She soon realized that making up her own stories was better than copying other people's, and she's been writing ever since.

Megan's award-winning short fiction has appeared in such diverse publications as *Hustler*, *On Our Backs* and *The Reaper*. Her novels include every genre of romance, from historical to steamy futuristic SF. In addition to her short erotic fiction for the Amber Kisses imprint, look for her other Amber Quill novels: *Riverboat Bride, Lonesome Bride, Convicted! and Love Match.*

Megan's current projects include a fantasy series, a futuristic trilogy and a dramatic suspense novel. Her dream is to have a movie made of every one of her novels, starring herself as the heroine and Keanu Reeves as the hero. Megan lives in the deep, dark woods of Pennsylvania with her husband and two monsters…er…children.

Learn more about Megan by visiting her website:
http://www.meganhart.com

*   *   *

Don't miss The Clear Cold Light Of Morning, by Megan Hart, available Winter, 2004, from Amber Quill Press, LLC

Perion Marrett's love fulfilled a prophecy and made Mason de Cimmerian the greatest magicreator in the land, but the high magic nearly tore him apart. Now only the love that granted him the power can keep him from succumbing to the thrall's deadly beauty. Perion's willing to give him all she has…

But will it be enough?

AMBER QUILL PRESS, LLC
THE GOLD STANDARD IN PUBLISHING

QUALITY BOOKS
IN BOTH PRINT AND ELECTRONIC FORMATS

ACTION/ADVENTURE

SCIENCE FICTION

MAINSTREAM

FANTASY

ROMANCE

HISTORICAL

YOUNG ADULT

SUSPENSE/THRILLER

PARANORMAL

MYSTERY

EROTICA

HORROR

WESTERN

NON-FICTION

AMBER QUILL PRESS, LLC
http://www.amberquill.com

776828